Beyond the Orchid House

Ruth Elwin Harris began storytelling when she and her brother were evacuated during World War II to live with their grandfather in his isolated Somerset house. "We led a very solitary existence," she says. "Not that we minded. We read a lot and made up stories to entertain each other. We both loved the house and were very happy."

It is that house, christened Hillcrest, which plays an important part in the Quantocks Quartet. "My grandfather bought it in the 1930s from three elderly sisters – all of whom had been painters. Their murals still remained on the stable walls. I used to think about those sisters and wonder about life in the village when they were young." From these thoughts came the author's books about the four Purcell sisters, the Quantocks Quartet: *The Silent Shore* (Sarah's story), *The Beckoning Hills* (Frances's story), *The Dividing Sea* (Julia's story) and *Beyond the Orchid House* (Gwen's story).

Ruth Elwin Harris has lived abroad at different times during her life. She spent three years in North America before her marriage, working in jobs as diverse as secretary, sailing instructor and stage manager for a theatre company, and at one time helped out at an orphanage in India run by Mother Teresa's nuns. She now lives with her family in North Yorkshire. Ruth has written stories for magazines and radio and is the author of *Billie: The Nevill Letters, 1914–1916*, a moving collection of World War I letters that she came across in the Imperial War Museum in London while researching the background for *The Dividing Sea*. Her first book in the Quantocks Quartet, *The Silent Shore*, was s

Also in this series

The Silent Shore (Sarah's story)
The Beckoning Hills (Frances's story)
The Dividing Sea (Julia's story)

Beyond the Orchid House

RUTH ELWIN HARRIS

WALKER BOOKS
AND SUBSIDIARIES
LONDON · BOSTON · SYDNEY

First published 1994 by Julia MacRae Books

This edition published 2002 by Walker Books Ltd
87 Vauxhall Walk, London SE11 5HJ

2 4 6 8 10 9 7 5 3 1

Text © 1994 Ruth Elwin Harris
Cover illustration © 2002 Rebecca Floyd

This book has been typeset in Sabon

Printed in Great Britain by Cox & Wyman Ltd, Reading, Berkshire

British Library Cataloguing in Publication Data:
a catalogue record for this book is
available from the British Library

ISBN 0-7445-8286-5

For Julia

Part One

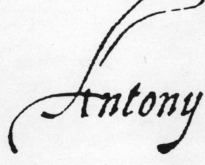

Antony

Chapter One

Mr Whitelaw frowned as he dug his knife deep into the bark of the tree. "Seen healthier ones than this before now," he grunted.

"I know," Gwen said unhappily. "What should I do? Cut it right back? Or grub it up? What do you think?"

After years of neglect the apple tree was a sorry sight, its branches, knotted and scarred, irremediably intertwined, the few leaves remaining curled and brittle. While neighbouring trees were heavy with fruit already beginning to flush, this one showed no signs of an apple.

The head gardener lifted his bowler hat and wiped his forehead with a large handkerchief. Gwen could feel the perspiration trickle down the back of her neck. The sun, high in the sky, cast no more shadow than a small circle round each tree. Its light had drained colour from the landscape; its heat silenced the wildlife. Only Willis's hoe made any sound as she stood watching Mr Whitelaw move from tree to tree. Willis was scratching the soil beyond the bramble hedge with uncharacteristic zeal. Trying to eavesdrop, no doubt, Gwen thought; anxious to learn in advance of any criticism

Mr Whitelaw might make.

"Don't know why you set such store on his opinion," Willis had said when told of Mr Whitelaw's visit. "We can manage well enough without the likes of him telling us what's what."

Willis had resented Gwen's taking control of the garden at Hillcrest on the death of her mother three years previously. Whether his resentment was due to her age – she had been thirteen at the time – or to her sex Gwen had never been able to decide. Whatever the reason, relations between them had never been good. She would have replaced him long ago had her sisters let her.

"He means well," Julia would say when Gwen raged yet again about Willis's complacency, while Frances pointed out that anyone else might turn out to be worse. "More expensive, certainly. Better the devil you know... We must have someone, Gwen. You can't manage two and a half acres on your own. Willis is all right."

So Willis remained at Hillcrest, and when in need of advice or encouragement Gwen went instead down the road to the Manor, home of Sir James Donne, to consult with Mr Whitelaw, Sir James's head gardener. Which was why Mr Whitelaw was at Hillcrest this morning, going from tree to tree in the orchard, examining each in turn and making notes. Gwen thought the orchard could be made more productive; she needed Mr Whitelaw's help.

The quiet was broken by the sudden *thwack* of croquet mallet meeting croquet ball on the other side of the sandstone wall. A whoop of triumph – from Antony, who else? – was followed by laughter.

Mr Whitelaw looked across at Gwen. "You should have told me you had friends in," he said. "I'd have come another day."

"It's all right," Gwen said. "It's only the Mackenzies – from the Rectory, you know. It doesn't matter. They spend most of their time here during the holidays."

She was conscious of the fact that Mr Whitelaw was giving up his morning to her. He would not be hurried, however, but continued to give each tree meticulous attention. His recommendations when he came to the end were both helpful and thorough. "Just one thing," he said when he had finished. "Grass could do with a cut. I'll send Jenkins up with a scythe."

"There's no need," Gwen said quickly. "We prefer it like this. Frances does, at least. She'd rather have the grass long, with plenty of flowers. For her painting, you know."

It was not fair to blame Frances when Gwen and Julia felt the same, but it was easier. The inhabitants of Huish Priory, unaccustomed until recently to having a painter in their midst – a professional painter, what was more, and female at that – regarded Frances as so extraordinary that any eccentricity of behaviour among the sisters at Hillcrest received less comment if attributed to her. Besides, Frances cared nothing for the opinion of others.

"Which reminds me," Gwen said now. "Frances wanted to have a word with you before you go. Would you mind? Have you the time?"

"Of course," Mr Whitelaw said. "A pleasure."

She took him from the kitchen garden through the gate in the sandstone wall to the flower garden, pausing for a moment to take in her favourite view of Hillcrest. Roses in the foreground clustered round the stone sundial, the flowers heavy, velvety, filling the air with their scent. Beyond, the lawn, studded with the white arches of croquet hoops, stretched up to the house. Apricot-painted walls, a roof of grey-green slates. Hillcrest. Solid, comfortable. Home.

The croquet players had retreated from the sunlight and taken refuge in the shade of the wisteria on the veranda where they were now lying in deckchairs or on the flagstones, refreshing themselves with Annie's lemonade. Purcells and Mackenzies, so close that they might have been one family – Frances, Julia and Sarah Purcell (Sarah with her nose in a book as usual) and Gabriel, Geoffrey and Antony from the Rectory across the road. Only Lucy Mackenzie was missing.

Frances saw Gwen standing with Mr Whitelaw at the gate, and came across the lawn towards them, dangling her sun hat from one hand. Her feet, clearly visible below her skirt, were bare, but if Mr Whitelaw saw them he gave no sign.

Not knowing why Frances wanted to speak to Mr Whitelaw Gwen was nervous, anxious that her sister should not offend with some casual remark. "Frances can charm the birds off the trees when she wants," Gabriel sometimes said, in the tone of voice that implied it was a pity she didn't want more often. Today, presumably, she did, for Mr Whitelaw was clearly charmed as she thanked him for the help and encouragement he had given Gwen over the past three years.

"I don't know what she would have done without you," she said, head tilted back, tendrils of chestnut hair curling round her face. "Or the rest of us for that matter. We'd have starved, no doubt."

"Her doing, not mine," Mr Whitelaw said. "She's a hard worker, your sister. I'd take her on my staff at the Manor any time."

He repeated his words when he said goodbye to Gwen at

the front gate. "Your sister's right. You've done well, Miss Gwen. Your mother'd be proud of you, no doubt about it."

"So that's Mr Whitelaw," Gabriel said when Gwen returned to the veranda. "What a nice man."

"Haven't you met him before?" Gwen was surprised. "I thought your family knew everyone there was to know in the village."

"Not if they don't come to church. Which he doesn't, so far as I'm aware. He must be chapel. Was he able to help?"

"Oh, yes." She gave a sigh of relief. "He always does. It'll take a couple of years, he says, but then I should have the orchard in as good shape as the kitchen garden. I've neglected it, you see. We've always had plenty of fruit, of course, but I knew we could do better. Annie says Mother was fussy about apples, and if she didn't like a particular variety she didn't give the tree any attention. There are a couple Mr Whitelaw thinks I should dig up. If I do that and prune the rest he says the orchard will be as productive as the kitchen garden, given time. Thank goodness."

Gabriel laughed. "You are wonderful, Gwen. So serious, always. And such a perfectionist."

"Let me help with the digging up," Antony said eagerly. The youngest of the Mackenzies, fifteen to Gwen's sixteen, he was enthusiastic about everything he took on, always bounding with energy. His face was still scarlet from his exertions at croquet, fair hair dark where it was plastered against his skin. "We'll organize it like a tug of war – first us and then you lot, taking turns. I bet we get the trees out of the ground before you do. Do ler's. It'll be fun."

Fun. How well that word described life at Hillcrest and the Rectory when Gabriel came home from Cambridge, where he was a fellow, and Geoffrey from school. Today was the first time the Purcells had seen Gabriel these holidays; he had returned only the previous evening from a visit to Germany.

"Staying with my dreary German professor," he said, making a face. Then he smiled. "But he has a charming young wife. And two lively sons, who took me up into the mountains and taught me how to walk in the Alps."

"Are the Alps any different from the Quantocks?" Frances asked. "Yes, of course I know they're higher, but apart from that?"

Sarah tugged at Gwen's arm. "Guess what we've decided to do tomorrow."

Gwen looked down at her youngest sister. "I can't guess. You tell me."

"We're going up to the Quantocks to see how far we can walk. We're going for the *whole* day, Gabriel says."

"We?"

"All of us. Me as well." She was bursting with importance.

"You can't call it a walk when there are eight of you doing it," Antony said. "It becomes an expedition then, not a walk. Why don't we pretend we're exploring the Alps? No, not the Alps. The Himalayas. Everest. We'll climb Everest, that's what we'll do."

"Really, Antony," Frances said. "How can you possibly pretend the Quantocks are the Himalayas? The top of the Quantocks is a ridge; Everest's a peak. Anyway, it's not settled that we're going. I still think it's too far for Sarah. Three miles across the valley, for a start, and then the climb up to the ridge, not to mention coming back again afterwards – she won't be able to do it. She's only eleven."

"I will. I will. And anyway, Gabriel's promised to carry me if I get tired."

"Why don't we stay at home together, just you and me?" Gwen said quickly, detecting a wobble in her sister's voice. "You can help me in the garden. We'll keep each other company."

Sarah stuck out her lower lip. "I don't want to stay at Hillcrest. I want to see the Quantocks."

"And so you shall," Gabriel promised. "Don't be so hard on the child, Frances. It must be rotten being so much younger than the rest of us. Let her come this once. We don't have to go far. As for you, Gwen, I'm not having excuses from you. We're all going, and that's that."

"What about Lucy?" Gwen asked. Lucy, the Mackenzies' only daughter, was expected by her parents to spend her time helping in the parish; the Purcells saw less of Lucy than they did of her brothers.

"I'll make sure she does," Gabriel said.

Frances laughed. "Really?"

"Care to bet?" Gabriel challenged her.

"Not if you're determined," she said.

Gwen, watching, would not have cared to bet either, knowing Gabriel's powers of persuasion. By the time the Mackenzies returned to the Rectory – Mrs Mackenzie had organized a tennis party for that afternoon – Gabriel had not only gained Frances's agreement to Sarah's inclusion in tomorrow's expedition but had persuaded the Purcells to provide food for the day as well.

"You know how it is. Annie's picnics are so much more delicious than the dreadful dry sandwiches Cook thinks walkers want."

Annie grumbled as she weighed out butter for pastry. "I never heard the like. Taking Miss Sarah with you, indeed.

How does Mr Gabriel think she'll keep up with those long legs of his? Tell me that. There'll be tears before sunset, you mark my words."

Sarah's eyes were anxious as she sat at the kitchen table watching Annie cut the fat into the flour. She knew that not even Frances would contradict Annie if Annie said no to tomorrow's expedition. For Annie was more than cook and housekeeper to the Purcells: she was one of the family. She had been with the Purcells for longer than any of them could remember; indeed, it had been her presence at Hillcrest that had persuaded Mr Mackenzie, the Purcells' guardian, to defy convention and let the four sisters remain in the house on their own after their mother's death in 1910.

Julia, always the peacemaker, smiled now at her youngest sister. "Why don't you go and ask Willis for some baby carrots, Sarah? They're always refreshing for a picnic." She waited until Sarah had left the kitchen before turning to Annie. "Do let her come," she begged. "You know how Gabriel dotes on her. He'll make sure she's all right. And it is true, what he says. She does get left out. If only she weren't so much younger than the rest of us." She looked across at Gwen. "You'll come too, won't you, Gwen?"

Gwen concentrated on the potatoes she was dicing. "I don't know. There's so much to do here. If we don't get the plums picked within the next day or two the wasps will eat the lot."

"That's just an excuse," Julia said. "One more day won't make any difference. We'll all pick when we get back. You know Geoffrey's always ready to help and I'm sure Gabriel won't mind if we ask him. Neither will Antony if we can persuade him that it was the Greeks' favourite occupation."

"I'll think about it," Gwen said.

She was still thinking when she went out at dusk to shut the hens up for the night. She had never been further than Dunkery St Michael, the village that lay below the Quantocks, though she felt that she already knew the hills well from Frances's many paintings of them. She was tempted. She would like to climb up the bracken-covered slopes, look down into the tree-filled combes and over the vale of Taunton Deane, see the scenes that she knew only in oils. But August was one of the busiest months when it came to cropping, and though she could work all day in the garden without tiring, she was no more of a walker than Sarah.

The smell of warm pastry lingered in the courtyard as she went by the open kitchen window. Tomorrow's picnic was already waiting on the marble shelf in the larder – hard-boiled eggs, lettuce and scrubbed carrots, tomatoes, plums, the first of the season's pears, straw wrapped, and, most delicious of all, Annie's meat pasties. A feast indeed. Did she really want to miss the fun?

Beyond the lamplit cobbles below the window it was darker than she had expected, the path up to the stables no more than a pale ribbon between the dark grass.

"*Boo!*"

She shrieked, recoiling from the figure that had jumped out at her from the blackness of the fig tree. "Antony!" She waited until the trembling had stopped. "Must you do things like that? Such a fright."

"Sorry." But his voice was unrepentant. "I've been waiting for ages. What have you been doing? I thought the hens had to be shut up before dark, so the foxes wouldn't get them."

"Yes, well. They make such a fuss about being shut up

these light evenings that I tend to leave them... I hadn't realized it was so late, as a matter of fact. What are you doing
here? Does your mother know?"

"Of course not. She thinks I'm in bed. I climbed out of my
bedroom window. I often do."

There was a swagger in his voice. She did not know
whether to believe him. "What happens if she finds out?"

"I've put a pillow down my bed so she'll think I'm fast
asleep. Come on – what about the hens? Can I help?"

It was so late that most of the flock had already put themselves to bed. They perched on bales of straw and the
remains of winter clamps in the stables, clucking together
like members of a parish working party. A quick count – not
easy in the darkness of the stable interior – was followed by
a hunt over the brow of the hill for the missing birds. Antony
shooshed the flapping and cackling recalcitrants through the
grass with shouts loud enough for Annie to hear from the
kitchen.

"That's done," Gwen said as she shut the stable door and
dropped the bar in place. "It's surprising how much easier it
is when there are two of you. Sarah helps when the days are
shorter, but she went to bed ages ago. Now – what do you
want?"

"Are you coming tomorrow? You are, aren't you?"

"I don't know. I haven't made up my mind."

"I don't understand you, Gwen." He sounded exasperated. "You don't ever leave Hillcrest."

"I do, sometimes."

"Not often."

"No. Well. There's so much to do always." She knew that
no explanation would satisfy Antony. The youngest of an
affluent family, he could never understand what it had been

18

like to be suddenly orphaned, left with an uncertain income and the fear that Hillcrest might no longer be theirs. And though problems of income had been sorted out long ago and life at Hillcrest was now secure, Gwen's compulsion to keep the kitchen garden productive and the larder and store cupboard filled still remained.

"You know what it is?" Antony said at last. "I think you're frightened."

"Frightened?" She was astonished. Outraged too. "Don't be so silly. Why should I be frightened?"

"I don't know. It's the only reason I can think of, that's all. And Gabriel said something, once... Because you don't leave Hillcrest, Gwen. Oh, I know Lucy doesn't leave the Rectory much either, but that's not because she doesn't want to. Mother expects her to help in the parish, that's why."

"Is she coming tomorrow?" Gwen said.

"Of course. Gabriel promised she would, didn't he? Everyone's coming. Except you, that is. You must, Gwen. Please."

"Is that why you're here? To persuade me?"

"I was afraid from what you said this morning that you might not. I knew it would be easier to make you see how important it was if I talked to you alone. That's why I waited till now."

"Important?"

"To me it is. I want you to come."

She was baffled. "Why?"

"Because I like doing things with you. It wouldn't be any fun without you."

He meant it. He wanted her. She felt a flutter in her stomach. It mattered to Antony that she should be there. How extraordinary...

"Well... Perhaps I will, then."

"'Perhaps' isn't any good. You must promise."

She took a deep breath. "All right. I promise."

"It will be wonderful." She heard the smile in his voice. "I know it will. The best day of our lives. You'll see."

Chapter Two

Gwen had not taken to Antony at their first meeting. He had been twelve when she and Sarah arrived for lessons at the Rectory study the morning after their mother's funeral, a thin-faced small boy with sharp, inquisitive eyes that watched every move the two sisters made. Gwen had been mortified to discover almost at once that Antony, though a year younger than her, was very much brighter. Worse, Mr Mackenzie was a classicist and taught his son accordingly, while Gwen's main interests, botany and art, were not highly regarded. In addition Antony was a practical joker and a tease. Gwen, with no experience of boys or their behaviour, did not know how to cope. Though she liked and admired Mr Mackenzie – love would not be too strong a word – she came to dread Rectory mornings. When her formal education came to an end a year later, with the agreement of Mr Mackenzie and Frances, Gwen's relief had been not so much for the end of her lessons, but for the release it gave her from Antony's presence.

Strangely, their relationship changed immediately. Outside the Rectory study they were equals; indeed, in the garden she was his superior. His cleverness no longer disconcerted her as it once had. She had grown accustomed to his teasing. They were no longer companions thrown together by age and propinquity but real friends.

Even so, it surprised Gwen that her presence on the Quantocks walk should matter so much to him. Lying in bed later that night, she pictured him climbing out of his bedroom window, sidling through the churchyard, well out of sight of the Rectory drawing-room windows, secreting himself behind the broad-leafed fig tree at the corner of the stables to wait for her to emerge from Hillcrest. She told herself that his wish to see her had been no more than an excuse for the adventure he was always seeking. She did not mind. She was still flattered.

When, next morning, sounds of the Mackenzies' arrival sent her hurrying downstairs, she found herself hesitating in the passage outside the kitchen, unexpectedly shy. She waited a moment before opening the door. Antony looked up from stuffing food into his rucksack and grinned across at her. She blushed.

There was scarcely a soul about when they set off. A housemaid folding back the shutters of a downstairs room in the Manor, Bill Roberts at work in the forge; no one else. Bill looked up at the sound of their footsteps, his face lit from below by the flames of the fire he was tending. "Good to see 'ee back, Mr Gabriel. Will 'ee be playing in the Milverton match come Saturday?"

Gabriel stopped. "Yes, of course. Milverton, is it? We'll give them a drubbing again this year."

Lucy walked beside Gwen. "Are you as surprised to find yourself here as I am to be here? Gabriel wasn't sure that you'd come."

Gwen smiled. "I couldn't not, when everyone else was going, could I? What about you? How will the sewing circle manage without you this afternoon?"

"Perfectly well. Silly, isn't it? Mother thinks I should be around to pour out the tea afterwards, but anyone there would be delighted to be asked to do it."

"It'll be much easier for us than it was for Hannibal," Antony was telling Sarah. "The Quantocks aren't as high as the Alps, for one thing. And it's summer, so there won't be any snow. There usually is snow on the Alps, I think, even in summer. It was the snow that made it so difficult for the elephants. They aren't used to snow, Africa being hot. India too. I wonder which country they came from. The elephants, I mean."

"Listen to him," Lucy said. "He lives in a different world from the rest of us."

The Somerset lanes were still cool, their high hedges shading walkers from the rising sun. Once the party reached Priory Common, however, the road was open and the sun hot on their backs. They were walking in pairs now, Gabriel deep in conversation with Sarah, Frances with Lucy, Geoffrey striding beside Julia. Only Antony rushed ahead to shout from a distance at the geese on the common, then waited for Gwen to catch him up.

"You don't have to wait for me," she said.

"I know, but I want to."

Beyond the railway line that ran from Taunton to Minehead the tree-covered slopes of the Quantock Hills rose up from the valley floor. Gwen began to pant as the path grew steeper.

"You can't be tired yet," Antony told her. "We've still got miles to go."

"I'm not," Gwen said indignantly. "I can dig in the garden for hours without getting tired. I'm not used to hills, that's all."

Antony bounded ahead, grabbed hold of a sapling with one hand and stretched out the other to pull her up. "Isn't this fun?" he said. "Good old Frances. We wouldn't be here without her."

"It was Annie, really. We couldn't have come if Annie hadn't said yes."

"I don't mean that," Antony said. "I mean the walk was Gabriel's idea and he'd still be in Germany if it weren't for Frances."

"Why? What's Frances got to do with it?"

"He's in love with her."

She stared. "Gabriel? In love with Frances? I don't believe it. Has he said so?"

"Didn't you know?" He sounded astonished.

"Of course I didn't know. Anyway, it's not true."

"It is, I'm sure it is. Think about it, Gwen. The way he looks at her, the things he says, the fact that he's at home now. Other summers he's either spent in Germany or wandering round the countryside on Fabian business. Besides, he reads Horace to her. He wouldn't do that if he wasn't in love." And when she was still unconvinced, he added, "Horace, Gwen. Love poetry."

"That doesn't mean…"

"Geoffrey thinks the same as me."

She tried to collect her thoughts. "But Frances isn't interested in that sort of thing."

"Perhaps that's why he's come home. To make her interested."

"But there wouldn't be any point. She's always said she'll

never get married, ever since her first year at the Slade, when her professor told her you couldn't be a painter and a wife. You know Frances. Her work's more important to her than anything else."

"Gabriel might think he has more influence than her professors now she's left the Slade," Antony said.

"Well, I don't know," Gwen said. She didn't want to contemplate such a possibility. "I think you're just being fanciful. I don't want to talk about it. Tell you what – I'll race you to the top."

She lost, as she knew she would, but at least the scramble to reach the ridge meant that the subject of Frances and Gabriel could be forgotten. And indeed the view was enough to distract anyone. It stretched for miles, across the valley to the Blackdown Hills, the Brendons and Exmoor, while across the sea the sun glinted on the coastal villages of Wales, the smudged horizon hinting at far-off mountains beyond.

And indirectly it was that amazing view that was responsible for changing what had been intended as a one-day walk to an overnight expedition. Sarah, frowning into the distance, wanted to know if the Bristol Channel was the sea. She had never seen the sea, she said. Immediately Gabriel, always indulgent where Sarah was concerned, determined to take her to the sea. "There's a beach at the end of the Quantocks... Yes, I know it's the Bristol Channel, but it's as good as the sea."

He would not listen to the Purcells' insistence that they had lived by the sea when their father was alive and stationed at Plymouth. "She can't remember it. That's the same thing." Nor did the distance dismay him – eight miles to the coast from where they stood, much too far for the time available. They could find a barn in which to spend the night, he said; send telegrams to Annie and the Mackenzies to assure them of the party's safety; return by train to Dunkery St Michael the following morning if Sarah was still tired; and if Frances were really worried he would see Annie on their return and take the blame on himself.

There was no doubt what most members of the party wanted to do. Sarah was dazed with delight at the very idea, Antony begged Frances not to be a spoilsport, Julia pointed out that as Annie's picnics were always so generous there would be no need to worry about food for the evening, while Lucy, the one person who might have been expected to object, merely said wistfully that it would be nice. As for Frances, responsible for her younger sisters, she agreed almost without argument, to their astonishment.

Julia, acting as quartermaster, suggested they should picnic there on the ridge. "We couldn't have a better view, and if there is a bit of a breeze, well, that would be welcome in this heat."

While she and Geoffrey divided the food into two, picnic and supper, Lucy came over and sat down beside Gwen. "You don't mind, do you?" she asked. "About leaving the garden for longer, I mean. What about the greenhouses and the hens and all that? Will Annie be able to see to everything?"

"I hope so," Gwen said. "Perhaps Gabriel could say something in the telegram. Annie'll remember the hens all right, but she might not think of closing the greenhouses, and Willis certainly won't do it before he leaves. He's probably spent the day smoking in the stables, with me not there to keep an eye on him." She surprised herself by her lack of concern. What did it matter if the greenhouses remained open? She was enjoying herself too much to care. "What about you?" she asked Lucy. "Will your mother mind your not being home?"

"I expect so," Lucy said, but she smiled.

"You don't sound very concerned," Gwen said.

"I don't think I am. It will have been worth it. I feel ... oh, I don't know ... free."

They lay about on the soft grass for a while after finishing their picnic, before setting off along the ridge. Antony led the way, chanting large chunks of *The Ancient Mariner* as he zigzagged across the ridge in front of them. Once started, he could – and often did – spend hours on end declaiming poetry. Greek, Latin, English, the language did not matter. He became drunk with the power of words, the rhythm of the lines, and went on, seemingly for ever. Sometimes Gwen wondered whether he held the entire *Golden Treasury* in his memory.

He came back to her at last, weaving his way between the whortleberry bushes.

"I bet you've never slept in a barn," he said.

"I don't suppose you have either."

"I have, you know. Oh, all right, then. Not a barn. I've slept out in the open though, lots of times." He saw her expression. "I have. Well, not lots. A few."

"When?" she said. "Where?"

"At home. You know that bit of grass by my rabbit hutch at the bottom of the garden? Geoffrey and I slept out there. Two summers ago, it was. We did it for a lark. I bet him he wouldn't, so then, of course, he had to. It was fun. You wake up very early if you sleep out in the open because the sun's hot on your eyelids. It's wonderful. Everything's sparkling because of the dew and the birds are singing and you're ravenously hungry... We persuaded Bertha to smuggle some food out of the kitchen for us when Cook wasn't looking, because we couldn't wait for breakfast."

"Didn't your parents mind?"

"They didn't know. Not until Hilda sneaked. Just the sort of thing Hilda would do. Mother was furious, of course. Which is why Geoffrey won't do it again. He can be awfully feeble, Geoffrey can. *I* still do it sometimes, when there's moonlight, but I make sure there's a bolster down my bed so no one can tell I'm not there. You'll understand how I feel after tonight."

"We're not sleeping out in the open, though. Gabriel said something about a barn."

"I know," Antony agreed, "but that's a sop to the grownups, isn't it, for when we get back. And to Frances, I suppose, who probably wouldn't have agreed otherwise."

"Was that what made her agree?" She had been surprised by the ease with which Frances had been persuaded. Headstrong in her own behaviour Frances might be, but she was invariably circumspect where her sisters were concerned, holding herself responsible for their well-being. Gwen had expected her sister to insist they return home for the night. That she hadn't made Gwen wonder whether there was, after all, truth in Antony's observations about Frances's relationship with Gabriel.

"Anyway," Antony said airily, "we might not find a barn, and then we'll have to sleep in the open. Which will be much nicer."

But Gabriel had had a particular barn in mind when making the suggestion. Gabriel, who spent much of his time at home walking the surrounding countryside, knew the Quantocks well. When shadows began to lengthen in the valley below, he led them down from the sunlit ridge through bracken and gorse towards the beginning of fields – "Marco Polo returning to civilization" was how Antony described their descent – until they came to a barn sheltering under a semicircle of trees. There was straw inside to sleep on – Sarah's eyes were already beginning to close – and a stream nearby, its water clear and refreshingly cool against the skin of tired long-distance walkers.

Antony was anxious to explore.

"Don't get yourself lost then," said Gabriel, about to set off with Frances to seek the farmer's permission for the use of his barn, and to send telegrams of reassurance to the Rectory and Hillcrest. "And don't be too long. I don't want to have to send out search parties when I get back."

"I'll stay with the stream," Antony promised, knotting his bootlaces together and hanging his boots round his neck. He rolled his socks into a ball and stuffed them into a trouser pocket. "Come on, Gwen. We'll be intrepid explorers setting out to find the source of the Amazon."

Geoffrey hooted with laughter. "The Amazon's *huge*, Antony," he said. "The biggest river in the world. This is just a stream. And a pretty small one at that."

"The Amazon must be small when it starts. Oh, all right. We'll pretend it's the Nile. The Nile's better anyway. Egypt's hot. Like today. Anyone else want to come? No? Ready, Gwen?"

They set off, stumbling along the stony bed, but before long the water, seeming at first so reviving to hot and dusty feet, quickly became numbingly cold. Gwen protested and said she wanted to put on her shoes and stockings. "We can walk beside the stream. That's almost as good as being in it."

Reluctantly Antony agreed. He dried his own feet with a grubby handkerchief before handing it to Gwen to do the same. "I expect you're right. My feet are so cold I can't feel them, as a matter of fact. You can't walk on frostbitten feet. Another five minutes and we'd have been doing a Commander Oates. 'I'll just be gone a little while.' Poor old Gabriel would have had to send out a search party after all. Except I suppose if we were in the Antarctic the stream would be a glacier and we wouldn't have been able to paddle. And if it was the Amazon we'd have impenetrable forest coming down to the river's edge, which would take us days to hack a way through. Just as well it's the Nile. The Nile has sandy banks. Very easy to explore."

"I can't see any sandy banks here," Gwen said as they began to climb. Sometimes she wondered whether Antony could tell the difference between fantasy and reality. Not infrequently she had difficulty following or understanding his wilder flights of fancy. Yet she thought that was one of the things about him that made him the most intriguing of the four Mackenzies.

The path grew steeper as the stream descended in a series of miniature waterfalls. Gwen began to pant. "Walking and climbing are quite different from digging, aren't they? My calves are beginning to ache."

"It's like cycling," Antony said. "You'd be surprised how stiff I was after my first bicycle ride."

"I didn't know you had a bicycle."

"Not one of my own. George Cross's. He lends me his whenever I want it. And don't, for goodness' sake, say anything to anyone at home. Not even Bertha. You know Mother. She still worries about the effects of scarlet fever, although it's years and years since I was ill. She'd probably say cycling's bad for my heart or something equally stupid and forbid me to do it. She won't worry if she doesn't know."

"I suppose not." She was curious. "What does it feel like, cycling?"

"Tremendous. Much faster than walking. Particularly downhill. It's *wonderful* downhill. Like flying, I should think. It's easy to pretend one's a bird. Tell you what. You can come with me one day, if you like."

"But I haven't got a bicycle."

"We'll share George's. You can sit on the crossbar and I'll pedal."

Climbing was becoming difficult, stony path, tussocky grass and whortleberry bushes growing indistinct in the fading light. Rhododendron bushes had begun to encroach, throwing branches across their way. Antony stopped.

"I think it's too difficult to go any further," he said regretfully. "It's probably time, anyway... Let's sit for a minute, before we start back."

Gwen was glad of the rest. She had no idea how long it was since she and Antony had left the others but she was surprised to discover how dark it had become in the vale below. Only the sky was still clear, tinged with lines of pink on the horizon.

"You're pleased you came, aren't you?" Antony's voice was anxious.

"Up here, do you mean?"

"Today. Leaving Hillcrest."

"Yes," she said, as though she had only just realized, "it's been wonderful."

"I wasn't sure you'd come, you know."

"But I promised."

"Even so, I was afraid you were angry with me, you see. For saying you were frightened. You were angry, weren't you?"

"I don't know." She thought back to their conversation

31

the previous evening. "I think I was more surprised than angry. Then, afterwards, when I was in bed and started to think..." She hesitated, suddenly wanting to confide yet reluctant to reveal so much of herself.

"Yes?" he prompted. "What about afterwards?"

"When I thought about it..." She took a deep breath. "I think you might have been right."

"Right? About leaving Hillcrest?"

"Yes."

"But why?"

"It's so stupid," she said.

He put his hand over hers. "You're not stupid, Gwen. Tell me."

"Promise you won't laugh?"

"What do you take me for? Of course I won't laugh."

She remembered how often she and Julia had exchanged confidences in the darkness in the days when they had shared a bedroom long ago. Why should it be easier to reveal secrets when the listener's expression was invisible? She said, "In case something dreadful happens while I'm not there."

There was amazement in his voice. "Something dreadful? But, Gwen, why should it?"

She began to shiver. "Because it has before. Twice."

He put an arm round her shoulder. "When?"

The shivering grew worse.

"It's all right," he said. "I'm here. You can tell me, can't you?"

She nodded. After a while she said, "The first time it happened was a long time ago. I don't know how old I was. Mother refused to talk about it afterwards, so even now I don't know the date, not even the year. I suppose I could ask Annie, but it's not something... Anyway ... we were living at Hillcrest. We always did when Father was at sea. One day Mother told us we were going to stay with friends. For a holiday. Not her, just the four of us."

Antony waited. "So?"

"Mother put us on the train for Plymouth. Annie came with us to see we were all right. The friends were naval friends. We'd known them when we lived in Plymouth. They had a house by a river. It was lovely. It's strange, the things you remember. I can see it all so clearly in my mind. In pictures. Like photographs, in a way. That's how I know Sarah was wrong when she said she hadn't seen the sea. I can see her knocking down sandcastles with a spade. There were wonderful rhododendrons in the garden. Huge they were, with white and pink flowers. It must have been May, I suppose, or early June perhaps. It was very hot. I can't remember any rain at all." The pictures were still so vivid that had she had paints and a brush in her hand she could have transferred them instantly to paper.

"Go on," Antony said.

"Well ... Annie met us at Taunton station. When we got home, Mother told us Father was dead. She'd known all along. She didn't want us around while she got used to the idea. At least, I think that was it."

Antony's arm held her close. She could feel the warmth of his body against hers. "I'm so sorry," he said.

"It was such a contrast, you see. Us having fun, when all the time back home ... and Mother was different after that. It's difficult to describe how exactly. She was always laughing before. She didn't any more. Annie says the life went out of her when Father died."

Beside them the stream rippled over the waterfalls and burbled down towards the valley.

"You said it happened twice," Antony said. "Was the second time...?"

"Mother. Yes. We went back to school after Christmas. Not Sarah, of course, she was still at home, but the rest of us... I didn't believe it when the headmistress had Julia and me into her office and told us. We'd only been back at school a week or so and Mother had been fine when we left. Quite jolly, for her, over Christmas. She planted a tree on our last morning, because it was 1910 and the beginning of a new decade and she and Father always planted trees to celebrate special occasions. Only, it was raining and she got a chill and it turned into pneumonia. Well, you know all about that. That was when your father became our guardian. The thing was, I kept on thinking that if only I'd been home I wouldn't have let her die. Father I couldn't help but I'd have *made* Mother live. I shouldn't have gone away." There was a long silence. "You probably think that's stupid," she said at last.

"I don't. Of course I don't. I'm just ... I never realized. Oh, Gwen, I am so sorry."

"Well ... it all happened ages ago now. It was just what you said last night sort of stuck in my mind and I lay awake thinking and wondering if perhaps that was why..."

"It can't happen again, now that both your mother and father..."

"It could. I thought it was going to happen to Frances, when she was away at the Slade and Sarah had measles so badly. Do you remember? I nearly wrote to Frances, as a matter of fact. Your mother decided with Annie not to tell her because she'd only worry but I knew Frances would never forgive herself if anything happened to Sarah."

"But, Gwen, Sarah wasn't going to *die*."

"I know she didn't, but we didn't know at the time."

"I knew. I always know what's going on at home. It's just a matter of listening... No one thought she was *that* ill."

"Well, you were right as it happens. It gave me a fright, all the same."

He gave her a little shake. "Listen, Gwen. Nothing's going to happen to hurt you ever again. I won't let it."

He sounded so certain she could almost believe him. Slowly she began to relax. "And you don't think I'm stupid?"

"Of course not. I'm just sorry..."

She leant against him. She had forgotten how comforting it was to be held so close, so firmly.

"I tell you what we'll do," he said. "We'll have little expeditions, just you and me, without telling anyone else, until you get so used to leaving Hillcrest it won't worry you ever again. Would you like that?"

"I think I might." She began to sniff. "Oh dear."

"Here. You'd better borrow my hanky."

The handkerchief was still damp from drying their feet, but she blew her nose with it nevertheless. "I don't know why I'm being so silly."

"You're not. I just wish you'd told me ages ago."

They sat in silence. The flush of sunset had faded into grey. A solitary star stood out in the sky above.

"Are you all right now?" Antony said at last. "Only I think we ought to be getting back to the others. I'd rather be there before Gabriel and Frances return from the farm."

She let him pull her to her feet. Her legs felt fragile, as if she had been ill. "It's strange," she said. "I feel ... different, somehow. Light-hearted, almost. You won't tell anyone else what I've told you, will you?"

"Course I won't. Cut my throat if I do, and hope to die."

Chapter Three

The strangeness of her surroundings kept her awake far into the night – the blackness of the barn's interior and the unidentifiable sounds, the discomfort of straw bedding that scratched and prickled, so different from the softness of a feather mattress, the presence of others lying so close. Antony was restless in sleep. He threw his arms about and muttered unrecognizable words. Latin, perhaps, or Greek – she could not tell. She had been comforted by his understanding earlier that evening, but now, lying awake while everyone slept, she began to regret those confidences. Would he laugh at her when daylight came, tease her as he so often did?

He gave no sign of doing so next morning. He paddled through the stream, threw water over Geoffrey, walked with Lucy to the farm where Gabriel had arranged they should breakfast. A table had been set between house and stream, the same stream presumably that Gwen had explored with Antony the previous evening, but wider here and deeper, with ducks paddling in it and preening their feathers, while the farmer's wife bustled to and fro from the kitchen with jugs of milk, pots of tea and coffee, and loaves of bread.

"Gosh, I'm hungry," Geoffrey said, and set to almost before Gabriel had had time to say grace. Gwen was amazed by the Mackenzies' appetites, Antony's in particular. Bacon, eggs, mushrooms, fried bread, he wolfed the lot and when he had scraped his plate clean cast longing eyes over to hers.

"Do you want that bacon, Gwen? Shall I finish it for you?" He smiled at her as he transferred the thick pink rashers from her plate to his, a reassuring, conspiratorial grin. Gwen gave an imperceptible sigh of relief. It was all right. He hadn't changed. He would keep her secret. She grinned back at him, knowing that her smile was as wide as his.

The heat was as intense when they set off as it had been the previous day. Fields glimpsed through farm gates shimmered as in a mirage – brown, overripe wheat stretching into the distance, golden stubble with clover flowers making a crimson carpet between the stalks, ploughed red earth transformed by drought into pale dust. It was a relief to reach the shade of a wood. The path twisted and turned between trees and began to descend. The smell of salt in the air grew stronger with every step.

Antony, leading the way, looked back at Gwen. "I've just realized," he said; there was surprise in his voice. "You're my favourite person to be with." He caught his breath as he began to slip on the steep slope, skidded the last few yards to the beach and only kept his balance with difficulty. He was laughing as he held out a hand but when she stood beside him on the pebbles he became suddenly serious. "I mean it," he said. "My favourite person by miles."

They looked at each other. Then, with shouts of warning and mirth, the others came slipping and sliding down the path to join them. The moment was lost.

They walked over rocks and pebbles towards the water-line. "I'm sorry it's so pebbly," Gabriel said. "Minehead has wonderful sand but it's too much to expect Sarah to walk that far."

"Never mind," Antony said. "She's seen the sea. That's all that matters. Do you see the land on the other side of it, Sarah? That's red dragon country."

Sarah stared at him open-mouthed. "*Real* dragons?"

"Of course not real dragons," Frances said quickly. "Honestly, Antony! Must you frighten the child?"

Antony, laughing, was unrepentant. "It's a great place for fossils, this," he said. "I don't know what you lot are intending to do but I'm going on a fossil hunt. Come on, Gwen."

Gwen scarcely knew what fossils were, let alone what they looked like, but she clambered over the lower slopes of the cliffs behind him. She had never seen such extraordinary cliffs, the lines of their formation slanting upwards, defined in the rich colours of an artist's palette – viridian greens, blood reds, cobalt blues.

"They were formed in the Jurassic Age," Antony said when she remarked on it. "Millions of years ago. That's why there are fossils here."

She watched him tap and poke and prod. "What are fossils, exactly?"

"They're ancestors of living things."

She blinked. "What do you mean?"

"Well, they're bits and pieces of plants and animals that lived millions of years ago. Before there were any humans on earth."

"And they're just lying about? From millions of years ago? I don't believe you."

"Not lying about. Buried in rocks and pebbles and things. In special rock. You can't find them all over the country, just in certain places. Here, for instance. Lyme Regis too. I keep on trying to persuade Mother to take us to Lyme Regis on holiday but she always insists on boring old Budleigh Salterton."

The extraordinary range of his knowledge never ceased to amaze her. She felt herself ignorant in comparison. "You always know so much about everything," she said.

"I don't," he said. "Not really. You know much more about art and painting and painters than I do. It's just that I read a lot. Anything I can get my hands on – well, you've seen all the books there are in the Rectory. You can't help learning things if you read, but it doesn't mean much. A ragbag of knowledge, Gabriel calls it. He says I should read in more depth, but I don't think he's right. I think I should be finding out about all sorts of things at the moment. There's years ahead when I can go deeper into things. It's like my poetry. I don't know yet what sort of poetry I want to write so I've got to experiment. Try everything. I do know quite a lot about fossils as a matter of fact. They fascinate me. Ah." He reached forward, picked up what looked like a pebble, studied it and gave a sigh of satisfaction. "Just think. This was living and moving and eating, millions and millions of years ago. It's hard to take in, isn't it?"

"What is it?"

"This? It's an ammonite."

"A what?"

"An ammonite. A mollusc. You know – like a snail. Here."

Carefully he laid it on the palm of her hand. She felt it, turned it over. She tried to hide her disappointment. "It's only a bit of rock."

"It is now," he agreed, "but it was a living creature once upon a time. Look at it more carefully."

She held it in her hand, studying the pattern of whorls, the delicate lines that marked the shell. "It is beautiful," she admitted at last. "The sort of thing you feel you should draw in pen and ink. Paint wouldn't be any good. It would be too heavy, and spoil it."

He held her hand and folded her fingers over the stone. "There," he said. "It's yours now."

She was overwhelmed. "Don't you want to keep it?"

"I'll find another some other time. Or ask George Cross – he comes here quite often to look for fossils to sell. The money helps pay for bits and pieces for his bike. No. I want you to have it to remind you of today."

"Well..." She could not find adequate words. "If you're quite sure." She played with it, smoothed its surface with her fingers. "And it really is old? Millions of years? You're not teasing?"

"You know I don't tease about things that matter. Millions of years. Hundreds of millions probably."

"It gives you a scary feeling inside, doesn't it, thinking of so long ago. I mean, we don't count at all, do we?"

"That depends who you are. It's hundreds of years since people like Plato and Homer and Virgil were alive but people still go on reading what they wrote. I envy them that. Art too. Well, you know about that, with Michelangelo and the Sistine Chapel and Rome and Florence and everything. Even today ... think how Frances goes on about Cézanne and Matisse. Who knows? Perhaps people will be admiring her painting in five hundred years' time. Or reading me."

"You?"

"I'm going to be a poet when I grow up."

He crouched beside her, looking up into her face. Long, fair hair, ruffled by the breeze; drops of moisture resting on the bridge of his nose; particles of sand smeared on one cheek. And the blue eyes, piercing, intense.

"Didn't you know?" he said. "I thought everyone knew." He smiled, stood up and flung out his arms. "Not any old poet, either. A great poet."

She felt shivers run up and down her spine. She could not take her eyes from him.

And suddenly she knew. Sitting on the rocks at the edge of the beach at St Audries she saw her future, understood the reason for her existence, recognized her destiny. She would marry Antony. She would look after him, support him, encourage him. She would help him become a great poet.

She told no one of that moment on the beach. Who could she tell? Frances's views on marriage were well known. (Antony's supposition about Gabriel's feelings for Frances turned out to be correct. Later that year Gabriel asked Frances to marry him; Frances turned him down.) Julia would tell Gwen she was too young for such ideas. Sarah would want to spread the news. As for Annie – "That's nice, love," Annie would say. "Now then. What veg are we having today?" Far better to hug her knowledge to herself.

Antony was the last person Gwen could tell. Cleverer than her he might be, but instinct told her she was years older in experience of life and in maturity. She knew that he needed time to grow and develop without thought to the future. Years of education still lay ahead, first with his father and then at university. She wondered whether, following in Gabriel's footsteps, he would try for a fellowship at Cambridge. Unlikely, she thought. Antony was too solitary to enjoy the college community that his more gregarious elder brother so obviously relished. A grand tour then, to see the world and gather material for his poetry, before returning to Huish Priory to settle. Eight years at least, Gwen told herself, possibly ten.

Such a time span did not daunt her. Gardening during the past years had taught her patience, and there were things she could do in the meantime. Making plans was too specific a description of what went through her mind during the following months, dreams more appropriate; dreams, floating in and out of her consciousness during odd moments of the day and night.

That Antony would finally settle in Huish Priory Gwen did not doubt. There was room enough at Hillcrest for him to move in when the time came. Frances had made a studio for herself in the stables but they were large. There was room left for a study for Antony, a library too. Indeed, the coach house and horseboxes might well convert into a dwelling place for them both. She could not see that there would be any need to leave Hillcrest. In any case she would still have her responsibilities in the garden – even more so, presumably, if Antony became part of the family.

She had no idea what sort of income poetry brought in. She suspected that poets might be like artists, their income uncertain, even non-existent. Though Frances now had an agent, a man called Denis Bond, she had yet to sell a painting, indeed was reluctant to do so, thinking that her work was not yet good enough. Tennyson presumably had earned sufficient from his poetry to keep himself and his family, but he had been Poet Laureate. No doubt starting had been difficult, even for Tennyson.

Gwen accepted that she would have to contribute

financially to their partnership. At least she could provide sufficient from the garden to feed another mouth without difficulty. With her talent for drawing she determined to take up illustrating professionally. Frances would scorn it as commerce, but to Gwen, who for as long as she could remember had admired Dulac and Rackham above all other artists and had for years entertained Sarah by illustrating her favourite books, such a career seemed not only logical but right. If she worked hard under Frances's tuition (and Frances was a martinet where draughtsmanship was concerned), ten years would surely give her time to develop a style and establish her name.

Life at Hillcrest had acquired stability, as well as greater financial security, now that art school fees and London living expenses were no longer necessary. Frances had expected Julia to follow her to the Slade but Julia had refused. Like Gwen, Julia loved Hillcrest; she enjoyed running the house as Gwen did the garden. In any case, she said, she and Gwen could learn from Frances all that Frances had learnt at the Slade.

Antony had always spent much of his time at Hillcrest, either with Sarah or in the kitchen with Annie. Now he came over to see Gwen. Not that they did much together; the autumn was too busy a time in the garden and kitchen for that. But he brought his books with him and studied or scribbled near where she was working. Sometimes he helped her. Sometimes he lay spreadeagled along the branch of the medlar tree gazing at the ground below, or the sky through the leaves, for hours on end without moving.

"What are you thinking?" she asked him.

He looked at her as if she were in another world. "Just thinking," he said, after a moment.

Until now she had not realized what an anarchic life he led. He did what he wanted, went where he wanted. If he suspected people might object to any activity, he did not mention it. Because the Purcells had always been law-abiding, careful not to cause worry or concern to the Mackenzies, who out of the goodness of their hearts had taken on responsibility for them, Gwen found some of Antony's behaviour difficult to accept.

"If people don't know what you're doing," he told her, "they won't object. Or worry. In fact, looked at like that, you have a duty to keep quiet. Besides, I have to think about my work. A poet has to experience life." For a moment it sounded as if he were talking in capital letters. "A poet can't let himself be distracted by what people think."

Sometimes he sounded like Frances. It had never occurred to Gwen that Frances and Antony might have anything in common, but now she began to understand that when it came to their work their attitudes were similar.

She never asked to read his poetry. She had too little faith in her own judgement and too little knowledge – Tennyson, Macaulay and Newbolt were her only familiars – to feel she could make any useful comment. Help and encouragement in that field must come from Gabriel.

When winter came and the garden was less demanding, Antony taught her to ride George Cross's bicycle on the bridle paths between the blackberry bushes on Priory Common. He took her up to the Quantocks again, and to the Blackdown Hills, so that she could see the Wellington Monument, clearly visible from Hillcrest but never before seen close to. He took her into Taunton and treated her to a cream tea in Maynard's café, behaving as if he were accustomed to taking out girls every day of the week, but the break in his voice when asking for the bill and his uncertainty about how much to leave under the saucer revealed the truth. Watching him frown as he calculated the tip she felt waves of love sweep over her.

He looked up. Did he suspect her feelings? "You're all right now, aren't you?" he said.

"What do you mean?"

"You don't mind leaving Hillcrest any more."

She was amazed. "Is that why you've been taking me out all this winter?"

"Well..." He shrugged. "One of the reasons. Mainly it's been for the fun of going out. What I would really like to do would be to take you fossil hunting in Lyme Regis, but I think Mother and Father might object."

"I'm sure they would. Annie too."

"'Fraid so. We'll have to wait until we're grown up. Then I'll take you to Greece and Rome and Troy and tell you all about the ancient world."

She had not expected the revelation on the beach to change her, but it had done so without her being aware of it. It had given her both confidence and a purpose. Before, she had accepted life as it came; after, she determined to make of her life what she wanted.

Chapter Four

"It was a monoplane," Antony said. "It only had one layer of wings. Biplanes have two, one above the other. Well, it's obvious, when you think about it. I don't know if two layers mean biplanes are stronger. This looked as fragile as anything."

"It was a Blériot," George said, "with a Le Rhone engine. Eighty horsepower it said it was in the paper. Try and picture that, Gwen – eighty horses hauling an aeroplane over the sand."

At first meeting George Cross seemed an unlikely friend for Antony to have, yet outside the Mackenzies and Purcells he was Antony's closest companion, possibly his only real friend. Friends were difficult to make in a parish, Antony had confided to Gwen. "Living in a rectory's a bit like living in a leper colony. People don't want to know you. Well, they do, but then they get scared that you'll mention their sins to your father. Or else they think you'll be priggish. Have a halo hovering somewhere overhead, you know. So they keep away."

The idea of a halo anywhere near Antony was laughable,

if half the tales he told of his activities were true. Over the past months Gwen had come to realize that Antony divided his life into compartments, playing a different role in each one. In the Rectory he was the youngest son, brilliant but delicate. Unlike Mrs Mackenzie, Annie was not taken in. "You can't tell me that lad's health's worse than yours nor mine," she would say. "Uses it to get his own way, he does. Spoilt, he is, no two ways about it." But Annie herself was indulgent too, entertained by the clown and practical joker Antony became in her presence, though she was not above giving him a cuff round the ear if she considered it necessary. With Sarah, Antony became the magician, transporting her into a world of make-believe, the world of mythology and classical history that she knew from her lessons with Mr Mackenzie. Then there were the aspects of Antony that Gwen knew little about, his nightlife with the lads in the village when his parents fondly imagined him safely in bed.

With some people Antony did not play-act. Gwen was one, Gabriel another, George Cross a third. George, older than Antony, was already working as a clerk to an agricultural supplier in Dunkery St Michael. "Shan't stay there for ever," he confided to Gwen. "It's a step onto the ladder, that's all."

George was ambitious. He intended to become an inventor. Because he spoke with a soft West Country burr, slowly as if considering each word, it took Gwen time to discover that in his way George was as clever as Antony, but whereas Antony tinkered with words, George tinkered with machines. He rode his bicycle little; it was Antony who borrowed it, using it as a means of escape from the Rectory. George had found the bicycle lying broken and twisted in a ditch beside the Minehead road, he assumed as the result of a traffic accident. "I did look to see if there were corpses about," he told Gwen earnestly. "But there weren't. There weren't no blood on the road neither." Ever since, he had been repairing and improving it, often with the help of Bill Roberts at the forge, welding bits on to make it stronger, streamlining it to increase its speed. Yet it had been Antony who tested it, freewheeling down Porlock Hill with shrieks of excitement. George, terrified for his precious machine's well-being, had insisted on walking it down from the top. Sometimes Gwen wondered how often the bike would have been ridden, had it not been for Antony and his enthusiasm for excursions – like the one he and George had just made to Minehead to see an aeroplane that was being toured round the coastal towns by Monsieur Salmet, the Frenchman who owned it.

George and Antony lay in the meadow at the far end of Tinker's Lane, drinking cider and smoking as they told Gwen about their day out. It was May, the hedges heavy with elderflower, the grass with cow parsley and daisies. The stones of the shepherd's hut, abandoned now that the lambing season was over, were warm against her back as she leant against them while she sketched the two boys. She was envious; she had never seen an aeroplane.

"You wouldn't believe that it was strong enough to support a human being," Antony said.

"Let alone the engine," George said. "Why, that engine must have weighed a ton at least."

"I don't know that I would have dared go up in it," Antony admitted. "The struts looked as if they'd crack at the first puff of wind."

"You'd have gone up if you'd had the money," said George.

"Could anyone go up in it?" Gwen asked. "Did they? How much did it cost?"

"Four guineas." Antony made a face. "Yes, I know. I didn't expect it to be that much. I thought the ten and sixpence I got from the poem Gabriel sent in to the *Westminster Gazette* would be enough, but it wasn't. There wasn't time for more than one or two to have a ride, anyway, because there'd been trouble with the engine or something."

"I'd like to have seen it," Gwen said. "I wish I could have gone with you."

"There wasn't room for three on the bike. Tell you what. Why don't we go tomorrow, just you and me? He's supposed to be leaving Minehead and flying up to Weston tomorrow afternoon. If we went to Watchet we'd be able to see him fly over."

She lacked Antony's nerve. It was too far, she said. There wouldn't be time. Would they see anything? What would people say? And, anyway, what about George?

"I'll be working," George said gloomily. "You go. You can have the bike."

"I don't know. I'm not sure..."

Once an idea was in Antony's head he would not let it go. It was true he had lessons in the morning, he agreed, but if he and she left the moment they were over... The only person likely to object was Frances and, as she was visiting Gabriel and Geoffrey in Cambridge with Julia, she would know nothing about it.

"You want to see an aeroplane, you said. Well, then, you'll have to do something about it. An aeroplane's not going to fly over Hillcrest and flap its wings at you, is it, so you'll have to go to it. Mahomet and the mountain, and all that. You have to make things happen in this life, Gwen.

49

Besides, it's silly to miss an opportunity. You may never get it again. Come on. I thought you'd got over that business about not leaving Hillcrest by now."

"I have. Of course I have. Ages ago."

In the end they decided to take the train to Watchet to avoid any risk of missing the flight. The two of them dashed down to the forge the moment Antony had finished his lessons, collected the bicycle from Bill Roberts in whose care George had left it, and with Gwen sitting in the saddle and Antony standing on the pedals – more comfortable and quicker than with Gwen on the crossbar – cycled over to the station at Combe Florey.

The Esplanade was bustling with sightseers when they reached Watchet, all buzzing with excitement and many with binoculars sweeping across the sky. Somebody said Mr Salmet had been delayed, someone else that he was carrying a passenger. "He's promised to demonstrate over the town," said another. "That's why the schoolchildren have been given the afternoon off."

Within half an hour there was scarcely room to move on the Esplanade. People began climbing Cleeve Hill for a better view, while those on the pier were teetering dangerously near the edge. The minutes ticked by.

"What do we do if he's terribly late?" Gwen said – and at that moment a rocket whooshed up from the pleasure ground into the sky.

Antony had brought Mr Mackenzie's binoculars with him. "There he is," he shouted. "I can see him."

Suddenly Gwen saw him too. Or thought she did. A speck in the sky. Was it? It was. A speck, a dot. An ink blot now, growing larger, turning into the shape of a dragonfly. She could make out the body and wings, the struts as delicate as pen and ink lines against the grey sky. She could hear the hum of its engine. The crowd cheered. Antony cheered. She was shouting herself.

The aeroplane dipped, came up. The crowd was silent. The aeroplane dipped again. The sound of the engine stopped.

"He's going to water plane," said someone near Gwen.

"He can't," said someone else. "He hasn't got floats." Alarm sounded in his voice.

The tail went up. The dip turned into a dive. The aeroplane dropped. Nose first it went into the sea. The crowd gasped. A huge column of spray and steam marked the spot where it had disappeared.

Silence.

Gwen felt sick. "Is he dead?"

Antony's face was as white as his shirt as he searched the sea with his binoculars. "I don't know. I'm trying to see." Minutes passed. Then he gave a shout. "I can see him. No, I can't. He's disappeared. A wave... There he is again. It's him. I can see a head. Two heads."

"Told you he had a passenger," said the man who had talked about floats.

Antony thrust the binoculars into Gwen's hand. "See for yourself."

She had difficulty focusing. Then it took minutes to find the right place. First she saw one head, then a second. Shoulders appeared above the water. Arms waved. "Can they rescue them?"

The tide was on its way out. Only a narrow channel of water remained in the harbour. Someone called for a lifeboat. "Not enough time," cried another. "Tide's on the ebb. They're drifting."

"There's water by the east wharf," suggested yet another and then a cheer went up. Six men had launched a boat between the wharf and the pier and were now poling themselves down the channel, carefully, so as not to run aground. "For heaven's sake, pull," called a frantic spectator as the boat reached deep water beyond the pier heads.

The aeroplane was sinking, the two men in it barely visible. Gwen gave the binoculars back to Antony. "I can't bear to look." The scene, from the time the engine cut out, replayed itself in her mind, minute by slow minute. If only she had stayed at home. She knew they would never reach the men in time. In, out, in, out, went the oars, without pause. In, out. Her nails dug into the palm of her hands.

"Come on," cried Antony.

It seemed like hours, yet it took less than thirty minutes to rescue the men. Even then Gwen could not relax. When at last the aviator and his companion stepped onto dry land, dripping water onto the pier, she began to shake, as violently as if she had a fever.

In later years the aeroplane incident became inextricably mixed in Gwen's memory with the outbreak of war. Which was ridiculous, for almost three months separated the two, three months no different from those of any other summer. The garden flourished, blossomed and cropped. Elderflowers were turned into cordial, walnuts pickled, strawberries jammed. The sun shone on games of croquet and tennis. Yet there were similarities between the two incidents. Both were amazing in themselves; both contained the same elements of disbelief, drama – melodrama, even – and excitement, as well as overtones of tragedy.

Excitement there was in plenty, once war had been

declared. Sympathy for plucky little Belgium, invaded by a Germany who had apparently hoped to swallow France as well but found the mouthful too big, was quickly followed by a nationwide urge to do something to help. Men rushed to enlist, Gabriel and Geoffrey among the first. Bill Roberts went soon after, despite his recent marriage to Mary Hancock, and was quickly followed by so many others that the cricket team no longer existed and the village band only survived, though with lowered standards, because sons stepped into their fathers' shoes.

Willis went too, announcing the fact one Friday when Gwen handed him his wages. "I felt it was my duty to give my all to our king and my country," he told her, his mouth set in a self-satisfied smirk.

"I shall have to let you go then," Gwen said. "Are you intending today to be your last day?" She was amused to see disappointment show on his face. Did he expect her to grovel, to beg him to change his mind, tell him she couldn't do without him? Quite the reverse. The news filled her with elation. She could scarcely believe that something she had prayed for for years had happened at last.

Frances and Julia were appalled. The garden was too big, they said. They talked of the impossibility of doing without help, the difficulties of finding someone competent when anyone with an ounce of initiative had rushed to enlist. "How can we possibly manage on our own?" they wanted to know.

Gwen was impatient. "Of course we can," she told them. Now that she was free at last to do what she wanted she had no intention of taking on someone who might be as obstinate, as ignorant and as unadventurous as Willis. Better to do without a gardener than risk another Willis.

"I could help in the garden," Sarah volunteered. "I do anyway, but I expect I could do more."

"Good girl," said Gwen. She told Frances and Julia, who spent a large part of their time painting in the garden, that they too must do more than they now did. Then there were boys in the village who would be glad of some pocket money – Miss Ross, the schoolmistress, would recommend those reliable. There were the Scouts, too, to call on when extra help was needed. Growing food was war work, after all, and she had heard that the military hospitals around the country were crying out for eggs and vegetables. She would increase the number of hens, enlarge the vegetable garden, help supply them. Even if the war finished by Christmas, hospitals would presumably have to remain open to care for the wounded. No, Willis's departure was a cause for celebration rather than panic.

Down at the Manor Mr Whitelaw, like Gwen, was making changes. He came up to Hillcrest one afternoon with a basket of orchids for Gwen. "Sir James has closed down the orchid houses. We're growing vegetables instead. All except one house, which we're keeping for the best plants, for breeding once this war's over. Had to get rid of the rest. Thought you might like these."

She looked down at those in bloom. "They're beautiful. Do you want me to look after them for you?"

He shook his head. "They're for you. Thought you'd appreciate them. I've taken what I can fit in back home with me, but as for the rest..."

She thought of the glasshouses he had taken her round at the Manor, warm and humid. She thought of the numbers of men working in them, imagined their skills. "I don't know anything about looking after orchids, Mr Whitelaw."

"I've given you the easy ones," he said. "They'll be happy enough outside in the summer. You could keep them on a window sill in winter, at a pinch, if the greenhouse isn't warm enough."

"Well, if you're sure... Thank you very much."

He nodded. "Glad they've got a good home. Dare say you'd like to draw them."

She went with him to the gate. Leaves lay scattered over the road where schoolchildren had thrown sticks up into the trees to dislodge the chestnuts in them. A peacock screeched from the Manor garden.

"Don't like throwing things away," Mr Whitelaw said. "Particularly beautiful things like orchids. We need beauty in our lives. More than ever in times like this." He sighed.

She watched him until he had disappeared through the Manor gates before taking the orchids into her own greenhouse. She had always thought him such a practical man. It had never occurred to her that he might have a romantic streak.

Frances had always insisted that Julia and Gwen should keep regular hours with their painting and drawing, and did not see that the war should make any difference. In addition there were house and garden to run. Time had always been in short supply at Hillcrest. Now there seemed scarcely a moment in which to draw breath. When Gwen wasn't gardening she was attending knitting bees at the Rectory or sewing parties at the Manor, helping Antony organize fundraising events on the village green and a cricket league in aid of those wounded at the front. ("Though that's a bit of a laugh," Antony admitted, "when the only players I can get hold of are halt and decrepit themselves.")

Gwen was fulfilled. She had come of age – not in years,

maybe, but in experience. She understood what she was doing with her life, knew where she was going. She was happy.

Until Antony enlisted.

"But why?" she asked him. "You're under age. You had to lie to get them to take you. Why not wait until you're nineteen? You might be able to get into the Royal Flying Corps then, which is what you really want, isn't it?" Heaven forbid that he should join the corps, not if aeroplanes often fell out of the sky, but she would use any reason that might make him change his mind.

"I'm in the Royal Naval Division now," Antony said, "and glad to be in it. So that's that. Besides" – she sensed defiance – "if Gabriel can go off to war, then so can I."

"But your work," she said desperately. "Your poetry. What about that?"

"That's the whole point," he said. "Can't you see? I need it for that. I need the experience. Don't be angry, Gwen. I don't want you to be angry. I knew Mother and Father would be upset and I didn't imagine Julia and Frances would agree, or Annie, but I did think you'd understand."

She could not bear to quarrel with him at such a time, yet she knew she must protest. She was taken aback by the depth of her distress and did not understand it. She had been proud of Gabriel and Geoffrey when they enlisted, felt shivers of patriotic fervour run up and down her spine whenever she heard a military march, deplored Frances's tirades against jingoism, against bullies and hooligans, whether German or British, and was embarrassed by them. Why then should she be so against Antony doing his bit?

"How can I understand?" she asked him now. "Why

can't you wait? What's the hurry?"

"Because it'll be over by Christmas. You know that. Everyone does. It'll be too late by the time I'm nineteen. It's an experience I can't afford to miss. Imagine what it would be like, Gwen, if for the rest of my life I had to admit that I'd missed out on the one experience that everyone else had. I'd die of shame. Really I would."

"Why should everyone? Not everyone fought in the South African war. Colonel Sherwood's the only one I know."

"Oh, Gwen." He was impatient. "This war is different. This one's going to involve everyone. People at home. Look at you, growing stuff to take into the hospital. You're involved too."

"But you're going to be a great poet," she said desperately. "You shouldn't be running risks..."

"You can't go through life without risks. And that's part of it. The poetry, I mean. I think ... I don't know if I can explain, when I don't quite understand it myself, but I'll try. It's something Gabriel once said, about universal truths. If you're going to explore universal truths then you have to have experience. You have to dig into yourself to get at them, and if you've done nothing..." He broke off. "Do you understand?"

She shook her head. "It's the sort of thing Frances might say."

"I suppose it is." The seriousness fell away momentarily. He grinned like the schoolboy he had been until yesterday. "I've always admired Frances, you know, even if I do play her up. She rises to the bait so wonderfully, that's the trouble."

She tried to smile as she waited for him to go on. "You said ... dig into yourself?"

He was studying his hands. Well-cared-for hands, hands that had done little rough work in their life with their neatly tended nails and half moons clearly defined. Her own hands were always stained, from earth, from podding and shelling, with ink or walnut juice... What would his hands be doing in a few weeks' time?

"I don't know," he said at last. "Perhaps I just want fun. An adventure – a big adventure. Or perhaps it's more than that. I'm not sure. I'm going, anyway. I must. But I do want your approval." He turned her face towards his. "Please, Gwen."

It was the first time she had been kissed. She could not understand why she should cry.

Antony, last of the Mackenzies to enlist, was the first to go abroad. In February he came home for his last leave.

It was a difficult time. The Mackenzies, wanting to keep him to themselves, expected him to spend every moment with them at the Rectory. On the few occasions he came over to Hillcrest he was awkward, fidgety, his eyes always going to the clock. "I'm sorry. It's Mother. She's upset, you know. I really ought to get back. It's the least I can do."

Sarah had been lonely without his companionship during her lessons at the Rectory. She clung to him now, eager to tell him every detail of what she had learnt since his departure. As a treat he took her down to the stream to look for tadpoles.

"He's a kind lad," Annie said. "And don't say it's too early for tadpoles. We all know that, but he won't let on to the child."

When at last Gwen and he were alone she did not know what to say to him. "Is everything all right?" she said. "You don't regret enlisting?"

"Of course not."

Would he tell her if he did? Unlikely. Not her. Not her, of all people. She felt that she was separated from him by a glass barrier. It was as though his body was in the room, sitting in the chair facing her (what huge, ugly boots the army wore; how uncomfortable they must be), while in spirit he was still with his fellows at Blandford. Not knowing what to talk about, she took him out to the greenhouse to show him the orchids Mr Whitelaw had given her.

It was raw out of doors but the atmosphere in the greenhouse was pleasantly warm. She was overwhelmed by his presence as they stood there, by the touch of his uniform against her flesh, by the smell of it – more than anything else by his size. He had grown during those few months in the army, had become taller, broader, stronger. The schoolboy she had known for so long had become a man, the man she wanted to marry. She trembled with her need of him. Yet the barrier was still there. She wanted to break it somehow, to shatter it with her bare hands if need be. She wanted to talk of what lay ahead, to discuss their future together.

Instead she showed him the orchids. "Don't you think they're beautiful?"

He stood, looking down at them. What was he thinking? What was he seeing? The orchids, with their arching stems, their delicate blooms? Or something else, something that she could not imagine?

He sighed. "Beautiful? Yes, of course. Still... A bit frippery, orchids, don't you think, in times like these?"

And then he was gone.

Chapter Five

Gwen found letters to Antony difficult to write even before he went abroad. She had never been good at expressing herself in words. At school the Sunday letter home had been a weekly chore. Later, when Frances was studying at the Slade, it was Julia who wrote with news from Hillcrest, while Gwen merely added a postscript on her own activities in the garden and illustrated the whole with pen and ink drawings of the week's happenings.

She struggled with letters in the weeks following Antony's departure. She sensed that it would be a mistake to reveal her own feelings for him, yet that was what she most wanted to do. She did not know what else to tell him. Life at Hillcrest must be dull in comparison with his big adventure.

Antony himself wrote infrequently. Gwen told herself that she must be understanding. Battalion training and army exercises would leave him little free time, and his first duty was, after all, to his parents and his family. She knew, because Mr Mackenzie said as much, that Antony and Gabriel corresponded. The two brothers had always been close, despite the ten years between them. Now they had military life as well as their poetry in common.

She was grateful for those letters that he did write, but found them unsatisfactory. He was play-acting again. He had become a soldier – or rather, as a member of the Royal Naval Division, a sailor. He talked of *going ashore* during time off, despite being stationed miles from the sea in the middle of Dorset. When involved in an exercise round the ancient fort on the site of Badbury Rings he imagined himself as one of Arthur's knights, fighting – and defeating – the Saxons.

When he left England at the end of February his letters to her stopped altogether. He sailed from Avonmouth, after an inspection by the king during what he described as a *pitiless storm*. King Lear couldn't have suffered more, he told his parents, though whether he was referring to George V or the troops no one was sure. His battalion was heading first for Malta and then Egypt and the Dardanelles, part of a landing force sent to take Constantinople and open up the Black Sea to allow arms and supplies to reach the beleaguered Russians. The big adventure had exceeded his wildest dreams. He saw himself freeing Byzantium from the Turks, emulating Leander at the Hellespont, joining the Greek expedition to Troy. In letters to Sarah, which Sarah read aloud at the breakfast table, he wrote of Menelaus and Helen and Hector, of Achilles and Priam, people about whom Gwen knew little and cared less. Yet it hurt her that Antony should write of them to Sarah.

She received only one letter after his departure and that was from Egypt, describing a visit he had made to the pyramids. He sent her a stone scarab. *Surprise! Surprise! They had hugs in ancient Egypt too. No time for more,* he finished. *We're off to the Dardanelles.*

Two weeks later he was dead.

Had it been Gabriel or Geoffrey, both now moving step by fateful step towards the trenches on the Western Front, she could have accepted it. But it was not. It was Antony, in no danger at all that anyone had known; Antony, who had set out on a jolly spree, with sufficient provisions for only a couple of weeks after landing – *so you can see we're not likely to get involved in any serious fighting,* he had reassured his family – and the expectation of being back by the end of May.

Every morning Gwen woke to the joyous sound of birdsong, joyful herself at the prospect of Antony's return. Then she remembered. Hour after hour she lay sleepless in her bed, watching the dawn lighten her room, while the grandfather clock on the half landing below her door sounded the relentless passage of time.

She dreamt of Antony. She saw him in Egypt. *So much sand,* he had said, *and so dirty.* She pictured him cycling with George Cross round the pyramids. In her dreams the two boys were flying a borrowed aeroplane over the Gallipoli peninsula. She heard the engine cut, saw the nose go down, watched the plane drop into the sea, the wine-red sea. *It isn't any exaggeration,* he had written to Sarah. *It really is wine red.*

It was not only in her dreams that she saw him, but during her waking hours too. She would raise her head from the peas she was picking, or the carrots she was thinning, and there he would be, lying out along the lowest branch of the medlar tree watching her. But when she ran towards him the light would move, the leaves shift, and he had gone.

One day she glimpsed him sitting in the shadows of the potting shed and remembered how, years ago, he had found a chrysalis lying in the dusty earth of the potting shed floor. He had held it out to her. "Look," he had said.

She could see it now, the tawny shell lying in the soft-skinned palm of his hand. "What is it?"

"A butterfly."

She had been indignant. "Don't be silly. You're teasing me again."

"I'm not. It is a butterfly. Well, it will be. A red admiral, I think. It'll climb out of the shell and shake its wings and fly off into the sky, leaving the shell behind. That's what happens when we die. Didn't you know? Our souls leave our bodies and fly away."

At the time she had imagined her mother as one of the many butterflies that hovered over the herbs and flowers at Hillcrest and been comforted by the thought that she had returned to watch over her. If only she could be so easily comforted now.

She changed during that summer. She knew it, but was powerless to prevent it. She become impatient and irritable. She was short with Annie, impatient with Sarah.

Frances was shocked. "How can you be so cruel?" she demanded when Sarah, snapped at by Gwen for some trivial offence, had burst into tears and run from the room. "Think how awful it is for the poor child. She spent so much time with Antony. She must miss him dreadfully."

Don't you think I miss him? Gwen wanted to shout. Sarah hasn't had lessons with Antony for months, not since he enlisted. What about me? I loved him.

She said nothing. She went out into the garden instead, and dug furiously for an hour, turning over soil that had been turned over twice already, ramming the spade down into the red earth, heaving the clod up with a strength she barely knew she possessed, banging it down onto the soil's surface. In, up, down. In, up, down. Take that. And that. And that.

Anger consumed her. She would never have believed such anger possible. Anger with Antony. Anger with herself.

How could he have been so *stupid*? To enlist at sixteen, almost three years under age. To lie about it, what was more. Why should he risk his life when there were others who could liberate Constantinople from the Turks, celebrate mass in St Sophia for the first time for however many hundred years, when there were thousands who were soldiers, proper soldiers, rather than poets? Great poets had a duty, not to themselves but to the world. What point was experience if dying was part of it? Where were universal truths then?

The questions hammered on and on inside her skull until she thought she must go mad. How dared he waste his talent? How dared he throw away her love? Above all, why Antony? Others had survived. Why not he?

In time the anger she felt turned to guilt, guilt that she had not been able to save him. If she had tried harder to persuade him to stay at home... If she had spoken of her love, told him of her plans, would he have behaved any differently? And that last morning in the greenhouse ... why had she not said something, anything? She wept at the thought that he had gone to his death knowing nothing of her love for him.

Julia, who had been unsettled ever since Geoffrey's departure for France, left for London to train as a nurse. Gwen was not so much glad to see her go as relieved. For Julia knew how Gwen felt.

They had always been close, the four sisters, knowing that

their survival as a family depended on it, but closeness did not mean that they shared their secrets. Frances now was too wrapped up in her painting to notice Gwen's distress, Sarah too young. But Julia and Gwen had shared a bedroom when their mother was alive and exchanged confidences in the dark. Julia, always the most perceptive of the four where people were concerned and knowing Gwen better than her sisters, had sensed Gwen's feelings for Antony. She said little but she understood.

Gwen did not want Julia's sympathy. She did not want to have to smile and pretend that she was beginning to recover every time she saw Julia's eyes upon her. She wanted to be able to cry in the kitchen garden without risk of discovery. She wanted to be left alone.

Time might not heal, for all that people said it did, but at least it went on, with the inexorable progression of the seasons. Spring, summer, autumn ... the crops sown, grown, harvested and stored. The larder full. What did it matter that she felt so empty?

It was a year since Antony had borrowed George Cross's bicycle for the last time and cycled into Taunton to enlist. The anniversary of the date came and went. If only pain could be so easily left behind.

George Cross had offered Gwen the bicycle before he went overseas with the Royal Engineers. "It's yours already, sort of."

She refused. She wanted nothing to do with it. He did not try to persuade her. "I'm sorry about ... you know," he said.

The earliest of Mr Whitelaw's orchids came into flower. She had paid the plants little attention since Antony's departure, had not even been aware that a flower was developing.

Then, one morning, she went into the greenhouse and there it was.

"Beautiful, isn't it?" Frances said when she saw it. "A pity Julia's not here to paint it. You'll draw it, though, won't you?"

Gwen stared at the flower, its petals so delicate, so white, so pure. And overseas men were dying in their thousands...

"I can't bear orchids," she said. "Heaven knows why I ever agreed to take these on. Such ridiculous plants, somehow. So *frivolous*." And she gathered the pots up in her arms and swept past her astonished sister out of the greenhouse.

Over the past weeks Charlie Shattock, the lad who helped at weekends and in school holidays, had been building a bonfire in the corner of the kitchen garden. Dug-up strawberry plants, unwanted and diseased wood, the autumn's prunings, Charlie piled them high into the shape of a pyramid. His mother was making him a guy to put on the top, he told her. Gwen promised him a party on the night, said that he could be the one to set the bonfire ablaze. But it was she who struck the match, now, and watched the head fizz and flare between her fingers before pushing it into the straw at the bottom of the heap.

The straw crackled and glowed red. Above it twigs hissed in the heat. A flicker of flame, then smoke twisted upwards, grey, pungent. Too much leaf, still damp.

She watched without emotion, distanced from herself. She might have been watching a stranger perform some primitive rite.

A finger of fire curled round a blackcurrant branch, releasing the sweet scent of its leaves. The flames spread, grew, leapt into the air. Their heat burnt her cheeks. Slowly, deliberately, she picked up Mr Whitelaw's orchids. One by one she threw them on the fire. Can you see me, Antony? Do you see what I'm doing? Frippery, you called them. Frippery no longer.

The flames grabbed at each plant. Flowers and leaves turned brown, curled, shrivelled, disappeared. Gone. Not a trace of an orchid left. Satisfied, Antony? They came between us that last morning. They won't come between us again.

She had no idea how long she stood there, watching the flames dwindle and die, the embers fade from red to rose, from rose to grey. When at last she came to her senses, the sun had sunk beyond the elms, leaving their leafless branches in silhouette against the cream of the evening sky. She felt as light as the particles of ash still floating and turning in currents of air.

So that was life. People came, stayed briefly, went away. No good, then, placing your trust in people. Only land remained for ever. The red soil of Somerset and the stone walls of Hillcrest would be here centuries hence. Nothing else.

Part Two

Orchids

Chapter Six

Mrs Whitelaw paused outside the bedroom. One hand, finger knuckles lumpy with arthritis, rested on the door handle. Wisps of white hair fringed her anxious face. "I'm sorry to bother you, Miss Purcell," she said, "only he has been asking for you, you see. And ... he gets upset. It's his condition, the district nurse says."

"Please don't worry," Gwen said. "I'd have come earlier if I'd known he was ill. What's the matter, exactly?" A fall ... pneumonia ... a stroke – Mrs Gadd, sent as messenger, had suggested them all. That Mr Whitelaw wanted to see her was the one certain fact Gwen had understood.

"He was in his greenhouse. Last Monday, it was, and bitterly cold. You'll remember, no doubt. When he didn't come in for his tea I went out..." Her voice wavered. "And there he was, on the floor. Mrs Gadd helped me get him into the house, but he's been bad ever since. He'll be glad to see you. He's been worrying." She made a visible effort to pull herself together and smile before opening the bedroom door and ushering Gwen through. "Here's Miss Purcell come to see you, Alfred," she said brightly. "Isn't that kind?"

For a moment Gwen thought she had been shown into the wrong room. Such a display of flowers seemed more appropriate for a conservatory than a sickroom. Then she saw Mr Whitelaw. He lay limply in bed, propped up against heaped pillows, like a puppet she had once had as a child. His eyes were closed. One side of his face sagged. A bruise stretched from his forehead over one eye onto his cheek in an extraordinary palette of colour, purples and blacks merging through blue greens into a yellowing border.

Mrs Whitelaw bent over her husband. "Alfred?" She looked up at Gwen. "He's sleeping," she whispered. "Could you wait? He been restless today. I'd rather not wake him."

"I'm in no hurry," Gwen said. "I'd be happy to sit with him."

"I'll make us a nice cup of tea," Mrs Whitelaw said, and went from the room.

Gwen pulled a chair up to the bed. She tried to compose herself. Stupid to be so upset. Death came to everyone in the end. Mr Whitelaw had had his threescore years and ten, probably a good many more. His life had been spent out in the open, doing what he wanted, and doing it well. He had been highly regarded by all who knew him. What more could anyone ask?

It was not the prospect of his death that she found so upsetting as the sight of him lying helpless in bed. She tried to remember him as he had been in the past, the stalwart head gardener commanding the Manor estate and its outside staff, stern but kind, the man on whom she had relied so much in her youth. She failed. She could only see the limp, bedridden figure of an old man, as she listened to his stertorous breathing and watched the rise and fall of the sheet covering his chest.

Mrs Whitelaw returned at last with the tea. Mr Whitelaw opened his eyes, as though woken by the familiar sound of her footsteps. His gaze wandered round the flowers that surrounded him and eventually came to Gwen. Recognition was immediate. "Miss Purcell." His fingers clutched at the sheet in an attempt to sit up.

"It's all right, Mr Whitelaw," Gwen said. "Don't move. I'm sorry to see you like this."

Mrs Whitelaw supported her husband's shoulders with one arm as she slipped yet another pillow behind his head. "It's a favour he wants to ask you, Miss Purcell," she told Gwen. She picked up her husband's hand and held it in hers. "Take your time, Alfred. Miss Purcell's in no hurry. She'll hear you out."

He wheezed in his struggle for breath. "Orchids."

She looked at the flowers around her. "They're beautiful."

"Take them."

She felt the skin on her face tighten with shock. "But they're yours."

"No good to me now. You take them." There was urgency in the cracked voice.

"He wants you to have them," said Mrs Whitelaw. "He knows he can't look after them any more. You're the only one who could do it."

"Gave you some before," he said. "Years ago. Remember?"

There was a lump in her throat. "I remember."

"Take them," he said again.

"They mean a lot to him, his orchids do," said Mrs Whitelaw. "Like children, they've been to him. He'd be happy, knowing you had them."

73

What could she do? What could she say? I don't want them. I hate orchids. Do you know what I did with the ones you gave me? I threw them away. On the bonfire. I *burnt* them. Instead she said, "What about your wife? Doesn't she want to keep them?"

"Too much bother," Mr Whitelaw said, his voice little more than a croak.

"Oh, Alfred." Mrs Whitelaw was near to tears. "It wasn't the bother, really it wasn't. It was the responsibility. All that worry when you weren't here, wondering whether I was doing the right thing."

I must be firm, Gwen told herself. I must say no. Her heart thudded in her chest. So many memories, so unexpectedly provoked.

"He won't be happy unless you say yes," Mrs Whitelaw said.

Mr Whitelaw's gaze never left Gwen's face. His eyes pleaded with hers. She remembered all that he had done for her, for the family, in the past – time, seeds, plants, cuttings, advice, expertise, all freely given. She had left childhood far behind before she realized how august the position of head gardener was. Yet Mr Whitelaw had never treated her as anything other than an equal. What would the Purcells have done in the old days, had he refused their requests for help?

She looked round the room. Pots of orchids stood on every available surface – on the window sill and the mantelpiece, on the chest of drawers, beside a large leather-bound family Bible on the bedside table – their fragile flowers translucent where the pale afternoon sun filtered through the delicate petals. She tried to calculate how many there might be. Two dozen? Three? Surely she could find space somewhere – in Hillcrest itself, if need be. And perhaps they would not be too demanding. Had those ones not survived, years ago, despite a summer of neglect?

She took a deep breath and tried to smile. "Of course I'll take them, Mr Whitelaw. I'd be glad to."

"There's a cymbidium. Wife will show you..." One hand clutched at his chest, as if trying to pluck out the pain within. "Special. Look after. Yours."

She left as soon as she had drunk her tea. Exhausted by his struggle to talk, Mr Whitelaw had lapsed into semi-consciousness; there was no point in her staying any longer.

At the bottom of the stairs she promised Mrs Whitelaw she would call again the following day. "As for the orchids, there's no hurry, is there? It'll take me a while to sort out what needs to be done. Besides, the flowers are giving him pleasure."

Mrs Whitelaw was not listening. "He might still get better," she told herself, "but even if he does, I wouldn't want him in the greenhouse ever again. I wouldn't have an easy minute. Shall I take you there now, Miss Purcell, or do you want to see the rest of the plants another time?"

The dark hall went darker. It swam round Gwen's head.

"The rest?" Her voice seemed to come from far away. "I thought ... aren't they all upstairs?"

"Only the ones in flower," Mrs Whitelaw said. "Cymbidiums, mostly. The rest are in the greenhouse. It won't take a minute to show you."

The greenhouse was a lean-to at the back of the house, old and shabby. Its wood was rotting in places, the paint peeling. Straw had been stuffed into gaps between struts and the cracked glass. A strong wind might well bring the flimsy structure down on top of the plants it was supposed to protect. Gwen, remembering the rows of immaculate glasshouses that had been in Mr Whitelaw's charge for so many years at the Manor, felt a lump come into her throat.

"Mr Whitelaw hasn't been able to keep up with things for some time," Mrs Whitelaw said defensively. "That's why... Do go in, Miss Purcell."

Gwen went in. She looked round.

She was appalled.

Pots of plants filled every inch of shelf space. Baskets hung from sagging roof beams. Fleshy bulbs rose above clay rims, thin rhizomes pointed white fingers, angular leaves and stiff stalks stretched upwards, uniting together in a pattern of grotesque shapes, making a palette of dirty browns and yellowing greens.

Thoughts rushed into her mind, one after another. So many plants. She would need another greenhouse ... shelving ... heating. Somehow she would have to transport the plants here, as well as those in the sickroom, to Hillcrest. It would take days, if not weeks. She would have to involve Waite. And then, when all that had been done, when every orchid, a species she didn't like and didn't want, had been moved, set up and properly housed, she would have to learn how to look after them. She would be responsible for their care. For ever.

Mrs Whitelaw watched her. "He used to work on his sermons out here," she said. "Closer to God among his flowers, he always said he was. I never liked them myself. It was the worry, you see, having to look after them when he went preaching. In case something went wrong." Tears trickled down her cheeks. "If only I could have my time back I'd never complain. He could take on all the sermons he wanted, and I'd not say a word."

Gwen was astonished. "*Preaching?* Mr Whitelaw?"

Mrs Whitelaw nodded. "Lay preacher, he was. We're chapel, you know."

"I didn't ... he never said anything to me."

"I expect he thought it best not, seeing as how the rector was your guardian."

She thought rapidly. More important than the discovery of Mr Whitelaw's other occupation was the realization that his wife had sometimes cared for his orchids – indeed, must be doing so now. The damp floor, which Gwen had not noticed until this moment, showed that someone had been in earlier with a watering can.

"Do you think you could carry on looking after them for a while?" she said. "I know it must be hard, with your husband so ill, but taking all these on will mean a lot of organization on my part."

"I'll do it for a week or two," Mrs Whitelaw said. "Not too long, though. They'll need repotting soon. Not the ones in the house, they have to rest after the spike's been cut, but all these. I can't do the potting."

"Of course not. It's just that ... well, I'm going to have to think very carefully what to do."

"You will take them, won't you, Miss Purcell?" Her eyes were anxious. "You said you would."

"Of course I'll take them. I promised."

"There's fibre under the bench you can have for potting," Mrs Whitelaw said.

Gwen bent down to find a bale of unpleasantly tough-looking fibre. Beyond it a broken pot and shards of clay scattered over the gravel provided a poignant reminder of Mr Whitelaw's fall.

"They're there in the corner, the orchids he told you

about," Mrs Whitelaw said. "Cymbidiums, they are. Three of them. He brought them from the Manor. Fusses over them as if they were babies. Not that they've flowered yet. 'Another couple of years,' he said. 'Then we shall see.'"

But Gwen had had enough. She could take the claustrophobic atmosphere of the greenhouse no longer. "I must go, Mrs Whitelaw. I'll be in touch."

She sat in the car without moving after Mrs Whitelaw had left her and returned to the house. What have I done? she asked herself. What else could I have done? Nothing. She knew it.

It must be twenty-five years since their first meeting. Now he was going. His death would make yet another break with the past. She sighed as she started the engine. She was getting old, no doubt – in two years she would be forty – and set in her ways, but she hated change, and these days change seemed to be taking place all around her. She remembered the fascinations of the village forge as she drove past the unattractive garage that had replaced it, and said a prayer for Bill Roberts, the one-time blacksmith, who had died only last week of wounds received at Sanctuary Wood eighteen years before. An eccentric from the Home Counties had taken over from the Taskers at Clay Court, painting the front door an inappropriate scarlet which shocked Gwen every time she went by. Saddest of all was the Manor, boarded up since Sir James's illness had kept him in London. At least, Gwen thought, seeing grass encroaching on the once immaculate drive, at least Mr Whitelaw will not have to watch its gradual deterioration.

Annie was pouring boiling water into the teapot when Gwen came down into the kitchen at Hillcrest. "Here you are, love. Give it a moment to brew. You look done in. Upsetting, was it? Sit down now and make yourself comfortable."

The tart, fresh smell of rhubarb filled the room. Newly filled jars of jam stood on the dresser. Gwen sat down and wiped the steam from her spectacles.

"Thought I'd get on with it while you was gone," said Annie, rosy-cheeked from the heat. "The lad'll be here in a matter of weeks and you know how he likes his rhubarb turnovers."

She poured tea for them both, joined Gwen at the table and listened without comment to Gwen's account of her visit. "Not a bad way to go, when all's said and done," she said at the end. "The old man's friend, pneumonia. That's what they say."

"Mother wasn't old," Gwen said.

"Ah well," Annie said. "Your mother could be foolish, for all she was so clever. Planting trees in a rainstorm – asking for trouble, that was."

"I suppose so. Still... Oh, Annie, what am I to do? I don't want his orchids. I hate the wretched things. I haven't the time, and I can't afford the expense. They're a rich man's plant, orchids, not for people like us."

"Only one thing to do, then. Go back and tell him you're sorry; you've changed your mind."

"How can I? I owe him so much. You know how good he was to me in the old days. Never impatient, never too busy. I must have been a terrible nuisance at times, but he never sent me away. He taught me all I know about gardening. How could I refuse?" She remembered his previous gift of orchids and wondered for a moment what part guilt over her treatment of those had played in her agreement to accept these.

"Well, then," Annie said. "That's it. You've decided. Grin and bear it, that's what you must do."

"But the expense, Annie."

"There's money laid by. We're not spendthrift in this house."

"We may well have to be, with an orchid collection," Gwen said grimly. "I'll have to buy another greenhouse, for a start."

"What about the Rectory greenhouse? I doubt if that's used much."

"Too far away. Oh, I know it's only across the road and down the hill, but orchids need to be close at hand so that you can keep an eye on the temperature and humidity and things like that. And another thing. What shall I tell Waite? You know what he thinks about flowers. He'd have the whole of Hillcrest turned over to vegetables if I let him."

"Mr Waite does what you tell him," said Annie.

"I suppose so." She went over to the sink and held her mug under the tap. "It's the *expense* of the orchids that bothers me," she said. "And the time it'll take to look after them. There were so many of them, Annie. Why did Mr Whitelaw want that number? What did he *do* with them all?"

"I don't know, love. Mr Whitelaw always was keen on his orchids. Think of the displays he set up at the flower show every year. Out of this world, they were."

Later that evening, needing fresh air, Gwen went down to the kitchen garden. Spring was her favourite time of year. The red earth, broken down by winter frosts to a fine tilth, was as exciting to her and as challenging as an empty piece of paper or a blank canvas. Who knew what pictures, what patterns, would be drawn on it in the months to come? But this evening, skirting the brown liquid that trickled from the compost heap and the puddles left by the morning's rain, she felt oppressed.

What have I done? she asked herself. What have I let myself in for? Yet even as she asked the questions she knew that she could have acted in no other way.

She watched the rooks wheel above the elm trees, gathering together to repair last year's nests for this year's young. Annie was right. What was done was done. There was no point in having regrets. Perhaps, in time, she might even grow to like them.

Chapter Seven

Gwen's spirits lifted as she drove into Taunton station to meet her eldest nephew. Forget the orchids: Tony Mackenzie was coming to stay. No one could be down in the dumps when Tony was around.

She enjoyed being an aunt. An aunt several times over, for all three of her sisters had married, even Frances succumbing to Gabriel's proposals in the end. Three boys and two girls there were in the next generation. Sarah's two Gwen barely knew, for Sarah's husband was stationed in India, but Tony Mackenzie and Julia's Rowena and Andrew visited Hillcrest frequently, sometimes with their parents, sometimes on their own.

It had always surprised Gwen that Tony should be her favourite nephew when she and Julia's son had so much more in common. Andrew was quiet and self-sufficient, like Gwen; like her he drew and painted, though he preferred birds to Gwen's flowers. Tony, on the other hand, was everything that Gwen was not: loud, extrovert, brash. He opened a book only when made to do so, considered drawing and painting soppy, while his interest in nature was limited to beheading dandelions, gathering conkers and climbing trees, the larger the latter, and the more difficult, the better. If anyone was going to fall off a branch, trip into a garden frame, smash a cricket ball into the greenhouse, it was Tony Mackenzie. Yet it was Tony she preferred, though she tried not to show it. Because he was an only child? Or was it because she felt he needed affection, Frances and Gabriel being too preoccupied with each other to give him the attention Gwen thought he needed?

The London train was drawing in as Gwen reached the platform. She remained by the exit, searching in vain for her nephew's face among the disembarking passengers. It was not until the train had steamed out of the station that Tony appeared, socks concertinaed around his ankles, tie disappearing under his collar and shirt tail showing below his jacket. She kissed him. "I was beginning to wonder whether you'd missed the train," she said.

"I was up at the front," he said, "so I could talk to the engine driver when we stopped."

She put his suitcase on the back seat of the car and held the door open for him to climb in. "So," she said lightly as they drove out of Taunton and along the road to the coast. "Is that what you're going to be when you grow up? An engine driver?"

He shook his head. "Being an engine driver'd be boring. Just imagine having to drive up and down the same track all the time. I'm going to fly round the world when I grow up. I'll visit Aunt Sarah in India and then I'll go on to Australia. Did you know it only takes a week to fly from Australia to England?"

Gwen smiled. "I don't think I believe that."

"It's true," he insisted. "Someone did it last month. Seven

days and nineteen hours from Darwin to Lympne. Imagine that! Halfway round the world in less than eight days."

"I'd rather go by ship," Gwen said firmly. "Much more comfortable. I doubt whether your parents would think much of your flying round the world either. How are they?"

"All right. They send their love."

"Aunt Julia's coming down on Friday with Rowena and Andrew so you'll have their company for the weekend. I'm afraid I'm rather busy at the moment. I'm taking on a collection of orchids. Foolishly, no doubt."

"Dad told me. He said you didn't want them. Why take them on if you don't want them?"

"Because I was asked to, I suppose, by someone I didn't feel I could turn down. I expect it'll be all right in the end, but I must admit that I'm depressed about it all at the moment."

He twisted round in his seat to watch a motorcycle disappear into the distance. "Why, exactly?"

"It's going to mean so much work. And orchids are expensive to maintain. Many of them are semi-tropical, you see, so they need heat." She sighed. "Heat isn't cheap to provide. And then it's going to be difficult getting them to Hillcrest and housing them ... and when I've done that I really don't know how to look after them."

"Can't you find out?"

Gwen gave him an amused glance. "Of course I can. There are books, you know. And a magazine. It all takes time, though, and time's not something I have a lot of."

"I think Dad was right," he said. "You should have said no."

"Life isn't always as straightforward as you might think."

She turned off the open Minehead road into the high-hedged lane that led to Huish Priory. "That's enough about me and my problems," she said briskly. "What about you? Have you any plans for your stay? I'd better warn you – Grandpa intends to give you bridge lessons. He says at thirteen you're old enough to learn. They're expecting you for lunch, by the way."

"Good," he said. "I'm ravenous. It's been ages since breakfast." He gave a sigh of contentment as the car bumped over the bridge into the village. "I always know I'm back when we go over the stream." He glanced at the empty doorway of the Robertses' house as they drove by. "It seems funny not to see Mr Roberts sitting there," he said. "Is Willy still at the garage?"

"He was certainly there last time I took the car in," Gwen said.

He fell out of the car the moment Gwen turned off the engine, rushed down the slope to the house and into the kitchen, where he hugged Annie and devoured every one of the orange cheese tarts she had been foolish enough to leave out. Then he charged round house and garden "to make sure everything's just as I remember it" – as if it had been years since his last visit rather than three months – before taking his suitcase upstairs and emptying its contents over the floor of his bedroom. By the time he left for lunch at the Rectory, Hillcrest gave the impression of chaos.

"Boys!" Annie said fondly. "Ah, me. 'Tis good to have the lad back."

Over her own lunch Gwen continued to struggle with plans for housing the orchids. It worried her that she was making so little headway with the problem. She consoled herself with the thought that caring for them gave Mrs

Whitelaw something to do during her early bereavement, but feared that the day would soon come when Mrs Whitelaw would decide enough was enough. She was still occupied with her lists and diagrams when Tony returned from the Rectory.

"I'm back," he announced unnecessarily as he came through the French windows.

She smiled. "So I see."

"Are you busy? What are you doing?"

"I'm trying to work out how much space I need under glass for the orchids, and how to divide it up. Sir James had a different house for each variety they grew down at the Manor, I remember, to make it easier to look after. Fortunately Mr Whitelaw only had three varieties, and the cymbidiums and cypripediums can be grouped together – they're cool house plants. The cattleyas need much more warmth. I've been trying to work out how much space I shall need for each. More than I'm likely to have, I'm afraid. Don't sit on the table, love, it's not strong enough to support your weight. Mrs Whitelaw has said we can dismantle her greenhouse and bring it up here, but Waite thinks a lot of the wood's rotten."

"We were talking about greenhouses at lunch," Tony said, sliding off the table and throwing himself into an armchair with enough force to break the springs. "Grandpa said you could use his."

"I know. Unfortunately it's not practical. I need one close at hand, here, near the house."

"I thought he meant you to have it here. If you're moving Mr Whitelaw's greenhouse, can't you move Grandpa's too?"

"Well, yes. I didn't realize he didn't mind losing it

altogether. Are you sure that's what he meant? It would be marvellous. I'll take Waite over there this afternoon to discuss it. Thank you, Tony. What a good thing you came to stay."

It was with some trepidation that she told Waite she needed his help at the Rectory. Waite was a very different person from Willis – he had been a shell-shocked ex-prisoner of war when the Purcells took him on as a gardener after the war – but he could make his opinion felt. He might not use the word frivolous about orchids but it was obvious that that was what he thought of them. This afternoon, however, he clumped in silence with Gwen and Tony down the road to the Rectory.

"You go down to the greenhouse," Tony said, "and I'll get Grandpa."

"Hmm," Waite said when he reached it. "Better condition than that other one, at any rate."

He proved more positive than Gwen had expected, took measurements and made notes, helped by Tony, who hovered in the background, holding the tape measure when asked, while trampling its end into the muddy grass.

"Are you sure you don't mind my having the greenhouse?" Gwen asked Mr Mackenzie. "I'm very grateful, of course, but I don't want to deprive you..."

"I doubt whether Shattock has ever made full use of it," the rector said, with his kindly smile, "whereas I know you will. Perhaps we may look to you for tomatoes during the summer?"

"Staging's all right," Waite said. "So's the glass. Plenty of it too, unless the lad takes up cricket again." He glared at Tony, who opened his mouth to protest.

"I'll get Norton up from the village to help," Gwen said quickly.

Waite looked at her with disdain. "I'll do it myself, thank you," he said. "I was a joiner myself, once."

Gwen was surprised. Waite never talked of himself; she knew nothing of his past.

The fire had been lit in the living-room and tea laid by the time Gwen and Tony returned to Hillcrest. She watched in amazement as her nephew devoured the thick mustard and cress sandwiches, cream scones, two rhubarb turnovers and a huge slab of Annie's fruitcake. Where did the boy put it?

Afterwards, when he was sitting on the hearth rug gazing into the fire, arms clasped round his knees, unnaturally quiet and still, she began to worry. Had he made himself ill with such a large tea? "Are you all right, love?"

He nodded. "Can I ask you something?"

"Of course."

"You know I'm supposed to be here for a week?"

"Yes."

"Do I have to go home then? I'd much rather stay here for the rest of the holidays."

She hesitated, flattered but uncertain. "What would your parents say? You've been away at school all term. Won't they want you home?"

"They're coming down here at Easter, aren't they? We'll see each other then."

"Well ... I'm not sure. Annie and I would love to have you, you know that. But you're going into the upper school in September. Shouldn't you be doing some work towards that?"

"Oh, Aunt Gwen. Dad must have been going on to you.

He thinks I should spend the holidays with my nose in a book. He's always telling me that's what he did when he was a boy. Uncle Antony, too."

"Ah." A non-committal reply. She thought, not for the first time, how difficult it could be for an outsider, looking in on a family, able to see both sides but take neither.

"Dad expects me to be like Uncle Antony, you know," Tony said, "but I'm not. I don't like books, for one thing. They're boring. I'd much rather be out in the open, doing things." He looked across at Gwen, his face flushed from the heat of the fire. "What was Uncle Antony *really* like, Aunt Gwen? Was he as brainy as Dad always makes out?"

Gwen considered her words. She did not want to criticize Frances and Gabriel to Tony, yet both she and Annie had always thought it hard that having named their son after his dead uncle they should expect him to have inherited that uncle's talents. Tony had qualities of his own, different, undoubtedly, but as praiseworthy, surely, if only his parents could be brought to see them. It must be misguided, if not wrong, Gwen thought now, to load the unfulfilled expectations of one generation onto the shoulders of the next.

"I don't know, Tony," she said at last. "Yes, he was clever. At least, I thought he was, but as I'm not brainy myself perhaps I can't judge. Your father and grandfather thought he was, and neither of them are stupid so I expect they were right. As for what he was like ... it's a long time ago now. Don't think he spent all his time studying or reading, though, because he didn't. He liked being out of doors too. In fact" – she hesitated for a moment – "in fact he could be quite wild sometimes. He used to borrow George Cross's bicycle and disappear—"

"George Cross? Mr Cross at the shop?"

"No, no. George was killed in the war. He was a cousin of Mr Cross at the shop." That gave her a shock. Mr Cross was middle-aged, like herself. George Cross she thought of as a boy still. Difficult to think of the two as contemporaries.

"So," Tony prompted. "Uncle Antony would disappear."

"Yes. He'd go off on the bike for hours at a time. He wouldn't tell anyone where. He used to say that if people didn't know what he was doing they wouldn't worry. And as it wasn't nice for people to worry it meant that it was his *duty* not to tell them." She was smiling. "That's what he told himself anyway."

"Didn't he even tell Dad?"

"I doubt it. Your father was away at Cambridge most of the time."

"And no one found out?"

"Not usually. Sometimes they did, of course. Sometimes they had to be told. When he enlisted, for instance, but he didn't say anything all the months he was trying to get into the army in case your grandparents tried to stop him." He didn't even confide in me, she thought. That still hurt. "But usually ... there was one occasion when he and I went off to Watchet to see a flying demonstration. No one ever learnt about that."

"Really? Was it exciting? Did they loop the loop and do aerobatics, and things like that?"

"I'm afraid not. It was before the war; I don't suppose they knew about aerobatics then. As a matter of fact, it was a bit of a disaster. There was only the one aeroplane and it nosedived into the sea. The pilot and passenger had to be pulled out of the water by men in a rowing boat."

"What happened to the aeroplane? Did it sink?"

"No. We discovered later it was rescued by a steamer that

just happened to be in the area."

"And Granny and Grandpa didn't find out?"

"Not as far as I know. Nor did your mother, I'm glad to say. Fortunately she was visiting your father in Cambridge at the time. She took it for granted that I'd been in the garden all the time she was away. She'd have been very cross if she'd known, so don't you go telling her now."

His eyes sparkled. "Aunt Gwen, I never thought *you* could be wicked."

"That's enough about your uncle and me." She was already regretting her indiscretion. "Let's get back to you, and your wanting to stay. I'm happy to have you, you know that, but only if your parents agree. And, remember, I'm busy. I shan't be able to take you to the sea or the cinema while you're here. You'll have to look after yourself."

"I don't mind. I'll go and write home now." He bounced up onto his feet. He paused at the door and came back into the room. "Aunt Gwen?"

"Mm?"

"They're going to be a lot of work, these orchids of yours, aren't they?"

She sighed. "I'm hoping it won't be too bad once they're here. It's the thought of erecting the greenhouse and getting everything in place before I'm able to bring them up from Mrs Whitelaw's that worries me. It'll take so long. The fact that it's the busiest time of year, particularly in the vegetable garden, doesn't help either. Waite ought to be working in the garden, not doing joinery." She studied her nephew over her spectacles with some amusement. "What's come over you, Tony? It's not like you to worry about me."

"I've been thinking, you see. About my staying on, I mean. I could help, couldn't I?"

"Help? How?"

"With whatever needs doing. I did woodwork last year at school. I could help Waite with the greenhouses. And I know I don't know anything about vegetables but if you showed me I expect there's lots I could do in the garden."

"Well." She was amazed by the turn of the conversation. Amused too. She had never seen him so earnest. "It's very nice that you're taking an interest in all this. I don't know what to say."

"Say yes," he begged.

"Wouldn't you find it very boring?"

"Not if I can *do* things. Please, Aunt Gwen."

"I suppose we can try, if you like. We'll see how it goes."

He still hovered. "Aunt Gwen."

"What is it now?"

"Just one more thing, and then you can go back to your plans. I was wondering..." He paused, avoiding her eyes. "If I did help would you pay me? What I mean is, if I work proper labouring hours will you pay me labourer's wages?"

What an extraordinary conversation this had become. "I've no idea what labourer's wages are."

"I'll find out," he said.

She laughed outright. "You're not serious, are you?"

"Of course I'm serious."

"But why?" Such thought, such careful planning, was out of character. She was wary. "What's all this about, Tony?" she said. "Has your father stopped your pocket money? And if so, why?"

He shook his head.

"Why, then?"

"I'm saving up for something. I don't want to talk about

92

it yet because I know it's going to take ages. Years, probably. I didn't see how I could do it with only my pocket money to save from, but then, when you were going on about the orchids and what a lot of work they were going to be, and afterwards, at lunch, when Grandpa was saying the same, the idea came to me. Here I am on holiday, with lots of spare time, and here you are, with not enough. And Waite is going to need help, isn't he? He can't move two greenhouses all on his own."

"It wouldn't be impossible. He'll have to dismantle them first, then we'll bring the pieces up here in the car. It might not take long. In any case, are you strong enough? You're only thirteen."

He was confident. "I'm the strongest rugger player in the school. And I'm growing."

"You're not likely to grow much in the next three weeks," Gwen said, but she laughed.

"So you agree?" he said eagerly.

"I'll think about it. You'll have to get on with Waite – you realize that, don't you? I won't have him upset. You've caused enough trouble with him in the past."

"Not this time." He gave her a hug. "Thanks, Aunt Gwen. I'll work hard, I promise."

"Only with your parents' permission, remember," she said. "In writing, what's more."

"Don't worry," he said. "They'll give it. They'll be glad to have me out of the way."

"I'm sorry to have to say it," Julia said, asked for her opinion when she came down for the weekend with Rowena and Andrew, "but it's true. Frances only thinks of her painting, and if Gabriel's not preoccupied with the next book or the

93

college, then he's worrying about Frances being distracted from her work."

"I don't want them to feel I'm trying to take him away from them," Gwen said. "On the other hand, he does seem very keen. Waite's been impressed with what he's done so far, and you know Waite – he's not one to show enthusiasm."

"Better make the most of it, then," Julia said. "Gabriel's always saying Tony lacks application. I doubt whether he'll stick it for the rest of the holidays." She looked up from sewing a replacement button onto a blouse. "What do you think is behind it? It's not like Tony to do something without an ulterior motive."

How hard people were on the poor child, Gwen told herself, thankful that she had said nothing about Tony working for money. All the same, she thought, I'd feel easier if I knew what he wanted it for. Still, I do need his help.

"Are you being sensible about these orchids?" Julia said. "It seems to me that you've more than enough to do as it is, quite apart from the fact that we're none of us getting any younger. You should have told Mr Whitelaw thank you, but no."

"How could I, when he'd been so good to me – to all of us – in the past? There he was, dying. He needed to know they'd be looked after."

Julia gave her a smile, aware, slightly rueful. "You're impossible, Gwen. Well, if you need money to tide you over, let me know. I'm all right at the moment. I've got a couple of commissions for portraits on hand."

"You know you contribute enough to the upkeep of Hillcrest as it is. I couldn't take more."

"Don't be silly. You send up hampers every week, look

after the children whenever we ask, act like a hotel the way you take us in during the holidays. Doing the mending doesn't seem much in return. Besides, Hillcrest matters as much to us as it does to you. We need you here. And talking of Hillcrest, have you ever thought of getting a generator? I don't know how you can see to sew in this light."

"I don't sew," Gwen pointed out. "You do that. Anyway, I like lamplight; it's much kinder on the eyes. Besides, it's one of the delights of Hillcrest as far as the children are concerned – going to bed with a candle."

"That's true enough," Julia said, smiling again as she put down the mended shirt and picked up a stocking.

"I had a very strange postcard the other day," Gwen said, watching with admiration the neat darn that was appearing under her sister's fingers. "From Mr Cole – you know Cole, the greengrocer in Taunton? He said he'd always bought orchids from Mr Whitelaw, and now that I'd taken over the collection would I be interested in carrying on with the arrangement."

"How did he know you'd taken them on? And would you?"

"Mrs Whitelaw must have told him. Yes, I think I might. After all, orchids normally flower through the winter, so I'd have the summer to get used to them and find out how to grow them properly."

"You've grown them before, haven't you? I seem to remember some before I went off to France in the war. What happened to them?"

"Vegetable growing became more important," Gwen said quickly. "Supplying the hospitals – that sort of thing. In any case, I only had one or two plants. I neglected them rather." She took a breath. "Their cultivation's quite difficult, you know – to do well, anyway. I think I shall have to talk to Mrs Whitelaw about it. She might be able to advise me."

"Did Cole say how much he'd pay?"

She shook her head. "He just said if I was interested would I go in and see him next time I was in Taunton. I did wonder ... would you mind going to Covent Garden sometime, to find out what price orchid spikes fetch there? It might be useful to know."

"Not at all. I'll take the children. It would be fun." She laid the darned stocking on top of the other neatly folded clothes and gathered the pile into her arms. "Well, well. Just imagine – my sister, the flower seller. What do you want me to do with this lot? I trust you won't find anything else needing my attention while I'm here. Don't you and Annie *ever* do any mending?"

Chapter Eight

Cole & Son. Fancy gold letters spelt out the words on the faded green board above the shopfront. HIGH-CLASS FRUIT, VEGETABLES & FLOWERS said the small upright capitals beneath.

Gwen stood on the pavement, trying to summon up the courage to go in. She hated doing anything for the first time, and was nervous of meeting strangers. It was too late to change her mind. Besides, Julia would want to know what had happened, would raise her eyebrows if Gwen had to admit she had been too nervous to respond to the postcard. Taking a deep breath Gwen went into the shop.

The smell of moss and damp earth mingled with the scent of flowers. Buckets of narcissi, daffodils and irises stood on the stone floor, baskets of primroses and violets on the counter. Posies of mixed flowers floated in a large bowl of water, made up by someone with a poor eye for colour, Gwen thought as she waited for the salesgirl to fetch Mr Cole. There were no orchids anywhere that she could see – scarcely surprising so near to the end of the season.

"Miss Purcell? I'm Mr Cole. Good of you to come."

He was stocky, not much taller than Gwen, and grey-haired. Father Cole, presumably, rather than son. The drooping moustache gave him a lugubrious air. "I trust you didn't mind my writing," he said. His manner implied that it did not matter to him whether she minded or not. "Mrs Whitelaw gave me your name."

"I don't know that I can help," Gwen said. "I've not had much experience in growing orchids."

"Mr Whitelaw must have been confident enough if he gave them to you. They were like children to him."

"Well..."

"Known him long, have you?"

"Since I was thirteen. He taught me all I know about gardening." She did not like the way Mr Cole was looking at her, up and down, as if he had expected someone more formidable and was disappointed. She stood up straighter, tilted back her head. "I own three acres of garden, so I am an experienced gardener, even if I don't know much about orchids. And I paint. Flowers. Professionally."

She detected a subtle change in his manner as he stood by the counter, sucking the ends of his moustache. "They're not a steady market, orchids," he said. "Not by any means. Weeks can go by without any interest. Then there'll be a hunt ball, say, or a wedding and a banquet together, and I might be able to sell three or four. Spikes, that is. Not single flowers."

She nodded. "How did you go about it with Mr Whitelaw? Did you tell him what you wanted, and when?"

"I'd send him a postcard. Then he'd put what I asked for on the train and I'd collect it from the station. If that's your car outside I take it you could bring them yourself."

She tried to marshal her thoughts. She came into Taunton

regularly to put hampers of fruit and vegetables on the train for Frances and Julia. There would be plenty of room in the car for orchids as well. Inexperience was another matter. She would have to learn as she went along, but there was nothing wrong with that. She hadn't known anything about vegetable growing when she started, but had learnt quickly enough. The fact that she hadn't taken to Mr Cole on first meeting was irrevelant. "It might take me a while to get used to what you want," she said, "but if you gave me enough warning I could let you know what was in flower. We could work from there."

He grunted. "Mr Whitelaw was able to bring the spikes on or hold them back, according to need."

She would not make promises she could not keep. "I might learn how to do that in time, but I've told you, at the moment I haven't any experience."

They stood squared up to each other. His face was impassive; she could not tell what he was thinking.

"Are you interested?" he said at last.

"Yes," she said instantly, before she could change her mind.

"Right, then." He held out his hand. "We'll give it a try."

He accompanied her to the car. "A large garden," he said thoughtfully. "Could you supply me with anything else? I've a number of lady customers – flower arrangers, you know, with small town gardens and no flowers to pick of their own. They're always wanting fresh blooms, good quality ones that will last."

Was this a preliminary test to check her reliability? She thought of the cutting border at Hillcrest, always prolific, providing more than was needed not only for Hillcrest and her sisters but for church and the Rectory as well. And it was

99

still only April: there was time to make another sowing of annuals, particularly sweet peas. She could dig up and split dahlia tubers to provide extra plants. What sort of flowers did lady flower arrangers prefer? she wondered.

"Bring in a couple of buckets for the Easter weekend," he said. "We can see how they sell. Good morning, Miss Purcell."

She was giggling like a schoolgirl as she drove out of town. The whole incident was ridiculous. "My sister, the flower seller," Julia had said. Well, why not? It would be interesting to try something new and the money would be useful, heaven knows. Not only had she the cost of setting up and keeping the orchids to consider, but since last week Tony to pay too. Eleven pence an hour was the standard rate these days; he had shown her the page in the *County Gazette* which gave it. Her admiration and amusement at his initiative had not stopped her from beating him down to ninepence – he was only thirteen, after all – but even ninepence an hour would quickly mount up. She was relieved that Mr Cole had made no mention of payment. She must have a word with Mrs Whitelaw as soon as possible, as well as get Covent Garden prices for more than just orchids from Julia, so that she could bargain with Mr Cole too, if need be.

Tony was sweeping the courtyard when she reached Hillcrest. A row of shoes gleamed by the back door. "Waite said I could do the routine jobs while he got on in the garden," he said. "I've never cleaned shoes before. Annie had to show me how. He wants us to fetch the glass for the greenhouse this afternoon. It'll need washing before he can use it, he said."

The three of them went down to Mrs Whitelaw after

lunch. Waite had already brought back the wood of the greenhouse; only the glass remained to be collected. "Do take care," Gwen begged Tony as he and she wrapped each piece in sacking before putting it into the car, terrified that he might do something frightful that she would have to confess to Frances.

Mrs Whitelaw had no idea what money she might expect for orchid spikes. "Alfred gave it all to the chapel, you see. They paid for a new roof, did his orchids. Well, nearly all of it." She brightened up at the memory; there was pride in her voice.

Tony took his role as gardener's assistant seriously. He even took sandwiches to eat out in the stables with Waite.

Gwen was anxious. "Don't let him bother you," she told Waite. "He can eat in the kitchen perfectly well."

"Don't you worry, Miss Purcell," Waite said. "I've given him what for before now and I'll do it again if need be. He's all right, is Master Tony. He's growing up."

She was intrigued. Did they sit in silence? If they talked, what did they talk about?

"His experiences in the war," Tony said when she asked him. "He was in Mesopotamia first of all. At Kut, he said. When he came back from there he was sent to France. He hates the Turks. The Germans were all right, he says, but the Turks were awful."

Gwen was amazed. Waite never talked of his past life, not even to Annie, a sympathetic character if ever there was one. That he should talk to Tony, when there were so many years between them... Yet was it so surprising? She was discovering herself how companionable a thirteen-year-old could be. Sometimes she almost forgot that Tony and she were of a different generation.

Occasionally, however, as when they went up onto the Quantocks to gather moss for the orchids' repotting, Tony reverted to normal schoolboy behaviour, scrambling up slopes and sliding down them, to the detriment of his trousers, teetering along the tops of walls, trying to swing from the branches of one beech tree to the branches of the next and devouring Annie's picnic with a speed that made Gwen blink.

He gave a sigh of pleasure when he finished, rubbing sticky hands clean on his jacket. "Did you have picnics up here a lot when you were a girl, Aunt Gwen?"

She shook her head. "We didn't have a car in those days. Your mother came up here often to paint. And your father loved walking over the Quantocks. Do you know, Tony, I was thinking the other day, he may say he spent all his spare time with his nose in a book, but that's not how I remember him. I remember him walking for miles and miles. Twenty or thirty miles a day he'd do before the war, over here and Exmoor and the Blackdowns, without thinking anything of it."

Tony was quiet. "It's difficult to imagine, isn't it?"

"I suppose it must be." Could a child whose father was crippled ever visualize him as anything else? she wondered. She said gently, "Life's been very hard on your father, you know."

He nodded. After a moment he said, "What about Uncle Antony? Did he walk too? Or did he always cycle?"

"It depended on whether he could borrow George's bicycle. He did come up here sometimes, I know. There was one wonderful day when we all did, all eight of us together. Two days, in fact. We spent the night in a barn and then walked to the sea." Such wonderful days they had been, those days before the war ruined everyone's life.

"Aunt Gwen?"

She came back to the present. "Yes?"

"I said, what was Uncle Antony *really* like?"

"I don't know, Tony. It was all so long ago."

"Did you like him?"

"Yes, of course I liked him."

"Why of course? Rowena and I are cousins, which is the same sort of thing, isn't it, but I wouldn't say we're friends exactly."

"Oh, I see. Well, I liked him. I liked him a lot."

A band of pain ringed her chest. Loved him too, she thought, but what good was that, to him or to me?

The greenhouse was slowly taking shape. She and Waite had decided on a three-quarter span, the design that let in the most light, and the one, according to Waite, that made most use of the wood and glass available. She had had to supplement both but not with much, while the combined staging from Mr Whitelaw and the Rectory had provided all the shelving needed. The building took longer than planned, largely because Waite had one of his turns and was away for two days, but the result was better than Gwen could have hoped for. Standing inside the completed house for the first time, she realized that though still apprehensive about her competence she had accepted that she was now an orchid grower.

Tony helped her gather up the plants from their various temporary homes, some already at Hillcrest, scattered about the house on north-facing window sills, some being nervously cared for by the Mackenzies at the Rectory. Most were still with Mrs Whitelaw, however, and several journeys were needed to carry them back to Hillcrest.

Mrs Whitelaw grew more tearful with each visit. She clutched Gwen's hand when Gwen prepared to leave for the last time. "If there's anything I can do to help, you've only to ask. Not that I'm an authority like Alfred was, but you know that already."

"I know. And thank you for all your help. You'll come and see them sometimes, won't you?" She prayed that none would have died in the meantime.

"There's someone up beyond Bristol if you ever need advice," Mrs Whitelaw said. "A Mr Alexander. He had the best collection of orchids Alfred said he had ever seen."

Gwen smiled. "I'll remember that. Goodbye then, Mrs Whitelaw, and thank you."

Mrs Whitelaw nodded. She had shrunk visibly in the past few weeks. "It's so dreadful not to be needed," she said.

"Mama would be quite happy not to be needed," Tony observed as he and Gwen approached Hillcrest. "It would mean she could get on with her painting."

She thought about his words for the rest of the day. That there was truth in them, she knew, but it hurt her that he should see it. Should she try to explain? she wondered. Or was it wiser to say nothing? In the end she waited until evening when Tony and she went up to the hill crest to round up the hens for the night.

"You know what you said earlier, Tony, about your mother not needing people?" She tried to keep her voice light. "It's not true, you know. She wouldn't have married your father if that's how she felt, now would she? I know it's difficult for ordinary people to understand people like her, but painting's her life. She can't help it. That's how she is."

"She's started doing abstracts now," Tony said. "They're

weird. Even Dad's not sure about them." He dashed off after a hen that was squawking away in the wrong direction. "Come back, you *stupid* bird. Do you want a fox to come and bite off your head?"

She watched him zigzag over the grass in the dusk. How strange children were. Had she helped the situation, or made matters worse? And how could you explain the difference between talent and genius to someone who had never experienced the need to create?

Once the orchids were in place Tony helped Gwen instead of Waite. She sat him down to make a list of the plants she now owned – a rash move, she couldn't help thinking, when she considered the quality of his writing. "Try and write neatly, and do take care with the spelling," she begged. "Just copy what Mr Whitelaw has put on the label."

"What about this one? All it's got is a question mark. So's this. There are three altogether. One's bigger than the others."

"That's probably the strongest. I don't know anything about them, except that Mr Whitelaw bred them himself. They haven't flowered yet, so we shall have to look after them until they do. Mr Whitelaw was very insistent I should have them, so I suppose he thought they were special. We shall have to wait and see."

"What shall I call them, then? I know." He licked the pencil tip and started writing.

"Question Mark," she read, and smiled. "Why not? It's as good a name as any."

Once he had finished the list, more or less legibly, Gwen set him to chop up fibre for repotting – a task so unpleasant that she felt quite guilty, though he was better able to do it than she, his wrist being stronger. "What horrible stuff," he said, coughing in the dust he had raised. "It's terribly tough. What ever is it?"

"Roots of the osmunda fern. From Japan, I think. Orchids have very fleshy roots; they rot in ordinary composts. You have to be careful about overwatering, Mrs Whitelaw says. I think that's what frightens me. Suppose she comes up to admire her husband's orchids and they've all rotted away."

"Or died because you haven't watered them enough." He grinned at his aunt. "Go on, Aunt Gwen. You are funny. You're a wonderful gardener. Dad's always saying so."

"Is he?" Gwen said, astonished. "That's nice of him."

"Mrs Whitelaw was talking to you about spikes. What did she mean? Do orchids have spikes like roses?"

"No, no. A spike is the stem that the flowers grow on. You usually get seven or eight flowers on each spike. Each flower can be used on its own, in a bridal bouquet, perhaps, or on a corsage – you know what that is, don't you? It's a flower arrangement ladies pin to their ball gowns. They make good presents too. Aunt Sarah has orchids given to her when she sails for India. The flowers last for weeks, you see, which makes them suitable for long voyages. Though I don't know how they survive places like the Red Sea. I must remember to ask her sometime."

"It's very satisfying, isn't it, looking round all this and thinking that there was nothing here three weeks ago."

"I suppose it is." He's right, she was thinking. I can almost feel excited myself.

"Do you think Mother and Dad will be impressed by all we've done?"

"*You've* done," Gwen corrected him. "Of course they

will, even if they don't say so." She prayed that Frances and Gabriel would make the right responses. Perhaps she should have a word with them first. "I'm impressed anyway. I couldn't have achieved all this without you."

Chapter Nine

"False alarm," Tony said, coming disconsolately in from the veranda. He sighed. "I really did think it was them. They're dreadfully late. What do you think can have happened?"

"We don't know what time they left," Gwen said, "so we can't tell when they'll arrive. Don't worry, love. They'll come." She smiled at her nephew, noting the clean shirt and tie, as well as his slicked-down hair. She prayed that his parents would appreciate the effort he had taken over his appearance – and without prompting on her part. Even his socks were at the correct level, temporarily at least. Only his hands let him down. "Do you think you could do something about your nails?" she said. "I know I'm not one to talk, but your father's never dirtied his hands in his life and he does notice such things. It looks as if there's oil on your fingers. Have you been helping Waite with the mower?"

Tony crimsoned, muttered something unintelligible and rushed from the room. He was still upstairs when the sound of a car in the lane outside heralded the arrival of his parents. "They're here! They're here!" He crashed down the stairs like a small avalanche. "You will let me show them the greenhouse, won't you?" he cried as he disappeared out of the back door.

"Lord help us!" Annie exclaimed in the kitchen. "There won't be anything of the house left by the time we've got rid of the lad."

Gwen gave him time alone with his parents. When she joined them he was still jumping up and down as he described in minute detail every stage of the greenhouse's construction. "And *then*, when it was all finished, we had to fetch the orchids..."

Frances smiled at Gwen. "Doesn't he look well!" she said. "I'm sure he's grown inches. Has he worn you out?"

"If he has," Gabriel said, "she'll be much too polite to say so." He smiled at Gwen, transferred his sticks to one arm and gave her a hug with the other. "I hope he's behaved. No broken windows this time?"

"Oh, Dad!" Tony said in disgust, quickly adding, "Anyway, it doesn't matter any more. Waite's showed me how to fix glass. Now I can mend any window I break."

"I trust you don't think that gives you a free hand to do what you want with a cricket ball," his father said drily.

"He's worked terribly hard," Gwen said, anxious to divert attention from past misdemeanours. "I don't know what I'd have done without him. Are you tired? What sort of journey have you had? Come in and relax. I told your mother we'd give you tea before you went over to the Rectory, Gabriel, so she won't be expecting you yet."

She poured out the tea and sat back, wishing, as she watched the family together, that Tony did not feel the need to try quite so hard to please. He pressed sandwiches, fruitcake, second and third cups of tea on Gabriel and Frances, who looked as though they would rather sit back and talk. Impatience got the better of him at last. "Have you finished? Please come and look." He tugged at his mother's hand. "I want you to see what I've done."

Gabriel smiled as he watched them go through the French windows, but made no move to follow. "Everything been all right, Gwen? No problems?"

She knew what he meant. "He's been wonderful, really good company, and such a hard worker. Even Waite's been full of praise."

"It's nice to hear something favourable. His school report was dreadful. I could understand when I read it why he was so anxious to come here for the holidays. Devious, they called him. Frances was very upset. Deviousness could never be considered a Purcell trait. Rather the reverse, I'd have said."

"Tony – devious?" Gwen was shocked. "How can they say such a thing? Do you think the school's all right? I mean, it's the last word I'd have used about Tony. He's always so open with me." Except, she couldn't help thinking with a sinking feeling in her stomach, over his need for money.

"I'm afraid," Gabriel said, "that Tony and I are going to have to have a serious talk."

"Not on your first day," Gwen begged. "Let it wait. He's been so looking forward to your coming."

"We'll see. Now, are you going to show me these orchids of yours?"

She was amused by the reactions of her sister and brother-in-law, seeing them as typical of their different characters.

"You're mad," was Frances's opinion. "Not that I don't admit that all this is very impressive, but how you can contemplate taking such a lot on, I cannot imagine. Still, they'll be fun to paint. Let me know when they start flowering and I'll come down at once. In fact, there's something about them even now. Do you mind if I sit and paint in here while we're staying?"

Gabriel had greater sympathy for Gwen's point of view, understanding why she should feel indebted to Mr Whitelaw, but worried that she was taking on more than she could handle. "We're none of us getting any younger, alas. You don't want to wear yourself out."

Julia, her husband David, and Rowena and Andrew arrived for the Easter weekend sufficiently early for Julia to help Gwen in the choice of flowers to take into Taunton. Mr Cole had asked for daffodils, but such a late Easter meant that the daffodils at Hillcrest were almost over. However, narcissi were flowering in quantity, as were the tulips. Rowena helped with the bunching of lilies of the valley, anemones and primulas, while Julia suggested taking some plants from the greenhouse – streptocarpi, gardenias, the last of the freesias.

"I think he'd like those," she said. "They're the sort of thing people give to grannies and maiden aunts at Easter."

Gwen wedged the buckets between the seats of the car, thinking how fresh and colourful they looked. Refusing Julia's offer of moral support – "Thank you, but I'd rather do it on my own" – she set off for Taunton with some trepidation. She carried everything into Cole & Son with an assurance she did not feel.

Mr Cole greeted her with surprise, as if he had not expected her to turn up, expressed regret at the lack of daffodils but seemed reasonably pleased with the rest of her offerings, and said he looked forward to receiving more in due course.

Gwen drove home, still shaking, but triumphant, to find the family waiting on the veranda.

"What happened?"

"Was he pleased?"

"Did he pay you?" That was Tony.

Gwen was momentarily downcast. "I forgot to ask about that. How stupid. I was nervous, that was the trouble."

"It won't matter," Gabriel said. "Just present him with an invoice at the end of the month. It's probably the best way to do it, anyway. He'll realize then that he's dealing with a professional. It gives you the whip hand over prices as well."

Gwen laughed. "Me, a professional? How ridiculous."

She was entertained by the whole episode. Thankful, as well. Having had to spend so much money during the last month she found it a relief to know that cash would be coming in. Covent Garden prices quoted by Julia had come as a surprise – threepence halfpenny for a simple bunch of anemones, for instance, while lilies of the valley, which grew like weeds under the wall by the pear tree at Hillcrest, apparently sold at Covent Garden for up to two shillings a bunch. Selling flowers might not make her a fortune, but it would certainly help with the expense of the orchids.

Later Gabriel took Gwen to one side and pressed a couple of notes into her hand. "I know you'll say you don't want them. You're all the same when it comes to money, you Purcells, but I insist. Boys of his age are permanently hungry, and I'm not having you out of pocket because of my son's appetite."

"We do grow the food," Gwen protested.

"Even so. Buy something you want. Clothes. Things you

need for the orchids."

"I can't take your money," Gwen said. "You know that Frances contributes to Hillcrest funds."

"To Hillcrest's upkeep, that's all. Not to the upkeep of a hungry thirteen-year-old."

"It's not as if Tony's been idle. He has been working."

"I know, and I want to thank you for that. It's done him good. Frances and I were saying only last night how much more sensible he seems. More responsible somehow."

"I've enjoyed having him. He's been good company." She wondered what Gabriel would say if he knew Tony's true cost. Not that she regretted the outlay. She could not have achieved all that she had in the past month without Tony's help. Tony had benefited too. She knew that he had enjoyed his visit, despite – or perhaps because of – the hard work. He had said as much, before asking whether he could do the same during the summer.

"I'd love to have you, Tony, but your parents..."

"Please, Aunt Gwen. Just for a week or two? There'll be lots I can do. You know there will."

"Well... Perhaps we should discuss it nearer the time."

"It's just like old times," Mrs Mackenzie said, gazing with quiet satisfaction at the families gathered round the Rectory dining table for lunch on Easter Day. "The house seems so quiet these days with only the three of us here."

"Children have always married and moved away, my dear," Mr Mackenzie said as he set about carving the saddle of lamb. "It's the natural pattern of life."

"To the next village, maybe, or even the next town. Not to Cambridge and London."

"I'm still here, Mother," Lucy said. There was an edge to

113

her voice that made Gwen look up in surprise.

"At least we're near enough to come back often," Julia said quickly. "Imagine if we'd all gone to India."

There was another similiarity today with the old days, Gwen couldn't help thinking, as she listened to the three men deploring the present situation in Europe and remembered how Gabriel had talked in his youth.

"Conscription in Germany, Italian troops preparing to advance over the border..."

"Ah, yes," Mr Mackenzie said quickly, "but it's the Abyssinian border. Scarcely as important as the Belgian border, surely, or the French. At least the Maginot Line will prevent a recurrence of 1914."

"I'm not so sure," Gabriel said. "Germany wants her old territories back. If she can't get them by peaceful means..." He gave a despairing shrug.

"Germany's rearming her air force," Tony said. Seeing the surprised faces turned towards him he added defensively, "I've read about it in the newspaper."

"I'm glad to see you're taking an interest in current affairs," said his grandfather. "I'm afraid I'm growing old. I find it difficult to understand what's going on in Germany these days. This fellow Hitler..."

"It's all much exaggerated by foreign journalists," Gabriel said. "Or so I'm told by the German professor I used to visit before the war. On the other hand he does admit that he's turned his back on the world and retreated into the Bavarian mountains, where he goes for weeks without seeing a soul, so I'm not certain how much trust one should put in what he says."

"I didn't know you were still in touch with that family," Mrs Mackenzie said.

"I wasn't, until Ebert wrote to me last Christmas. A surprise, that. We hadn't had any contact since I left Germany in 1919. He didn't want me to think all Germans agreed with what Hitler was doing, he said, and insisted that ordinary life was going on as usual. He even invited me to stay so that I could see for myself. Extraordinary, really. Why should it matter to him what I think? Which reminds me, Gwen. Apparently he's building up an orchid collection in his eyrie. It's all he cares about, as far as I can make out. If you want to know anything about orchids, get in touch with him. He'll know everything about them. He was always thorough."

Gwen was amused. "Are you suggesting that I should take German lessons? Or are you offering your services as a translator?"

"You wouldn't need one. His English is perfect. I was very put out when I discovered that after the war. He'd always given me the impression he didn't know a word of the language. Heaven knows what he overheard in the old days. I always assumed I was safe talking to the family in my own tongue."

Easter was not only a religious festival and a time for family reunion. At the Rectory it marked a more sombre occasion, the anniversary of Antony's death. Every year the two families gathered round the churchyard cross, raised to the memory of all those in Huish Priory who had died in the war, for a brief service of remembrance, not only of Antony, but also of Geoffrey, killed in 1917.

Gwen had never been able to understand the need for anniversaries. Ten years, fifteen, twenty – what did it matter? The past was gone, like last year's summer, withered, faded. Out of last autumn's dead plant shoot this year's growth. She would have preferred to remember the occasion alone at Hillcrest, among the butterflies and the cordon trees that she had planted after reading Geoffrey's descriptions of fruit growing in France.

This year the morning was sunless and grey. A chill wind fluttered the hem of Mr Mackenzie's surplice as he stood, pale and gaunt, reading from the Gospel. "'Greater love hath no man...'"

Gwen kept her eyes firmly fixed on the letters incised in the plinth below the cross. Twenty-four names in all; twenty-four men gone for ever from a village of three hundred. Only names to Tony and Rowena and Andrew, but men to her, men whose faces she could see now as clearly as she had on the day they left the village for the last time: jolly Bert Hawkins, whom Annie had hoped to marry, handsome David Hancock, young Dick Chedzoy... She had been frightened of Dick Chedzoy as a child, she remembered, so swarthy, and threatening as she had imagined only a pirate could be. Her sympathies had been with the Germans he might meet – misguided sympathy, as it turned out, for it was they who killed him in the end. Poor George Cross, with the soft voice and slow smile, who had been blown up the week before the Armistice by the bomb he was trying to dismantle. Then there were the others whose names should have been there, but were not, like that of Bill Roberts, whose grave was so recent it was no more than a mound of red earth beyond the large yew. Above all, Geoffrey, quiet, kind Geoffrey, who might have married Julia had he survived, and become Gwen's brother-in-law instead of David Elliot, whom Julia had married after the war. And Antony. Always Antony.

She was cold. Her body ached. She looked up – and felt pain clutch her heart.

Antony.

Except that it was Tony, not Antony, who was watching her, his smile affectionate, amused, almost mischievous. "Dear Grandpa, how he does go on." She could hear the words as clearly as if he had spoken them aloud: the words Antony so often used when deploring the length of his father's sermons.

A strange thing, heredity. Plants reproduced year after year without change, yet family likenesses were greeted with surprise by each generation. Gwen had never seen anything in Tony of his dead uncle – not until now. In the past days she had several times glimpsed the Antony she remembered in his nephew: in mannerisms rather than looks, in the way he shook the hair out of his eyes, in his sudden stillness when his attention was caught, in the occasional teasing smile as if secretly amused by what she had said or done.

Was it Tony's curiosity about his uncle that had brought Antony to mind, she wondered, or the fact that today Tony was as old as Antony had been at their first meeting? Or was it only her imagination that had conjured up Antony's image?

"'And some there be, which have no memorial; who are perished, as though they had never been; and are become as though they had never been born; and their children after them.'"

The pain intensified. A life's promise, ended in a few minutes' fighting. The waste of it. The waste. What might Antony have done had he lived; what might he have become?

Honoured in his generation ... the glory of his time?

No one would ever know.

Chapter Ten

"Bright lad, your nephew," Jim Harrison said when Gwen took her car into the garage for a decoke before her London visit.

She looked at him blankly. "I beg your pardon?"

"He's all right, is your nephew," said Jim.

"Tony? Has he been here? He didn't tell me."

"Came down here most afternoons. Oh, not for long. Half an hour – an hour at most. Wanted to learn about engines, he said. I told him to hang around, watch what was going on. He and Willy Roberts got on like a house on fire."

"Well…" Gwen was at a loss for words. "I hope he didn't get in your way."

"Don't you worry, Miss Purcell," Jim said cheerfully. "Any trouble and I'd have had him out on his backside, quick as a flash."

"Yes, well. I'm sorry," Gwen said – feebly she couldn't help thinking. What would Tony do next? "I'll see it doesn't happen again."

Willy Roberts, Bill's eldest son, was changing the wheel of a van in the courtyard as she went out. He looked up and gave her a nod. "Afternoon, Miss Purcell."

Briefly she wondered what a twenty-year-old and a boy of thirteen could have in common. "Good afternoon, Willy. How's your mother these days?"

"Not too good. Don't do nothing but sit and wish Father were still here."

"I did ask her whether she'd be prepared to give us a hand with the ironing at Hillcrest. We could do with some help and it would get her out of the house. Besides, Annie – Miss Sampford – would welcome the company. Could you persuade her, do you think?"

"I'll do me best," he promised.

Walking back up the hill, Gwen stopped on impulse and walked down the Rectory drive. Mr Mackenzie would be taking morning prayers at the school, Mrs Mackenzie still planning the day's meals with Cook. With luck she would be able to talk to Lucy on her own. She could. Lucy came out onto the front doorstep.

"Tell me," Gwen said. "When Tony was here during the holidays, what time did he come over to you?"

"When he'd finished work with you, I suppose. Half past fourish? I know we had to put tea back till after five so that he wouldn't be late. Why?"

"I made him stop work at three thirty," Gwen said. "I didn't want to be a slave driver. I thought he should have some free time – and time to spend with you and your parents as well."

"Three thirty?" said Lucy. "He certainly didn't come over as early as that. What do you think he could have been doing?"

"Jim Harrison's just told me that Tony went down to the garage every afternoon. You didn't know anything about it?"

"I knew nothing. How strange. Why the garage?"

"He told Jim he was interested in engines."

"Interested in engines? Tony?" There was disbelief in her voice.

The school's verdict returned unbidden to Gwen's mind. *Devious*. No. Not Tony. Surely not Tony.

"I'd better not say anything to Mother and Father," Lucy said at last. "They'd only worry. Will you mention it to Frances when you write? Or say something when he comes down in the summer?"

"I don't know. I might see what Julia thinks when I'm staying with her next week."

Twice a year Gwen drove up to London to stay with Julia, taking with her the bedding plants she had grown for Julia's window boxes and tubs. Though she enjoyed herself once there, she always dreaded the visits beforehand. She did not like being away from Hillcrest, and she hated long-distance driving. This year the orchids made her even more reluctant to leave.

"I rue the day you took them things on," Annie said, frowning over Gwen's detailed instructions for their care. "A worry they've been from the start. Besides, 'tis Mr Waite sees to things outside, not me."

"And he will this time, of course he will. He'll look after the orchids when he's here during the day. It's just that if the greenhouse gets too hot before he arrives he'll find it hard to get the temperature down. It isn't much extra, Annie, really it isn't."

"Hmm," said Annie with disbelief.

Waite was equally put out, though he said little. His mouth set in a thin line. "If I'm looking after them orchids

I shan't have time to plant out the brassica."

"It's only for three days, Waite."

There was another problem about staying with Julia: what to wear. Gwen had never given much thought to her dress – what was the point, when most of her time was spent in the garden? – but she recognized that London was smart. Even Julia, who at Hillcrest dressed casually and never wore make-up, wore clothes in her own home as stylish as any, thus causing Gwen agonies of indecision as to what she should pack for her stay. This year she had even wandered round dress shops in Taunton after making a delivery of flowers to Cole's, in an attempt to find something new, but had baulked at paying forty-two shillings for a dress she knew she would rarely wear. She reassured herself with the thought that the shortness of this month's visit – two nights was as long as she felt able to leave the orchids – meant there would be little time for entertaining or going out. Perhaps there was something to be said for orchids after all, she decided as she drove across the open landscape of Salisbury Plain.

She reached Julia's house by late afternoon, surprised as always after a long journey that she had reached her destination without accident or misadventure. ("Why are you so tense?" Julia's husband, David, used to ask when teaching her to drive. "Try to relax." A command impossible to obey.) Andrew was returning from school as she drew up outside the house, looking so hot and uncomfortable in his grey flannel suit that Gwen scarcely recognized the child who hid himself in hedges and crawled over the ground while birdwatching in Somerset.

His face lit up at the sight of the car. "Aunt Gwen!" he shouted as he ran towards her. "How are you? How's

Hillcrest?" The words tumbled over each other in his hurry to get out the questions. "Have the house martins hatched? What's happening to the orchids? Can I help with your things? Goodness, what a lot of plants."

"They're for your window boxes. It would be wonderful if you could help take them down to the basement."

"It won't take me a minute," he said as he folded down the front seat and scrambled into the back of the car. In fact it took rather longer for him to pass the seed trays and pots of plants to Gwen on the pavement, and longer still for the two of then to carry everything down the steps to the basement. He was just crossing the pavement with the last pot of marguerites clasped to his chest when Julia came out from the house.

"I thought I heard voices... Oh, Andrew, *must* you do that in your school uniform?"

"It's all right," Gwen reassured her. "It's only earth. It'll brush off when it's dry."

Pleasure at Gwen's arrival quickly replaced worry about dirty uniform. "Come along in. Are you dying for tea? How was the journey?"

"All right," Gwen said, sinking into an armchair and wondering, as she invariably did at the end of a journey, why she had worked herself into such a state before its beginning. "The country looked wonderful. I really do think spring is my favourite time of year."

Andrew was eager to drag her upstairs and show off the stuffed owl that was his latest acquisition. "It's wonderful," Gwen said, inwardly shuddering at the thought of finding that watching you in the middle of the night.

"I've decided what I'm going to be when I grow up," he told her, solemnly. "I'm going to be an orni ... ornithologist."

"That sounds interesting. Though I'm not quite certain what an ornithologist does."

"Neither am I, not exactly, but I think he draws birds."

Rowena insisted on helping Gwen unpack, pirouetting across the bedroom as she did so, eager to demonstrate the latest steps she had learnt in her ballet class. Nowadays her feet seemed to be permanently set at a quarter to three, and her conversation dotted with extraordinary names, most of them ending in "ova". There were times when Gwen felt embarrassingly ignorant. She looked Gwen's dress up and down as she hung it up in the wardrobe. "Haven't I seen this one before, Aunt Gwen?"

"You know you have. You see it every year."

David, pale and tired, arrived home late for dinner. "I'm sorry. I'm sorry. Something cropped up at the hospital. You know how it is. Lovely to see you, Gwen. How are the orchids?"

"They were all right when I left. I hope nothing dire's happened since."

"And the flower selling?"

"That's all right too. Amazing, really. Mr Cole buys everything I take in. I was very glad that I was able to quote the Covent Garden prices Julia had sent me. It meant I could bargain. Not that he agreed immediately, even then. He told me I couldn't expect London rates in Somerset."

"I'd have thought there was something in that," David said.

"Well, yes, except that anything sold at Covent Garden has had to travel for goodness knows how long, whereas everything I take in has only travelled seven miles."

"So?"

"We compromised. In fact, I thought I did rather well."

"Good for you."

There was admiration in his voice. Gwen herself had been surprised by her temerity in standing up to someone she suspected might have bullied her, had she not had the prices in her hand.

"I've found someone else who might be interested in buying your orchids," Julia said.

"Really?"

"A Mrs Meyer. She runs a flower shop near here. Not your run-of-the-mill flower shop, I might add. She arranges flowers for big displays and special occasions, that sort of thing. I paint some of her arrangements now and then. She does the ones for the consulting-rooms at Harley Street; that's how we met. She's quite a character. I was telling her about your orchids and she said that if you had any to spare... I hope you don't mind, but I promised you'd go and talk to her. The shop's called Maximilian's Floral Decorations. I don't know where the Maximilian comes from."

"It's her husband's name," Rowena said. "He's a refugee. They both are. He hasn't been able to find work in England, and they've run out of money for food, so his wife's had to go out to work. She's always been good with flowers, so that's what she decided to do..."

"Really, Rowena," Julia said. "You're worse than Sarah for making things up. Mrs Meyer has been living in England for years now, long before there was trouble in Germany. In any case, she's Viennese, and Vienna's in Austria, not Germany. Don't they teach you any geography these days?"

Gwen was amused. "Rowena's become very serious all of a sudden," she said after her niece had gone up to bed.

Julia sighed. "Everything's so dramatic where she's concerned. I'm beginning to wonder whether ballet lessons were a good idea after all. As for her interest in refugees, that's my doing, I'm afraid. David asked me to have a couple of them round for a meal. The husband's a professor of medicine David's known for some time; he and David work in the same field. In fact it was David's department who helped him and his wife come here when he was sacked from his university for being Jewish. We don't usually let Rowena stay up when we have visitors but this time I did. The wife doesn't speak English and Rowena learns German at school; I thought she might be able to help keep the conversation going. It was a sticky evening even so. Rowena's been intense about refugees ever since. She's trying to raise funds at school to help. And it is dreadful. This chap's a potential Nobel Prize winner, according to David, but works as a lab technician, because that's all the hospital can afford to pay him."

"It sounds extraordinary," Gwen said. "You can't sack a university professor because he's Jewish, surely?"

Julia shrugged. "You can in Germany apparently. Both Klee and Kandinsky have been dismissed from their posts, if you remember."

"That's different. It won't stop them painting, will it? In fact, it'll give them more time. Which reminds me – how's your painting going?"

Julia's preference had always been for portraiture, though in the past she had painted still lifes as well. Nowadays she concentrated on portraits of children, and at the moment had several commissions to paint school-friends of Andrew. Earnest small boys gazed wide-eyed from the canvases she brought out to show Gwen. "It's a wonderful age, eight to ten," she said. "They're so serious. And so confiding – their mothers would die if they knew how many family secrets were being let out during the sitting." She painted other children too, down at a Settlement in the East End of London, where she helped run the Mothers and Babies Club. No formal portraits these, but quick sketches and colour washes done whenever she had a free moment.

"I've been painting flowers again," she told Gwen. "For Mrs Meyer. We have an agreement. I paint her arrangements whenever she wants, and she lets me have any flowers left over at the weekend to take down to the Settlement. The mothers love them; they don't have much colour in their lives, poor things."

Gwen sometimes suspected, but never asked, that a good proportion of the contents of Julia's weekly hamper from Hillcrest found its way to London's East End.

Next morning Julia helped Gwen empty window boxes and tubs of spring bedding and replace them with flowers brought up from Hillcrest.

"You are good to spend so much of your time on this when you've got more than enough on your plate with the orchids," she said. "Don't ever feel that you have to do it, though, will you? We can always buy plants, if need be. And don't forget, you're calling on Mrs Meyer this afternoon. I promised I'd send you along."

Gwen walked past Maximilian's Floral Decorations the first time, despite Julia's directions. She had been looking for a grander version of Cole & Son; it never occurred to her that the huge plate glass window with nothing but an alabaster urn behind it, spilling flowers and foliage in a waterfall of greens, creams and whites, could front a florist's shop.

Having discovered her mistake and retraced her steps, she stood in front of the window, staring at the flowers in amazement. They gave the impression of an Old Master painting rather than a flower arrangement. It was not only their profusion she found so remarkable, but their variety – creamy rhubarb flowers, heads of cow parsley, anthurium and strelitzia leaves – and the way they were put together, with different kinds of clematis spilling over the rim and onto the floor. How did it all stay in place?

"Chicken wire," Mrs Meyer said. "See," and she gently moved the foliage apart at the back to reveal wire netting fixed over the mouth of the urn. "We put that there first, and make sure it is hidden before we finish."

She was shorter than Gwen and stout, with ginger hair, streaked with white, that stood out from her head like a halo. Her speech was heavily accented, her gestures expansive, as she welcomed Gwen with every indication of pleasure. "I have been so looking forward, Miss Purcell... Come in. Do come in. We will go through to the back so we can talk."

Anything less like Cole & Son would have been hard to imagine. The shopfront was open and uncluttered, the walls whitewashed, the floor black and white square tiles. Half a dozen arrangements, presumably awaiting collection or delivery, stood on the counter, all as idiosyncratic as the one in the window and, like it, including flowers and foliage that Gwen would never have considered suitable for an arrangement – foliage from shrubs, flowers from the hedgerow, even weeds... Unsuitable, possibly, but wonderfully striking.

Two girls were working in the back room when Gwen was ushered through, one at the sink – "Sylvia," Mrs Meyer said, waving an arm in her direction – and one flattening rose stems on the draining board – "Patricia." The scent of the roses floated over to Gwen as she stood looking around her.

127

Floral paintings by Dutch Old Masters decorated the walls. A high table stood in the middle of the room. Mrs Meyer sat down on a stool, pulled up another and gave it a pat. "Come, Miss Purcell." She rolled the r. "Tell me about yourself."

Gwen felt a strong desire to giggle. She had expected a straightforward business discussion, such as she had had with Mr Cole. She had imagined nothing like this. "I don't know where to start."

"You are Mrs Elliot's sister. And you have a collection of orchids."

That made it easier. She told Mrs Meyer how she had come to take on the collection and explained about the need for money, however little, to help pay for the cost of their upkeep. So sympathetic was Mrs Meyer that Gwen found herself revealing far more than she had intended, confessing her ignorance of their cultivation ("though I am learning, of course") and her fear of betraying Mr Whitelaw's trust. "I'm sorry," she said at last. "I'm talking too much. I don't know why I should tell you all this."

"No, no," Mrs Meyer said. "I am interested." She always needed orchids, she said. "For the ships, of course – Southampton, Tilbury – but also for patients. Here, we are near Harley Street. There are nursing homes. And hotels in this area, too."

Gwen began to feel alarmed. Mrs Meyer sounded far more demanding than Mr Cole. "I'm very inexperienced," she said. "I don't even know how many spikes I'm likely to have. I wouldn't want you to get the wrong impression."

But Mrs Meyer patted Gwen's knee and said she didn't think she was getting the wrong impression. She was prepared to wait and see, she said. She talked about transport, advised Gwen about packing orchids for travel. When she mentioned payment Gwen was surprised to hear herself say that she would leave Mrs Meyer to decide the price. She did not doubt that Mrs Meyer was as businesslike as Mr Cole, but she liked and trusted her. She was prepared to argue with Mr Cole, where she was not with Mrs Meyer.

She was just deciding, reluctantly but not wanting to overstay her welcome, that it was time to leave when Mrs Meyer said, "You will stay for tea," and sent Sylvia out to buy cream cakes.

Over coffee and cake the conversation became more general. They discovered a mutual interest in the work of Gertrude Jekyll, in flower painting and in particular the Dutch Old Masters, with their mixture of flowers and fruit. "They cheat, though," Gwen said. "My sister – not Julia, but another one – was very keen that we should copy Old Masters when we were young. I remember trying to copy that de Heem you have there and being terribly disillusioned when I realized he couldn't possibly have painted it from life because there were flowers and fruit from different seasons in it."

"I have a confession to make, Miss Purcell," Mrs Meyer admitted, forking the last crumb of gateau into her mouth. "It is not only your orchids that interest me. Tell me about your garden." She wanted to know the plants Gwen grew, the varieties of trees and shrubs that flourished at Hillcrest. She made large arrangements, she said, like the one in the window, arrangements for hotels, for business firms, for conferences. Although she could, and did, buy flowers from Covent Garden, "they have nothing there that is unusual. Covent Garden is for florists. But I am not a florist. You must not call me a florist. A florist is someone who says sweet peas must have gypsophilia and carnations asparagus fern." She raised her hands as if in horror. "*Pah!* No, I am an artist, like you. I paint pictures with flowers. I will show you."

She opened a drawer in the table and pulled out paintings which Gwen immediately recognized as Julia's work. Unlike Gwen's meticulous studies, Julia's paintings of flowers were fluid watercolours where colours and shapes ran into each other. These were of arrangements, like that in the window, presumably Mrs Meyer's work in the past.

"Your sister paints when I ask her," Mrs Meyer explained, "so I may show the arrangements to possible clients. Some people don't like, you see. They say, you can't use this flower or that flower…"

"Like cow parsley?" Gwen suggested, remembering the alabaster urn.

"Like cow parsley," Mrs Meyer agreed. "So then I know they will not like what I do. So sorry, I say, but you must find a florist. Plenty of florists in London, you won't find it difficult, but me, I am a decorator. Floral decorations, that's what I do. Look at those paintings, Miss Purcell. See what you think."

Gwen went slowly through them, admiring Julia's skill, but admiring even more the originality of Mrs Meyer's choice of colour and shape and form.

"It is difficult for me, living in London, to find the material I need." Mrs Meyer was watching Gwen closely. "Foliage especially. Now, you have a large garden, so Mrs Elliot tells me, and you are an artist. You see there in the paintings the sort of thing I like. Would you be interested in sending material up from the country? I leave it to you to send what you think best. And sometimes I tell you. Next week, I might say, I do a large decoration for a room that is yellow. Then you go into your garden, into the country too, perhaps, and pick what you think I might like. What do you say?"

Gwen did not have a moment's doubt. "I'll do it," she said.

"It's ridiculous, really, the way one thing has led on to the next," she told Julia, after describing her visit. "The orchids. Mr Cole. And now this. I think this is the most unbelievable of all."

"Do you mind?" Julia said. "I know Mrs Meyer can be very persuasive but I can easily tell her you've changed your mind if you'd rather. I'd hate you to feel I'd forced you into taking on more than you want."

"You haven't, you haven't. Mrs Meyer's wonderful. I can't wait to go round the garden and see what she might like. She's opened my eyes to all sorts of ideas. It'll be a tremendous challenge. I'd much rather deal with her than Mr Cole, to tell you the truth."

Julia smiled. "Hampers for Frances and me. Now hampers for Maximilian's. You'll find yourself hiring a train next. Perhaps you should stay on for the Chelsea Show. You might get some ideas and you know we'd love to have you for longer."

"I must get back. I daren't leave Waite for long."

"You underestimate Waite, you know. He's very competent. You should give him more responsibility. He'd cope."

"Waite and I are all right as we are," Gwen said firmly. "We understand each other."

"All right," Julia said mildly. "I was only trying to help. Let me know how you get on with Mrs Meyer. And be sure to tell me if there's anything I can do. You don't think it might be a good idea to have a telephone installed?"

"Last year you wanted an Aga. Then electricity. Now it's a telephone. What next will you suggest?"

"If you had your way you'd still be rubbing two sticks together to cook over a fire in the courtyard," Julia said, laughing. "No, but seriously, that old range..."

"We like it. We're old-fashioned."

"We could club together as a family to buy it for you. You know that the cost of home improvements comes out of the trust."

"Annie and I can manage," Gwen said firmly. "If I want an Aga I'll buy it myself."

"You're hopeless," Julia said, but she smiled. "I'll see what Annie says when I come down in July. Oh dear. I do wish Somerset wasn't so far away."

There had been frost in the West Country during her visit to London. She glimpsed blackened fruit blossom on the drive down, told herself that frost in Somerset during the third week of May was impossible and discovered she was wrong before she had had time to step from the car.

"Killed off the runner beans, it has," Waite told her, in the tone of voice that implied he held her absence responsible.

"They'd be the first to go. What else? What about the French beans?"

"Gone too. Not those under cloches. They survived."

In fact, as she discovered after she and Waite had gone round the garden together, Hillcrest had escaped lightly, no doubt due to its position on top of the hill. Several apple trees in the orchard had been touched, and three rows of half-hardy annuals lost, though the loss of the latter was her own fault for planting them out too early in an attempt to increase flowers for the market. She noticed that Waite had already cleared the dead beans which were lying in a bedraggled jumble on the compost heap, forked through the soil and sown their replacements, and, despite his words before her departure, had also found time to plant out the brassica. She remembered Julia's words. Perhaps she should give him more responsibility.

She told him – nervously, knowing his attitude to flowers – about her visit to Maximilian's Floral Decorations. "It's quite different from Cole & Son. It sounds ridiculous, I know, but it's more like an art gallery. I thought London and Taunton would combine rather well. What one wants the other doesn't. It's foliage that Mrs Meyer's really interested in and we've no shortage of that."

"Be a good thing to get that wild bit under control," he said. "It's been needing a good prune for the past twenty years."

"You're not laying your hands on that, Waite," Gwen told him. "Leave it to me. I've no doubt that if you had your way you'd clear the ground altogether and plant it all out with potatoes."

There was a glimmer of a smile on his face. "Dare say I would," he agreed.

Chapter Eleven

During that summer Gwen's flower selling flourished. Mrs Meyer could not have enough of the material Gwen sent, writing ecstatic letters in florid handwriting that Gwen could barely decipher. Mr Cole was more difficult.

"Nice flowers," he said of a bucket of marguerites she took in. "Pity they're all white. How about some coloured?"

She could not believe that a florist could be so ignorant. "Marguerites aren't coloured," she told him. "They're white. Always."

"Then dye them."

She stared. "What did you say?"

"Stick 'em in coloured water. Cochineal. Ink. That sort of thing. Let 'em suck up the colour."

"But that would be cheating."

He grunted. "Don't see why. Try it. I'll pay."

She realized then, if she had not already done so, that he was a businessman above all else. Mrs Meyer was an artist, like the Purcells. That moment decided her priorities. Mr Cole provided her with her bread and butter. In return she would supply him with what he wanted, within limits –

dyeing being beyond those limits. Her interest, indeed her pleasure, revolved round the needs of Mrs Meyer. She welcomed Mrs Meyer's money – who wouldn't? – but she would have supplied her for no more than expenses had she been asked. Her satisfaction came from thinking and planning, from picking and choosing the colours, textures and shapes, from imagining what Mrs Meyer might make of the material with which Gwen was surrounded. In return, and to help stimulate her imagination further, Mrs Meyer sent Gwen Julia's watercolour sketches of the arrangements that satisfied her best.

There were problems with Waite, as Gwen had expected. He was outraged at her decree that flowers on the rhubarb should be allowed to develop. "Everyone knows flowers weaken the plant. You'll get stems not worth the having."

"But the flowers are such a wonderful creamy colour, and a nice solid shape. Just the sort of thing that goes down well at Maximilian's."

"You know Miss Sampford likes her rhubarb wine. How's she going to make that without a full crop?"

"There's still plenty left in the store cupboard. Oh, all right, Waite. As you wish. We'll just keep the flowers on the plants at the end of the row and divide in the autumn for extra next year."

Meanwhile she continued to cope with the orchids. She was still anxious and uncertain – did this plant need dividing now or should it be left? Should she cut here? Or there? How big should its pot be? – and would have welcomed a mentor, but her confidence was growing. She gained satis faction from the sight of the glasshouse interior, with its careful arrangement of plants and hanging baskets, the blinds at last in position, and surprised herself by the excitement she felt when she thought the unnamed cymbidium was developing a flower spike. Her disappointment when she realized that the spike was no more than a new growth was intense.

That particular orchid was Tony's first concern when he arrived with Frances and Gabriel on their way back from a fortnight in South Devon.

"How's Question Mark, Aunt Gwen? What's Question Mark doing?"

"Not much, I'm afraid. We're going to have to wait another year at least before it flowers."

He stood in the doorway of the orchid house. "Oh, Aunt Gwen!" he said. "What a lot you've done since I was here."

She enjoyed his appreciation. "It does look better, doesn't it? It's amazing how a semblance of order improves the appearance of things. That's what Annie always told us when we were your age. 'Keep the place tidy,' she'd say. 'First impressions count.'"

He was looking round him, standing on tiptoe to peer into the baskets hanging from the roof beams. She noticed how much he had grown since his last visit.

"The house is only just big enough for them all, isn't it?" he said.

"That does worry me sometimes," she admitted. "You can't have plants too close, particularly in a humid atmosphere, without risking infection."

"Like people. We had measles at school last winter. Did I tell you? Not me though, worse luck."

She laughed. "Don't wish measles on yourself."

He went from pot to pot, peering closely at each plant. "Poor old Question Mark," he said when he reached it. "It is being a bit slow, isn't it?"

"Mrs Whitelaw says it takes seven years for an orchid to flower. Unfortunately she doesn't know when Mr Whitelaw bred Question Mark so we can't tell whether it's slow or not."

He grinned at her. "It makes me feel really proud, knowing I've had something to do with all this. Can I work for you again while I'm here? We spent a few days with the Merediths on the way back from Devon and I helped Hector with the harvest. It's done wonders for my muscles. Just feel them. Digging will be easy now."

She smiled, surprised by the extent of her pleasure at having him with her again. "You know what I always say..."

He smiled and said the words with her. *It depends on your parents.*

"If you don't mind having him," Frances said when asked. "It will at least mean Gabriel can get on with his book."

Gabriel said he would be glad of the solitude. "Writing's being difficult. I'd like to get away from thrillers, at least for the moment. I can't help feeling it's irresponsible to concentrate on such things when the world's in such a mess. What do you think?"

Gwen, who couldn't have found Abyssinia on the map and certainly hadn't understood the details of the crisis, hesitated. "There's nothing you can do about the world, is there?" she said. Then, remembering how when young he had joined the Fabians for that very reason, she added, "Not now, anyway."

"You don't think it's one's duty to do *something*? The pen is reputed to be mightier than the sword, isn't it, though I can't say I've noticed its might in my time. Rather the reverse, I'd say."

When she read Gabriel's thrillers Gwen often had the feeling that there was more to them than appeared on the surface, if only she had the intelligence to see it. Once, when a spate of reminiscences and autobiographies harking back to the war began to appear in the bookshops, she asked Gabriel if he were going to produce one himself. The look he had given her was cryptic. "Oh, but I have. It's there, in all my books, if you care to look. Chaos, lurking underneath..."

So she said now, feebly, she couldn't help thinking, "Well, perhaps."

"Thinking about Germany, reminds me," Gabriel said. "I hope you don't mind, but I mentioned you and your orchids to Professor Ebert. You know, this professor of mine in Germany. He keeps writing to me and I run out of things to say in reply. I'm certain the postal service is censored and orchids seem sufficiently innocuous as a subject."

"Heavens, Gabriel. Are you sure your thrillers aren't taking you over?"

The summer holidays always gave Gwen pleasure. She enjoyed the family comings and goings, liked finding children in unexpected places – falling over Rowena curled up with a book in the shade of the catalpa, or Andrew watching a yellowhammer from an unstable home-made hide. She appreciated Julia's help with the fruit picking and making of jam, and enjoyed the exchange of opinions between the three sisters on painting and drawing, as well as the discussion on their very different work. Frances was concentrating now on abstracts, strange, dark paintings in thick oils. While she admired their power Gwen couldn't help regretting the loss of Frances's landscapes. "I'll come back to them eventually,

I expect," Frances said, "but with a different approach. Come on, Gwen. You know one can't stand still. Every artist has to develop."

However enjoyable family visits might be, Gwen always relished the quiet that came with their end. Julia and her family returned to London; Frances and Gabriel to Cambridge. Tony waved his parents goodbye with what seemed to Gwen inappropriate high spirits.

"That's them gone," he said as the sound of their car faded down the hill. "Now it's just you and me, Aunt Gwen. Isn't that nice?"

He worked hard during the rest of his stay, taking on his own shoulders the task of digging and manuring new borders to increase the area available for market flowers the following year. Gwen, surveying the result of his labours, felt he deserved a reward and suggested taking a picnic up onto the Quantocks the afternoon before his departure. "I could do with some moss, but that won't take long to collect. How about it?"

"Well ... perhaps."

"Or we could go to Minehead. Would you rather do that?"

He hesitated. "Grandpa did say something about one last bridge lesson."

Gwen was disappointed by his lack of enthusiasm. "I'm sure Grandpa wouldn't mind changing that to the evening."

"I'll think about it."

Lucy, visiting Hillcrest to fetch tomatoes for the Rectory, overheard. "I'll come with you, if you want company," she offered. "I'd be glad to get away for an afternoon, to tell you the truth, and it's ages since I've been on the Quantocks."

Gwen would have preferred Tony's company, but a treat

was no treat if it had to be forced. "You have only to say if you change your mind," she told him.

She looked for him before setting out, wanting to give him a last chance, but he had disappeared. "Said he was taking the afternoon off," Waite told her, without looking up from the frames he was cleaning. She expected to find him at the Rectory when she arrived, but Lucy was sewing vestments alone in the drawing-room. Silver-framed photographs of Antony as a boy stood on the table beside her chair. Glancing at them Gwen saw her nephew in his gaze.

"No," Lucy said, "I haven't seen Tony yet, but then I wouldn't expect to. Mother's still resting upstairs, and the last time I looked into the study Father had fallen asleep over the *Church Times*. Tony'll come over in his own time." Carefully she laid the stole she had been mending over the back of a wing chair. "Shall we go?"

She leant back in the seat, stretched and gave a deep sigh as the car climbed through the beech woods on Cothelstone Hill. "It's such a relief to get away for a bit. To feel free."

"You know you've only to say if you ever want an afternoon off," Gwen said, surprised and a little guilty. It had never occurred to her that Lucy might like to accompany her on such trips.

The sackful of moss was quickly gathered. "There's no need to go straight back, is there?" Lucy said, after Gwen had stowed it away in the boot. "It's such a lovely day. Why don't we walk?"

It was warm but not too hot, a perfect day for walking. The ground felt springy and soft underfoot. Distant views disappeared into the haze, the Welsh coast no longer visible and the islands – Flatholme and Steepholme – like pencil smudges on the flat water. In the valley below, the patchwork pattern of fields was indistinct, the colours blurred as colours of the flower border blurred when looked at without glasses.

"Do you remember that summer before the war when we all came up here?" Lucy said.

"I was just thinking of it."

"It was wonderful, wasn't it?"

"Yes."

"And the night we had to spend in the barn because Gabriel wanted to show Sarah the sea. Do you remember that?"

"Yes," she said again. Close her eyes and she was back twenty-two years. The dark vault of the barn roof above, the tickling sensation of the straw underneath, the warmth of Antony's hand round hers, the sound of his breath as he lay beside her. And the next morning...

The familiar ache returned.

Oh, Antony. So clever, so amusing, mercurial, like the shooting star he had once showed her in the sky, opening her eyes to the world, encouraging and supporting her. Most important of all, loving her, loving her who was no Helen of Troy but ordinary, down-to-earth Gwen.

How could she ever forget?

They walked fast, without speaking. What Lucy was thinking Gwen did not know, or care. It took Lucy's plea for a rest to bring her back to the present.

They had brought a Thermos of tea and some fruitcake, which they ate while still on the ridge. The haze was clearing as the day advanced; they could see Exmoor to the south, and the Blackdowns, though the Wellington Monument was still little more than a line standing up from the horizon. On the slopes below, a stag emerged from the trees to sniff the air. A curlew uttered a mournful cry.

Lucy screwed the cap back on the Thermos and brushed the crumbs from her lap. "This may sound stupid to you," she said, gazing into the distance, "but I sometimes think that that walk was the pinnacle of our lives. Oh, I know it was another two years before the war really hit us with Antony's death, but somehow those two days up here, all of us together ... you felt anything could happen. Life was so full, so hopeful..." She gave Gwen an apologetic smile. "I'm not making much sense, am I?"

"You are, you are. I didn't know you felt like that too, that's all."

"I suppose I knew it wasn't likely to happen again. I mean, I had difficulty getting away from home even then. It's so long ago, I can't remember why now, but I do remember telling myself to make the most of the opportunity. You're so lucky," she burst out with sudden emotion, "all four of you. Oh, I know I didn't think so when I first knew you. I used to lie awake at night wondering what it must be like to be you with no one to look after you. I couldn't imagine life without Mother and Father. It wasn't until later that I envied you being so free. Frances going to art school; Julia nursing in the war. I'd have given anything to go with her. And now Sarah in India. Not that I've wanted to go to India ever, but it would be nice to know I could if I did. I can't. I'm stuck. I love Mother and Father dearly, but, well, here I am..."

Gwen searched for something to say. She had always thought Lucy as firmly rooted at the Rectory as she herself was to Hillcrest; she could scarcely believe what she had just heard. "I suppose we can't ever tell how life's going to turn out," she said. "And, anyway, I'm stuck too."

142

"But it's your choice. You could go if you wanted. Frances was anxious you should go to the Slade but you said no. You don't want to leave Hillcrest, that's all."

There seemed nothing she could say.

"We ought to get back," Lucy said at last. "You know how they are about my being away from the house for too long."

They were crossing the Minehead road when it happened.

Gwen had halted at the end of Dunkery High Street to let a bus go by and was gingerly emerging from between the high hedges when Lucy leant forward. "Watch that motorbike. It's coming much too fast." Her words ended in a shriek.

Gwen slammed on the brake. The engine stalled as the car skidded to a halt. The motorcycle swerved over onto the wrong side of the road, slanting until the knees of its riders seemed to touch the tarmac, righted itself and disappeared down the Huish Priory road with a roar of exhaust. The startled face of the pillion rider looked backwards before being hastily averted.

"Well." Lucy sounded breathless. "That was a close thing."

"Yes," Gwen said. Her hands were trembling, wet on the steering wheel. After a moment she took a deep breath, restarted the engine and drove slowly and carefully the two miles into Huish Priory.

She stopped at the end of the Rectory drive. Lucy did not move. Neither of them said a word.

"Did you think that was who I thought it was?" Lucy said at last.

"The motorcyclist?"

"The passenger." She waited. "It was Tony, wasn't it? With Willy Roberts."

"It might have been. Yes, of course it was."

"Did *you* know he was riding bikes with Willy?"

Gwen was indignant. "Do you think I'd have let him out of my sight if I had? I thought he was at the Rectory. He told me he was going to your father for a bridge lesson."

There was a long silence. The church clock struck the hour.

"Was that the first time, do you think?" Lucy said.

"That he's been out with Willy? I don't know. I didn't even know Willy had a bike. In fact it can't be his. He couldn't afford one."

"What would Frances say if she knew?"

"She'd kill me," said Gwen, and meant it.

"Then she'd better not find out. Which means not telling my parents. I'd rather they didn't know, as a matter of fact. They'd only worry."

Like me, Gwen thought, recalling with sinking heart the accounts of local traffic accidents that appeared with frightening regularity in the pages of the *County Gazette*. If what they had just seen was an example of Willy's riding...

"I'd better go," Lucy said at last. She stood still for a moment before shutting the car door. "You know, Gwen, if we're going to continue having Tony here on his own we'll have to sort out with Gabriel what he's allowed to do and what he isn't."

"The difficulty," Gwen said, "comes in trying to anticipate what he might do next."

"I know." She started to walk away, hesitated and came back. "Gwen."

"Yes?"

"What I said earlier. Up on the Quantocks. Don't let it go any further."

"Of course I won't."

Mary Roberts was sitting in the kitchen with Annie when Gwen arrived home. The room smelt of newly baked sponge cake and the ironing Mary had just finished. Clothes aired from the creel, folded sheets were neatly stacked on the table, while Mary and Annie shared a pot of tea. Gwen fetched herself a mug from the dresser.

"Bought it last week, he did," Mary said when Gwen brought up the subject of motorcycles. "Mechanics make good money these days, Miss Gwen. 'Tain't like it were in the old days, working out in the fields for pennies. There be a crowd of young lads meet in Dunkery of an evening and race through the lanes on their bikes."

"I see. Well, I don't think Tony is old enough to join them. He's only thirteen, and I'm quite sure my sister wouldn't want him riding round the countryside. Do you think you could have a word with Willy? Tell him to refuse to take Tony if Tony should ask."

"Willy dursn't want a young lad like Master Tony with him of an evening," Mary said with conviction.

"Thank heavens for that," said Gwen.

"He's wild, is my Willy." Pride sounded in Mary's voice. "Like his father were, afore him."

Gwen blinked. She remembered Bill Roberts in the years before he had been wounded. Blacksmith, cricketer, trumpeter, bell-ringer – the Purcells had looked up to him as one of the pillars of village society. "You can't mean it," she said. "Bill, *wild*? Surely not."

"No holding him when he'd got the drink in him. Him and them Chedzoys ... the rumpus they'd kick up in the New Inn. And the fights. He were a great fighter, were my Bill. Isn't that right, Miss Sampford?"

Annie smiled at Gwen. "There was a lot went on in the village you girls didn't know about."

"There seems to be a lot I don't know about these days as well," Gwen said grimly. "Just wait until Tony gets home."

Tony was whistling when he returned to Hillcrest. "Hello, Aunt Gwen. Did you have a good time? Grandpa says I'm getting really good at bridge. He still won't let me play for money though. I keep telling him that matchsticks aren't the least bit exciting, but he won't listen."

"Always money, isn't it, Tony?" This is ridiculous, she told herself. I'm not letting this situation go on any longer. "What *are* you saving for, Tony? A motorbike?"

He was instantly still. "You saw us?"

"Of course we saw you."

"It was the first time," he said. "Willy only got the bike at the weekend. He gave me a ride so I could see what it was like."

"And what was it like?" Her voice was sharp.

His eyes were wary. "All right."

"Dangerous, wasn't it? You nearly came off."

"But we didn't."

"You haven't answered my question. Are you saving up to buy a motorbike?"

He shook his head. "I told you, Aunt Gwen. I don't want to tell anyone yet. I did promise you it's all above board, what I want. You shouldn't worry so much."

He didn't trust her.

Why should he? They were of different generations.

"It's a common fault with maiden aunts, I believe." She tried to make her words sound light-hearted, but inside she was desolate.

Part Three

Tony

Chapter Twelve

The orchids came into their own during that autumn and winter. From September until the following Easter Gwen was never without flowers – flowers to admire, flowers to sell, flowers to paint. Over the weeks her feelings towards the collection changed, so gradually, so subtly, that she was scarcely aware of it. She was won over by their beauty, fascinated by their variety, challenged by the difficulties in growing them well, but above all else she became obsessed by the painting of them. She had drawn and painted flowers since childhood – it had been a suggestion of Antony's that led indirectly to the publication of her flower books – but orchids were different from any other variety that she had portrayed, romantic and exotic where the rest were prosaic and commonplace.

A conversation with Gabriel in the Christmas holidays made her realize it had taken less than a year for her to become as absorbed in the collection as Mr Whitelaw had been when it was his.

She was fastening a cypripedium spike when Gabriel joined her in the orchid house. It was late afternoon, the light already beginning to fade. Beyond the glass roof the bare branches of the pear tree made a stark outline against the deep rose of the western sky.

"Don't mind me," Gabriel said. "I'm just pottering. A refugee from snakes and ladders in the living-room, if you must know."

He watched her working, sniffed this flower and that, and after a while said, "It's all right now, isn't it? You've accepted them."

"What do you mean?"

"You didn't want to take them on at the beginning, did you? It was a duty, not a pleasure. I think it's a pleasure now."

"I suppose it is. Yes, you're right. It is."

"You've changed, you know. You're confident. Much more confident. Not only with the orchids, but with everything. I couldn't have imagined your carrying on a business this time last year. Now you're the modern businesswoman, par excellence."

She laughed as she picked up the watering can. "I don't think I see myself in that role. Take care, or you'll get wet feet. Once I've damped down the house I've finished out here for the night. I'm afraid it's going to be snakes and ladders after all."

"No, seriously," he insisted. "You must be doing quite well, aren't you? Financially, I mean."

"I am, as a matter of fact. Not that I'll ever make a large income, but I have been able to afford extra help for Annie in the house and put up Waite's wages as well, which is nice." She put the can away under the bench, took off her apron and dried her hands. "I had a letter from your professor the other day," she said. "Strange, I thought, writing

150

to someone he's never met."

"What was he writing about?"

"Orchids. What else? He wanted to know which ones I grew. He offered advice – which was kind of him. I shall have to write back, of course, though I've no idea what I can say. Would you like to help? Oh, and he said he was interested in my painting. Of orchids, presumably. You told him about that, did you?"

Gabriel nodded. "He always was an odd character. I don't know why he should want to write to you. Or to me, come to that, when we've been out of touch for so many years. It's not as if we ever cared for each other."

"I thought perhaps he didn't know anyone else who feels as he does about orchids. I can understand that. There. I've finished. Shall we go back to the house?"

He did not move. "I didn't realize how beautiful they were," he said. "I always thought they were overrated, but now, when you see them like this..."

"I know," Gwen said. She stood by his side, as little able as he to find words that might do justice to the flowers' delicate beauty. Only in watercolour was she able to express how she felt. Above the shelves the orchid spikes reared and arched, the colours of their flowers – the mauves and pinks, the creams, the greens and whites – merging into one colour, reduced by the half-light to the same ghostly pallor. And though she had described the letter from Professor Ebert as strange, in some way it had not seemed strange at all, but familiar. In his descriptions of the orchids he remembered growing wild and luxuriant around him during his South American childhood she sensed an underlying feeling, a passion, that she could recognize beginning to grow deep in herself.

*   *   *

Though Tony had spent most of the Christmas holidays with his parents and grandparents, he escaped from the Rectory whenever he could to help Gwen in the glasshouse, chopping fibre, cleaning pots and washing and grading crocks.

"They're funny things, orchids, aren't they?" he said. "I mean, they do the opposite of everything else. If you look at the plants out there in the border, well, they're not doing anything, are they? They're resting."

"Dormant, it's called," Gwen said.

"All right. Dormant. Then, in the summer, they grow and flower at the same time. Whereas orchids, when they look ... dormant, they're really growing, you said, and when they flower, like now, they're resting. It seems very strange to me."

"They're like tulips. Or daffodils. Any bulb, in fact. After a tulip has flowered, the bulb has to renew itself, gather food – grow, in other words – or else it won't have the strength to flower the next season. Tulips are like orchids in other ways too. In the seventeenth century they were so popular they became incredibly expensive. The bulbs which produced the most elaborately marked flowers used to change hands for hundreds of pounds. A sort of showing off to your neighbours, you see. Like orchids in the last century. One orchid was sold for a thousand pounds in the eighteen eighties, I believe."

"Really?" He considered that information for a while. "How much do you get for a flower, Aunt Gwen?"

"It depends on the variety and the condition of the flowers. On the time of year too. You get more before Christmas, for instance, and then the price goes down towards Easter. I'm getting up to two pounds for a good cattleya spike at the moment. A bit less for a cypripedium, and ten to fifteen shillings for cymbidiums."

"You're talking about flowers, aren't you? What happens if you sell a plant? How much would you get then?"

"I don't know. That's a different business altogether. If you want to sell plants you breed them yourself – hybridizing, it's called – and hope you produce something outstanding. Question Mark's a hybrid. Mr Whitelaw used to do a lot of hybridizing when he worked for Sir James Donne, Mrs Whitelaw told me. He named the best after Sir James's daughter."

"That's fame, isn't it? Will you call one after me?"

She laughed. "I'm not going to start breeding."

"Why not?"

"There's a limit to what one can fit into one's life, Tony. I'd rather spend my time painting."

"I suppose that's because you're a Purcell," he said. "You're like Mama. It's all she wants to do."

Andrew admired Gwen's orchid paintings when he and his family came to Hillcrest at Easter. He sat in rapt silence watching Gwen apply the first washes to her drawing of a yellow frilled cymbidium. "The colours are really wonderful, aren't they?" he said when she paused for a moment to rest. "They're so bright, but they're not gaudy at all. The way they merge into each other reminds me of birds' feathers."

Gwen took off her glasses to rub her eyes. "Why don't you try painting one yourself?" she suggested. "Flowers are much easier to paint than birds, you know. They don't move."

"I know. I still prefer birds though, thank you."

She smiled at him, thinking how different he was from his boisterous cousin. "I've had an invitation to visit Germany to paint orchids. I can't help feeling that it would be a bit ridiculous to travel all that way just to paint flowers. What do you think?"

He considered. "I think it would depend on how beautiful they were."

"But I wouldn't know that till I got there, would I?"

"I suppose not. Are you going?"

"Of course not. I'm too busy here."

"Have you ever been abroad, Aunt Gwen?"

She shook her head.

"Neither have I, but we're going this summer, Daddy says."

"Brittany," Julia said when asked. "We thought it might help Rowena with her accent. She says we should go to Germany to look for refugees, though I don't know what she thinks we could do with them if we found any. Smuggle them home in the boot of the car, I dare say. Anyway, she's having to put up with Brittany."

That Rowena was still interested in refugees Gwen had quickly discovered when she came to her in the garden on her first morning at Hillcrest.

"Aunt Gwen?"

She looked up from the dahlias she was planting. "Yes?"

Rowena hovered on the grass at the edge of the border. "Can I ask you a favour?"

"What is it?"

"You know that picture in my room at home, the one Mummy made out of pressed flowers for Christmas when I was little?"

"I think so."

"We thought, well, Janet and I did – Janet's my best friend – we thought if we made pictures like that we could sell them. To make money, you know."

Gwen looked at her over her spectacles. "Gracious me, Rowena. Does flower selling run in the family?"

"I don't know." She sounded uncertain, as if she feared that Gwen might be laughing at her. "This isn't like you and Mrs Meyer, Aunt Gwen. We won't be keeping the money. We'll be doing it for the refugees – you know, people like Daddy's professor. School has a summer fair next term, you see, and we thought if we had a stall and made things to sell – all sorts of things – we could give the money to them."

"What a good idea." The next generation certainly did not lack initiative when it came to fund-raising. The four Purcells might have known all about conserving their money but it had never occurred to them to go out and increase it. Gwen was torn between amusement and admiration.

"The thing is," Rowena said earnestly, "we don't have anything to make them with. The pictures, I mean."

"Ah," said Gwen. "I understand. You want me to provide the dried flowers."

Rowena danced across the border to hug her. "Aunt Gwen, you're wonderful."

Painting had to be put aside for the holidays, but Gwen did not mind. After a wet winter, spring had arrived at last. The mimosa was out in the bed by the wall, the buds of the wisteria beginning to burst beside the veranda, those of the clematis open over the pergola. Tony was working with Waite, Frances painting in the wild part of the garden – "before you send it all up to Maximilian's" – Gabriel talking politics to whoever would listen, deploring Germany's march into the Rhineland. Life was busy, with a different busyness from that of the term-time but just as pleasurable.

155

Andrew joined Tony and Waite in the garden to help sort out the compost heap. It was Waite's idea. He wanted to collect the liquid seeping out from under the heap into a tank, to dilute and use as additional fertilizer. Gwen took out his mug of tea mid-morning, together with milk for her nephews, and stayed to watch them dig and breach and dam. They looked more like small boys having fun with waterworks at the seaside, she thought, than the hydraulic engineers Tony claimed they were. Thin, red worms wriggled in the compost that had been scattered during the digging. Hens clucked and squawked and flapped underfoot as they pecked at the unexpected feast. There was compost smeared over Tony's trousers, mud on Andrew's face. As for Waite, Gwen had never seen him so jolly.

"I'm impressed," she told him that evening as he wheeled his bicycle out of the stables on his way home. "I've always thought that that liquid was good stuff going to waste, but it never occurred to me we could do anything about it. What gave you the idea?"

He gave her a cryptic look. "Flanders," was all he said.

The following Monday Tony stumped into the kitchen in his wellington boots to announce that Waite had failed to arrive. "He must have gone on one of his benders over the weekend."

"I do wish you wouldn't use that word," Gwen said. She sighed. Waite's turns, though infrequent, always seemed to come at the worst possible time. She wondered whether the mention of Flanders the previous week had brought back memories which he needed to drown. On this occasion she felt herself partly to blame: by putting up his wages she had given him the extra money to spend on drink.

She went up to the stables with Tony. Waite used the part of the building that had housed the horses in the days before the Purcells came to Hillcrest. The place was dark, shaded by the fig tree outside the window, and smelt of oil and earth and sacking. Garden tools, cleaned and oiled, hung on pegs in the harness room, Waite's thick mackintosh cape beside them, his heavy boots on the floor beneath. In one horse stall stood the lawnmower, in another the upended wheelbarrow. Everything was clean, nothing out of place.

"Not a sign," Gwen said. "Not that I expected anything really."

"You don't need to worry, Aunt Gwen," Tony said. "I can take over. And Andrew won't mind helping, I know. He'll do what I tell him."

Waite did not turn up the next day or the next. Gwen was perturbed – his turns had never before lasted longer than three days – as well as irritated by his thoughtlessness in getting drunk when there was so much to do.

Gabriel too was concerned. "You don't think he's in trouble?"

"Waite? In trouble?" The possibility had not occurred to her. She had never been able to imagine the quiet, peaceable Waite drunk, and certainly could not visualize him disorderly or, worse, violent. "I wouldn't have thought so. Would you?"

"Would you like me to go to the police?"

She shook her head. "No. I'm sure there's no need."

She realized for the first time how little she knew about her gardener. That he lodged with two sisters in Taunton she knew, because he had once told Annie so. That was all. She did not even know his address.

"I don't think I should go home with you tomorrow,"

Tony told his father. "I'll stay and give Aunt Gwen a hand until Waite comes back."

"You will not," Gabriel said. "You're coming back with us. I don't think you realize how much more serious the upper school is than the lower. You're going to be in real trouble if you don't pass your exams this summer, let me tell you."

Tony grinned at his aunt. It had been worth a try, said his expression. As for exams, he would worry about them later.

Gwen smiled back. "Shall I see you here next holidays?" she asked him.

He hesitated. "I think the Merediths want me to help with the harvest," he said at last. "Perhaps I can do both. I'll let you know."

The day after the families' departure Gwen was mystified to receive a letter addressed to her in spidery handwriting she did not recognize.

The writer signed herself Adelaide Glover. She apologized for bothering Miss Pursell but felt that Miss Pursell should know: Mr Waite was not too good at the moment.

Gwen showed Annie the letter. "At least now we've got his address. Should I go and see him, do you think? I don't want to interfere but on the other hand I do employ him. Can a hangover last this long? Or might he be ill?"

"They want your advice," Annie said. "They don't say so, but that's why they've written. I'm sure of it."

Gwen drove into Taunton that afternoon.

It was nearly seventeen years since Waite had arrived at Hillcrest's back door, an emaciated ex-prisoner of war, looking for work. He had heard, he said, that she wanted a gardener. Could he apply?

He had no experience ("Dug trenches," he said when asked), no references, was obviously shell-shocked and looked too frail to stand up to a light wind, let alone the south-westerlies that gusted over the brow of the hill. Why had she taken him on? At the time she assumed it was because she saw in him someone as unlike Willis as it was possible to be. Later she thought his admission that after his experiences in Germany he had determined never to be dependent on others for food had been the deciding factor. She recognized in him something of herself.

She had never regretted taking him on. Over the years he had straightened and filled out, gained strength, eventually got over the shell shock. Only one weakness remained. Occasionally, every twelve months or so, he would have what he would describe afterwards as "one of my turns". He would be away for one day or two, very rarely three, before returning with sallow face and trembling hands, looking as if shell shock had overcome him again.

It had taken time for the truth to dawn.

Julia was tolerant. "You've no idea what memories he has," she told Gwen. David, a surgeon in France during the war, suggested that the occasional alcoholic binge might even be good for those who had experienced the horror of life in the trenches. "Banish the nightmares temporarily," was how he put it. Gwen knew she could not afford to lose Waite. Trained by her, he had become the gardener she wanted. She had to turn a blind eye to his turns.

The address was in an area of Taunton unknown to her, the house one of a terrace built in red and yellow brick. In the distance a cluster of boys kicked a football up and down the road. Three girls stopped their skipping to watch Gwen

159

get out of the car. Across the road a net curtain moved against the window.

The two Miss Glovers, small, with wispy, greying hair, were older than Gwen had expected. Their appearance, the way they held their heads and moved, reminded her of two bright-eyed sparrows. Their relief when she introduced herself was palpable. They took the basket of vegetables she had brought with her, twittering their thanks, and ushered her into the front room, where they left her to go and make tea. The familiar bronze plaque commemorating a dead soldier hung on the wall by the fireplace. Among the china pieces on the mantelpiece stood a studio portrait of a boy in khaki, his expression a mixture of hope and uncertainty. A shabby picture postcard of a French square, the name of the town blacked out, had been tucked into its frame.

"That's our Billie," the younger Miss Glover said, pride in her voice, when she returned with the tea tray. "He was our baby brother." She answered Gwen's unspoken question. "Hill 60. He'd been out less than a month."

Yes, Gwen thought. I remember Hill 60. Hill 60 followed Gallipoli.

The elder sister removed a purple crocheted cosy from the teapot and poured out the tea while the younger asked after Gwen's orchids and Tony. Waite was obviously more communicative here than he was at Hillcrest, Gwen thought, trying, but failing, to picture him in this over-furnished room, sitting large and awkward among the little tables and china flowers. Did he sit with the sisters in this room every evening and converse until the need for alcohol overcame him?

"We didn't know what to do for the best," explained the younger Miss Glover. "He's never been ill for so long before.

He won't let us call the doctor, you see. There's nothing a doctor can do, he says. It's just a matter of..." she paused, lowered her voice, "sweating it out."

Gwen was mystified. Did you sweat out a hangover? "I thought ... what is the matter, exactly?"

"It's some kind of fever," said the elder. "The first time he had it was when he was in Mesopotamia during the war, so he says. It comes back now and then."

"He doesn't like us going into his room when he's ill. We did go in this time. He seemed ... confused, really. We weren't sure he knew who we were. That's when we wrote to you."

Annie had been right. They wanted to be told what to do, particularly if it meant going against Waite's instructions. But Gwen did not know what to tell them. This was more serious than drink. She had misjudged him. She put down her teacup. "Should I go up and see him?"

There was no reply to her knock. She tried a second time before pushing open the door and going in. She was struck at once by the contrast to the cluttered room downstairs. Wardrobe, chest of drawers, one chair, a bedside table supporting a water jug and glass – that was all. No pictures, no souvenirs of France. Or of Mesopotamia either, come to that. No bottles, no whisky.

Waite lay in bed, eyes shut, shivering. Though the north-facing room was cool, his face glistened with sweat.

She sat down. He gave no sign that he had heard her come in. "Waite," she said quietly. "It's me. Miss Purcell. I've come to see you. Is there anything I can do?"

His eyes opened. He looked across at her, expression blank. Recognition came suddenly. "Miss Purcell." He tried to pull himself into a sitting position, felt for a handkerchief, realized he was not wearing a jacket. "I'm sorry. Please, a

161

handkerchief. Top drawer."

She pulled out the dressing-table drawer and took out a handkerchief. Beside the ironed and neatly folded pile lay a medal. Waite mopped his face. Surreptitiously she glanced back at the medal. A cross, the ribbon silver and mauve – how extraordinary.

Waite pulled the sheet up to his shoulders as he mumbled apologies. "I'm sorry. You shouldn't... What day is it?"

"Friday."

"Friday?" Alarm sounded in his voice. "It can't be. I didn't know. I'll be back. Tomorrow."

"Don't be stupid, Waite. You're in no condition to cycle seven miles, let alone work at the end of it. Don't worry. We can manage." She hesitated. "Is this what always happens when you're away?"

He lay back against the pillow, as if exhausted. "Not as bad."

"Shouldn't you see a doctor?" Was it a matter of money? "I'll pay."

He shook his head.

"Well." She was at a loss. She felt she should do something to help but had no idea what. And it was obvious that she was embarrassing him by her presence, as much as she was embarrassing herself by being there. "If you're quite sure there's nothing... I'll tell Miss Glover to let me know if I can help. And don't come back until you're really fit."

Downstairs the tea things had been cleared away. The Miss Glovers stood with their backs to the fire, beside the silver-framed photograph of Billie. They at least were grateful for her visit, thanking her for coming and promising to let her know if there was anything they thought she should know or could do.

I should have called before, Gwen told herself as she drove back to Huish Priory, before remembering that until their letter arrived she had not known their address. Not that that's any excuse. I should have asked questions, found it. But her predominant emotion was amazement. Waite an officer? Surely not. Yet she knew that the Military Cross was awarded to officers only.

"I'm sure it was," she told Lucy. "It looked exactly like Gabriel's."

"I don't see why you're so surprised," Lucy said. "Waite may not be a heroic figure, exactly, but there's no telling what he was like in the war. The most surprising people..."

"It's not that so much. It's ... well, it makes me feel so awkward. How can I start ordering an officer about?"

"You've been doing it for sixteen years," Lucy said, "and he hasn't objected yet."

"I know. All the same..." She sighed. She disliked discovering that things were not what they seemed. It gave her a feeling of insecurity.

There was one relief.

"Thank goodness I put up his wages," she told Annie.

Chapter Thirteen

Waite's expression was blank.

"Why didn't you tell me?" Gwen, at first determined not to mention the Military Cross, had finally let her curiosity get the better of her.

He shrugged. "Medals were ten a penny in 1918."

"I'm sure you must be mistaken. What did you get it for?"

"Doing what I was told."

"You might have said you were an officer when you applied for the job."

"I was only a temporary gentleman." His tone was ironic. "If that's all, Miss Purcell, I'd better get on. There's a lot of catching up to do."

"Don't try to do too much on your first day. You don't look as though you've properly recovered."

Although she would not question Waite further she was still intrigued. "What did he mean, temporary gentleman?" she asked David during her spring visit to London.

"Not public school," David said. "He must have come up from the ranks – made it simply because everyone else had been killed. What was his regiment?"

"I don't know. He's never talked about the war. I wish I hadn't found out. It makes things very difficult. I feel so awkward telling him what to do."

Julia made it clear that she thought Gwen was fussing unnecessarily. "I don't see why. You've told him all these years. I'd carry on as you always have done, if I were you."

It was what Gwen was trying to do. Waite hadn't changed, after all, merely her knowledge of him. Strangely enough, that knowledge made her more confident at leaving him in charge during her visit to London, so much so that this year she stayed long enough with Julia and David to visit both the Academy Summer Exhibition and a fortnightly show at the Royal Horticultural Society.

She turned down Julia's offer to take her shopping for clothes.

"There's no point. I don't lead the sort of life that needs anything smart. WI meetings and meals at the Rectory are the only social occasions I have. And staying with you, of course. Which reminds me – I suppose you wouldn't give a talk to the WI in August? It won't be a full meeting because of the harvest, but the committee decided to get together anyway. People look forward to it, you know. Lucy wondered whether you'd like to tell us about your work at the Settlement. She said we could have a collection afterwards."

The thought of addressing a Women's Institute meeting would have appalled Gwen, but Julia accepted the invitation without hesitation. Julia was prepared to do anything that might help her club, as Lucy had known when sending the invitation. Indeed her talk went down so well when the time came that at the end of it five pounds eight shillings and sixpence was collected for the Settlement's Mothers and Babies Club, for Julia to spend as she thought fit. She had brought

165

drawings she had made of mothers and small children at the Settlement for people to see, as well as sketches of life in London's East End. As a result two members offered to take in any mother or child in need of country air and food for a week during the holidays and several others showed interest. There was general agreement during the tea break that though farming was going through difficult times, at least in the country children were reasonably well fed, whereas it was obvious from Julia's drawings that in cities this was far from the case. When members rose at the end of the meeting to join in the singing of "Jerusalem", the "green and pleasant land" had taken on new meaning.

Julia was touched by their unexpected concern. "How kind everyone was. Fancy offering to take people into their homes. I couldn't believe it."

"Shall I pass your name on to Jane Milne in Dunkery?" Lucy asked. "She's secretary there. I know they're always looking for speakers. It's a bigger branch than ours; you might get more offers from them."

Gwen was impressed by her sister's performance, by Julia's confidence and her fluency, as well as by the response she had received. "I think you're wonderful. I don't know how you have the courage to stand in front of so many people and just talk."

Julia thought nothing of it. "You could do it too, if you had to. If you feel really strongly about something... Somehow you don't think of yourself then."

Hillcrest was quiet over the holiday season. Frances and Gabriel were spending the summer in Provence, where Gabriel planned to finish his novel undisturbed, while Julia and Rowena and Andrew visited for less than a week before

166

joining David in London to drive over to Brittany.

Gwen missed each one of the family, but it was Tony's absence that made Hillcrest so empty. He was spending the holidays with Mary Meredith, his godmother, and Hector, her son. *Aunt Mary said she could do with my help for the harvest,* he had written to Gwen during the summer term, *and I didn't like to say no. Besides, I enjoy working with Hector. Can you manage without me? I'll try and get away early so I can spend a few days at Hillcrest. Dad's making me have a week's coaching before I go back to school, have you heard? He wasn't very happy about my report so perhaps it's a good thing he's gone to Provence with Mama or he might make me do school work all through the holidays.*

She could manage, of course she could manage, but she was surprised to discover how much she missed his company all the same. She missed his noisy presence round the house, his bounce, his curiosity, his enthusiasm. She missed the younger outlook, the way he showed her things from a different angle. She had hoped they might take a picnic to the seaside, explore the Blackdown Hills and visit the Wellington Monument. Stupid, really. She acknowledged it. A boy a year older, as Hector was, must be infinitely better company than a maiden aunt.

Her greatest regret over Tony's absence centred round Question Mark. At first she had damped down her excitement; she had had too many disappointments in the past to risk disappointment again. But in the past few months she had learnt to tell the difference between flowering spike and shoot, and as the days passed she knew without doubt that this was the year Question Mark would flower for the first time.

Letters for Tony arrived at Hillcrest from Frances and

Gabriel, which Gwen forwarded on to the Merediths, along with letters of her own. She heard nothing from Tony himself, apart from a couple of uncommunicative postcards, but that did not surprise her. He would tell her his news when he called in, as she was sure he would, on his way back to Cambridge. He would be able to see Question Mark then.

She was in the apple store one morning, clearing out debris from last year's crop and preparing the store for the autumn's harvest, when she heard a car drive up Tinker's Lane. She paused in scrubbing a shelf and listened. Engine idling, footsteps, the sound of the wood scraping over the earth... She came out into bright sunshine to see Frances and Gabriel drive through the gates. She ran down the slope to greet them, shooing hens out of the way.

"What a wonderful surprise! What are you doing here? We thought you were in Provence."

"We were. We've come back early. We decided we'd been a bit hard on Tony." Frances looked sheepish. "I know he's happy with you and with the Merediths, but all the same. All work and no play... So we decided to take him down to Devon for a few days before he starts on his coaching. Gabriel will be able to work there and I can paint. It's the week of the regatta. With luck Tony'll be able to crew."

Gabriel reached for his sticks and eased himself out of the car. "How is he? Not been any trouble, I hope."

"He's not here. He's with the Merediths. We haven't seen him all summer."

"Really? I thought he was dividing his time between you both."

"They're short of men, apparently, and need his help with the harvest."

Gabriel looked surprised. "How strange. We had a letter

from Mary the other day and she didn't say anything. Oh well. We can stop off at Winsford and pick him up. It isn't much out of the way."

"You'll stay the night, won't you?" Gwen said. "It's too late to drive on today. Come in and tell me how the book's going. And the painting – are you turning Provençal Roman arches into abstracts these days?"

She tried to persuade them to stay longer – she thought they both looked tired after so long a journey – but they insisted on leaving the following morning. "We can relax once we get to the cottage," Frances said from the car, "but we need to be there before the start of regatta week if Tony's going to get a place on a boat. I would like him to have some fun before he has to get down to his books. Gabriel won't stand any nonsense this time."

"Poor Tony," Gwen said. She shut the car door and stood back. "Give him my love. Mary and Hector too. Annie and I have missed him this summer. So has Waite, believe it or not. Oh, and you will spend the night here on the way back, won't you? It won't be any trouble – I'll leave your beds as they are."

"We'll think about it," Frances said. "I'll drop you a line."

They were back in a matter of hours. Without Tony.

"He wasn't at Winsford. He hasn't been there all summer."

Gwen felt her heart lurch. "What do you mean? He must be. He told me he'd be there."

"Well, he isn't. Mary said he was here, with you."

"But ... the Merediths needed help with the harvest. I'll show you his letter. He hoped he'd be able to get away in

169

time to stop off here on his way home. That's what he said."

"And he told Mary he couldn't leave you because you needed so much help in the garden. He hoped to visit her too. Just for a couple of days."

"I don't understand," Gwen said. She looked from Frances to Gabriel and back to Frances. "Where is he?"

"We don't know," Frances said. She collapsed into the wicker chair on the veranda. "You don't know. Mary doesn't know. None of us has the faintest idea."

"Do you think..." Gwen hesitated, began again. "You don't think he's run away? Because of the coaching?"

"He didn't seem particularly upset when Gabriel told him he'd arranged it. Did he, Gabriel?"

"More mulish than upset, I'd have said. He may not work but he's not stupid. He must have seen it coming. He made the mistake of thinking that because he'd been picked to play cricket and rugby for the school I wouldn't mind him failing his exams. A lamentable error of judgement on his part."

"What should we do?" Gwen said. "Will you tell the police?"

"Lord, no," said Gabriel. "Not at the moment, anyway. Not until I've thought things through."

"Please, Gwen, don't breathe a word at the Rectory," Frances said. "You know Mrs Mackenzie. She'll say it's all my fault because I'm a rotten mother."

"Don't be absurd, Frances," Gabriel said. "Of course she won't. Though it's probably as well to keep quiet, all the same. We don't want them to worry."

"I don't suppose it ever occurred to him we might worry," Frances said bitterly.

"Of course it hasn't," Gabriel said. "Why should it? He thinks we're comfortably settled in the south of France,

170

believing him to be here or at Winsford. I don't doubt that he'll turn up at Cambridge on the day we're due to arrive home from Provence. Darling, I'm sure he's all right. Hector would have said something otherwise."

"*Hector?*" Frances said. "Does Hector know where he is?"

"Almost certainly, I'd say."

"Then why didn't you force him to tell you?"

"I don't know what else I could have done, other than take my sticks to him." He gave Gwen a rueful smile. "I couldn't help admiring the lad. He swore he hadn't the faintest idea where Tony might be, while insisting that he was all right. 'You don't need to worry, Uncle Gabriel, really you don't.' I suppose we'll just have to put our trust in that."

A sudden thought occurred to Gwen. "What happened to the letters?"

"What letters?"

"Yours. From Provence. I sent them on to Tony at Winsford. I wrote to him there myself."

"Mary didn't say anything about letters," Frances said, "and I didn't think to ask. I'd forgotten about them, to tell you the truth."

"He sent me a couple of postcards," Gwen remembered. "Wait a minute. They're inside, on the mantelpiece." She returned with them in her hand. "Pictures of Exmoor. A Winsford postmark on both. It is Tony's handwriting, isn't it?"

Gabriel took the cards from her and studied them closely. "This supports the conspiracy theory," he said. "Hector must have been acting as postman, passing letters to and fro. Everything planned to the nth degree. Bad luck that we had to spoil it by coming back too soon. I'm torn between admiration and wanting to throttle the boy."

"I just want to know that he's safe," Frances said desperately. "He's only fourteen. Anything could have happened."

"He looks older than fourteen." Gwen tried to console her. "Behaves older too. Really he does." It's all my fault, she thought. She would never forgive herself if anything had happened to Tony. Dreadful pictures darted through her mind. Tony lying ill ... unconscious in a ditch... She tried to recall past conversations, then wished that she hadn't. "You don't think he might have gone abroad?"

Frances turned her head sharply. "What makes you say that?"

"Well ... he did ask me about Gabriel's travels in Germany before the war. Last Easter I think it was. Or it might have been Christmas." Had Tony brought up the subject? Had she? Or had it arisen by chance during talk of the German professor? In any case, was Tony likely to spend money on travel when he was saving so hard? Gwen swallowed. Perhaps travel had been his ambition from the beginning. It would take years to save sufficient, he had said when asking for work, but he could not have foreseen then the steady, regular income she would give him.

"I hope you told him that I'd left school at the time, and had a place at Cambridge to come back to." He looked at her more closely. "Are you serious?"

"It was just an idea," she said miserably.

"I think it unlikely," Gabriel said, after a moment's thought. "How could he finance it, for a start? You know what he's like with money. It slips through his fingers."

"He wouldn't need money for Spain," Frances suddenly said. "Oh, God, that's where he's gone. He's fighting in Spain."

172

"Spain? Fighting?" Gwen was astounded. "What do you mean?"

"There's civil war," Gabriel said. "Frances—"

But Frances had burst into tears. "You know the Cornford boy disappeared for weeks without anyone knowing where he was. He turned up in Spain in the end."

"John Cornford's been involved in politics for as long as we've known him," Gabriel said. "Tony's utterly different. I doubt whether he could tell the difference between a communist and a fascist. Darling, don't cry. Please don't cry. He'll be all right. I'm sure he'll be all right."

But Frances sobbed on and on, while Gwen sat in silence, wondering whether she could say nothing or, if she had to speak, exactly how much she should reveal.

She waited until Frances stood up, muttered something about tidying herself up and stumbled into the house. Gabriel let her go. "She's overwrought and tired. Give her half an hour and she'll feel better."

From across the road came the sound of Mr Escott's cows gathering for the evening milking. Nearer at hand a thrush tapped the shell of a snail against a stone. The shadows of evening were beginning to creep over the lawn.

"Gabriel."

"Mm?"

"I feel a bit guilty. Very guilty, in fact."

He gave her a faint smile. "Without reason, I'm sure."

She shook her head and swallowed. "I didn't like to say anything in front of Frances, but... Oh dear, this is difficult. The fact is, Gabriel, Tony has got some money. Quite a lot, I'm afraid. I've been paying him, you see. For the work he's done for me."

Gabriel sat very still. "Since when?"

173

"The beginning. You must understand," she said quickly, "I couldn't let him do it, not regular work – hard labour, a lot of it – without giving him *something*."

"So ... Easter last year then. Right?"

She nodded.

"How much did you pay him?"

"Well ... labourer's wages."

"But, Gwen, you haven't that sort of money to throw around. Or you hadn't when you started."

"I know. That's why I started selling flowers. Quite funny really, when you think about it." But what was happening now wasn't in the least funny. "I needed the money to pay for the orchids, as well as for Tony, but I needed Tony to help get the orchids set up. A kind of circle really. So when Mr Cole wrote and asked if I was interested in selling him orchids, well, naturally I said yes. That's how it all began. And of course, once Mr Cole had begun buying, then I had money to pay Tony. And that led to Mrs Meyer and more money..."

"Was this Tony's idea, or yours?"

She stalled. "What do you mean?"

"Did he ask you to pay him? Or did you suggest it?"

"Well ... he suggested it, originally. I was happy to do it, Gabriel. Don't think he didn't earn it. It's just now, not knowing..."

"Did he ever tell you what he wanted it for?"

"No. I did ask, but he wouldn't say. He did tell me that it would take a long time and he'd be grown up before he'd saved enough."

"I see."

"I'm sorry," she said miserably.

"It does put a rather different complexion on things,

I must admit. How much do you think he's saved?"

"I don't know. I could work it out." Why hadn't she insisted on knowing? Why hadn't she refused to pay him unless he told her what it was he wanted? "Do *you* think he has gone abroad?"

"I don't know. I'd say it was unlikely. He's never shown any interest in the continent up until now."

"That's another thing, Gabriel. I know you don't think so, but I've always thought Tony was quite interested in politics, myself. Lately, anyway."

He looked at her. "Spain?"

"Not Spain," she admitted. "Germany. He's talked quite a bit about Germany – the way they've been rearming and the fact that they've got more aeroplanes than we have. And the new kind of roads – I forget what they're called."

"Autobahns."

"That's it. They seem to have made a big impression on him. He says they've been built straight and wide to make it easy for the German army to reach the frontier. I'm afraid I didn't pay much attention. You've always gone on about Germany, so I just thought it had rubbed off on him. Besides, I've always assumed no country would be stupid enough to want war after last time. It wasn't until Frances said that about Spain..." Her voice trailed away.

"I still think Spain's unlikely," Gabriel said. "As for Germany ... I don't know. I'm very much afraid we shall just have to wait and hope he returns when he's due. Frances will find that harder than I."

They refused her invitation to stay – "You could go up to the Quantocks for the day and paint. You know you'll only fret back at home" – saying that they must return to Cambridge

175

in case Tony had left a message with a neighbour or friend.

"We'll send you a telegram as soon as we have any news," Frances promised, getting into the car.

Gabriel put an arm round Gwen's shoulders. "Don't blame yourself," he said.

But she did.

She waited until the sound of the engine had faded into the distance before going in search of Waite. She found him blanching celery on the far side of the vegetable garden.

"Tony's disappeared," she told him. "No one's seen him these holidays. I suppose you haven't any idea where he might be?"

Waite gripped the celery in one hand while fishing in his apron pocket with the other. "The lad's said nothing to me."

"His mother's frightened he's run off to join the fighting in Spain."

He tied a broad band of raffia slowly and deliberately round the celery stems, before straightening his back. He looked her in the eye. "I'd be surprised if he has," he said. "Don't you worry, Miss Purcell. He won't come to harm, won't Master Tony. He's a lad can look after himself."

Could he? she wondered. Could he?

She spent the rest of the day in the orchid house. She felt Tony's presence all around her. His efforts had helped put the house in place, transport the plants, fill the shelves. His admiration had flattered her at the beginning of every holiday. "What a *lot* you've done since I was here..." At times his interest had matched hers, his pleasure in the flowers been as great. Under the bench lay the original list he had made, the paper now curled, the ink faded, but the writing still clearly his, uneven and untidy. "Question Mark?" How he had laughed. "That's a funny name for an orchid."

Would he ever see Question Mark's flowers?

She occupied herself with washing crocks, preparing pots, tidying up the already tidy bench, her thoughts circling endlessly over possibilities of where he might be, what he might be doing, while she waited for the telegram Frances had promised, should there be news.

No telegram came.

Chapter Fourteen

Annie stood at the greenhouse door. "He's here," she said.

Gwen looked up from the cattleya she was studying. For a moment she could think only of her orchids. "Who?"

"The lad. Tony. Walked into the kitchen a minute ago. 'Hello, Annie,' he says, bold as brass. 'How are you?' Looks fit, I'll say that for him."

Gwen felt weak-kneed with relief. "What did you tell him? Does he know we've seen Frances and Gabriel?"

Annie shook her head. "Told him nothing. Said it was good to see him, same as I always do. I left him working his way through a loaf of bread. Starving, he be."

"All right, Annie. Go back, but don't say anything. I'll be with you in a minute."

She stood without moving. Anger took over from relief. Three days of fearing the worst. Three mornings spent digging the vegetable patch. "No need to do that, Miss Purcell," Waite had protested. "Leave it to me." "I must," she had told him. Ramming the spade into the baked earth, heaving the clods up, turning them over. And now here he was, walking into the house as if nothing had happened.

He was spreading bread thickly with apricot jam when she came into the kitchen, while Annie chopped windfalls for chutney. His face lit up when he saw her. He jumped up, came forward and gave her a hug. "Hello, Aunt Gwen!"

He had changed. He was taller now than she was. He had lost weight. There was a trace of down on his upper lip. His voice had deepened. But there was something more than physical change, something indefinable in the way he held himself. She watched him sit down and reach again for the bread. Don't shout at him, she told herself. Keep calm.

"You're looking very well," she said. "Very sunburnt."

"It's being out in the open that does it," he said. He cut himself another slice of bread, sawing at the loaf so that the end was jagged and slanting.

"How was the harvest?"

"Hard work. Fun, though."

"Finished now, is it?"

"More or less. Aunt Mary let me go anyway. She knew I wanted to see you before going home."

"That was nice of her. And of you. I'm flattered." She waited. At the speed he was eating, the loaf would be finished in a matter of minutes. "Didn't Aunt Mary feed you before you left? Or give you a packed lunch for the journey? That doesn't seem like her."

He didn't look up. "She probably would have, but I expected to get here by lunchtime. I hitch-hiked to save the train fare, but it took longer than I expected."

"I see. Still saving, are you?" She sat down on the other side of the table. "How are your parents?"

"All right, as far as I know. They're not exactly communicative when they're working, are they? It's hot, Mother

179

said. Which is what you'd expect of the south of France. She says Dad's living in the world of his book. Bit of a waste of money going to Provence at that rate, I would have thought, but still. Have you heard from them?"

"Yes. They were here the other day."

The words took a moment to sink in. He stopped eating. He stared at her. Colour, sunburn, both drained from his face. "Here?"

"Here."

"What were they doing here?"

"Looking for you."

He swallowed. "Did you tell them I was with the Merediths?"

"Of course. But you weren't, were you? You haven't been there all summer. As Aunt Mary told them when they arrived."

He looked down at his hands. Big hands. A boy's hands no longer. "Next week, they said. They told me they'd be back home at the end of next week."

"That's what they planned, yes, but then they felt sorry for you, having to work so hard through the summer, first on the farm and then here at Hillcrest. They thought you could do with a holiday too, before getting back for your lessons. So they left Provence early in order to give you a week's sailing in Devon."

He sat silent.

She stood up. "How could you do it, Tony? To them and to me? Didn't it occur to you that it was bound to come out? They've been out of their minds with worry, not knowing where you were or what you were doing. So has Annie. So have I. You *used* us, Tony, spinning so many tales and not one of them true. You deceived us."

"I didn't mean to. I was sure it would be all right. I didn't think you'd find out."

"Of course we'd find out. If not now, then later. We all keep in touch – or hadn't you thought about that? Well, I'd better go and put them out of their misery. Don't you dare move while I'm gone. I'm not having you leave the house until they arrive. Is that clear?"

He sounded alarmed. "I don't want them to fetch me," he said. "Please, Aunt Gwen. I'll hitch-hike home. I'll leave now."

"And disappear off the face of the earth once more? You will not. Look after him, Annie."

"Growing up fast, isn't he, your nephew?" Stephen Tuck observed as he passed a telegram form over the post office counter for Gwen to fill in. "Saw him through the window earlier this afternoon. Scarcely recognized him. Soon be as tall as his father."

"Yes," she agreed, making a mental note to take Tony over to the Rectory before his grandparents heard of his arrival from any other source, and wondering what story she could tell that would be close to the truth. As she filled in the form – TONY ARRIVED THIS AFTERNOON SAFE AND WELL WILL YOU FETCH – she realized that she had been so angry at his duplicity that she still did not know where he had been during the past weeks or what he had been doing.

He was washing dried fruit in the sink when she returned to the kitchen, while Annie creamed butter and sugar, the cut flesh of the abandoned apple slowly turning brown in the preserving pan on the dresser. Well, Gwen thought grimly, he hadn't wasted much time getting round Annie.

"Right," she said. "That's your parents informed. I imagine they'll drive down tomorrow to collect you. Now, my

181

lad, you'd better tell us what you've been doing with your-self all this time."

He glanced from Gwen to Annie and back to Gwen. Then he drained the dried fruit and brought it over to the kitchen table where he started drying it in a tea towel.

"I've been flying," he said at last.

Her heart lurched. For a moment she saw again in her mind the picture of an aeroplane dropping slowly, oh so slowly, into the distant sea. *"Flying?"*

"Well, not flying, exactly. I mean, I have been up in the air but only a few times."

She sat down. "You'd better tell us about it from the beginning."

He looked at Annie again. Had he told her already? "It's a long time ago, the beginning," he said. "Two summers – 1934, in fact. I was spending part of the holidays with Walker – a friend of mine from school. There was an airfield not far from his home. It wasn't much of a place, just a hangar and a couple of sheds. There were two pilots there, who took turns to take people up. Seven shillings it cost, for one flight. I hadn't got that sort of money, of course, and neither had Walker, but he persuaded his father to pay, so up we went. There was just room for two passengers sitting behind the pilot. It was" – he smiled to himself, reliving the moment – "wonderful. You can't imagine how wonderful. Like being a bird, I suppose. Everything looks so neat and tidy from up there, and the colours so bright. A bit like patchwork, somehow. It was summer, like now. Most of the fields had been harvested and some had been ploughed. It's amazing what you can see from that height – all sorts of things you'd never imagine. Roman roads, things like that. It's not just what you see, either. It's so exciting.

The wind tears at your hair, your face freezes, and your scalp aches and smarts. I didn't like banking at all, that scared me a lot, but bumps were great fun."

He stopped.

"So," she prompted. "This was two years ago. Before you started working for me?"

He nodded. "That's when I decided I must learn to fly. It was all I wanted to do. But it's expensive, you see. It's not just the lessons that cost money, though they do. The real trouble comes because you don't know how long it's going to take you to gain your licence. You don't want to have half a dozen lessons and then have to wait for weeks or months until you've saved up money for more. You want to carry on until you can pay for the lot. Mr Marshall – he was the pilot who took us up – said it was the only way to do it, and I could understand that. He said I was too young, anyway. So I decided that by the time I was old enough I must have saved enough. Only I couldn't think how to do it. We came down here at Christmas – the Christmas before last, that was. Willy Roberts said he'd show me how engines worked, which seemed a good idea. I didn't know whether aeroplane engines were like car engines or not, but at least I felt I was doing something—"

"Was Willy in this?" she interrupted. "Did he know you wanted to fly?"

Tony shook his head. "Not then. It didn't seem sensible to tell him in case he let on to his mother. In which case it was bound to get back to Granny."

At least he had shown some sense. "Go on."

"As a matter of fact," he said, "though I didn't tell Willy in so many words, I'm sure he guessed. He's not stupid, and it must have been obvious."

"I don't see why. If I didn't guess why should he?"

He looked from Gwen to Annie and back again. "I persuaded him to take me to an air show when I was down here last summer."

"An air show? Here? Where?"

"At Taunton. Musgrove Field. Well, there'd been one the previous week in Wellington, but Willy couldn't come to that because he was working. I was a bit worried that time, because I wasn't sure whether you'd noticed how long I'd been gone, so I persuaded Willy to take me into Taunton on his motorbike. He'd only just bought it, you see, and he was dying to show it off. He managed to get the afternoon off from the garage and we went together. Taunton was the show I really wanted to go to because it was Sir Alan Cobham. There was lots of flying – crazy flying, they called some of it. There was even a woman in a glider, looping the loop. Joan Meakin, she was called. Have you heard of her?"

Gwen shook her head. "You know I don't know anything about flying."

"She was amazing." His nervousness had disappeared. He was confident. "There were lots of aircraft to look at. And you could fly too. Only four shillings this time. I offered to pay for Willy but he wouldn't come up. I don't think he'd wanted to go to the air show really, but he'd let me persuade him. And of course we needed the bike to get back before you got home. So I went up on my own. The pilot wasn't as nice as Mr Marshall, but it was just as wonderful. You'd be surprised how small the Quantocks look from the air."

"Presumably that was the day Aunt Lucy and I saw you with Willy?"

He nodded. "We'd intended to get back earlier, but I'd had to queue for the flight, so wc wcre late. That's why we were going a bit fast." He paused, but she said nothing. "Anyway," he continued, "we all came down here for Christmas. Granny decided she couldn't knit me the usual sweater, because her hands were too bad, so she gave me money instead. Uncle David gave me half a crown at the end of the holidays and you did too. That started my savings, but after that ... well, I don't get very much pocket money and you do need tuck at school, particularly in the winter. I could see it was going to take years and years to save all the money I needed. I was quite depressed really. Then we came down here at Easter and you were depressed too, because you'd been given the orchids and didn't know where to put them... You know how Grandpa's always saying God moves in a mysterious way? That Easter I was sure he was right. I thought that God was moving, for you, as well as for me. It wasn't just the money, Aunt Gwen. I know that was why I started working for you, and I don't suppose I would have offered otherwise, but I really enjoyed doing it. I was interested. I didn't think I would be but I was."

"But the money helped?"

"Well, yes, of course it did. I don't want to be an old man before I've saved enough. Besides, it's pointless getting your licence if you can't afford to carry on flying afterwards."

He stopped. Annie tipped the dried fruit on top of the creamed butter and sugar and began mixing them in. She gave him an encouraging nod. "Go on, lad. Your aunt wants the full story. Better tell her what's happened this summer."

"Well." He took a deep breath. "I've been working at an airfield in Suffolk. I discovered the place last year, by accident, when I was out for the day on my bike. I stopped for a couple of hours and people were friendly, so I said to myself, why not try it this summer. I'd been saving hard so

I didn't feel too badly about spending some of it on digs. I didn't do much at first, sort of hung around, you know. I thought, if I could get my face known... And it worked. There were just a couple of pilots, and another man working on the ground, so there was plenty to do. They were glad to have me around, I think. I know they were, in fact, because in the end they started paying me. Not much, just a couple of bob a day, but it all helped. Mr Henderson, the one in charge, called me their ground assistant. I was pleased about that. It sounded rather good, I thought. Sort of official, don't you think?"

She nodded. How he's changed since last Easter, she was thinking. So self-assured now. "Go on," she said.

"I had hoped I might get a lesson or two without having to pay – you know, if one of the pilots hadn't got anything better to do. That didn't happen. I suppose it was a bit much to expect. And I did get up into the air, several times. If there was only one passenger wanting a ride they'd take me up too to add weight. And of course I learnt an awful lot just by watching. Like learning to drive, really. Do you remember how surprised Uncle David was by how much I knew, that time he gave me my first lesson? So I hope, when I do start, it won't take me too long..." He stopped. "I don't have to tell Mother and Dad all this, do I? They might not let me have lessons at all."

"They might not, indeed. In which case you'll have to wait until you're twenty-one, won't you?" She saw the shock on his face and for a moment was glad. It served him right. He hadn't the faintest idea of the distress he had caused. "I wouldn't, if I were them. Not so much because of what you were doing, but because of the deceit and the lies."

"That was your doing," he said.

"*My* doing?" For a moment she was speechless. "I don't believe it."

"It was. Don't you remember? You told me how Uncle Antony said it was a duty not to tell people things if it was going to make them worry. You admired him. You did, Aunt Gwen. You told me so. I was going to tell people in the end but not for a while. I had it all worked out. I'd wait until I'd got my licence, and then I'd fly over the house when Mother and Dad were in, and waggle my wings at them. Then, when I got home afterwards, I'd say, 'Do you remember that aeroplane flying overhead this morning? Well, it was me.' I thought they'd be pleased. It would show them I could do something."

"Oh, Tony." Such dreams, such wild dreams. She could not decide whether to laugh or cry.

He said little during supper. He was apprehensive, no doubt, and with reason. As indeed she was. Would Frances consider her partly responsible?

Tony picked without appetite at his apple crumble. "Will they be very angry?"

"You can't blame them if they are, after the worry you've given them. You should have told them."

"It wouldn't have done any good if I had. They wouldn't have let me do it."

He was right, of course. "Flying is *dangerous*, Tony."

"Not always, it isn't. If you do something stupid, of course it is. And if you do something difficult like aerobatics or flying round the world, then it can be. Not other wise. One of the Avro Cadets hit a haystack when Alan Cobham was at Dulverton. It didn't rise quickly enough, they said. The aircraft was in a bad way but the pilot was all right. He wasn't hurt."

Now that she came to think of it the pilot of the aircraft that had dropped into the sea had been back on dry land with his passenger within the hour, wet certainly, but otherwise unharmed.

"That's what they teach you to fly in, in the air force," Tony was saying. "Avro Cadets."

"Perhaps you should join the RAF. Then you wouldn't need money for flying lessons."

"I can't. Dad expects me to go to university."

"He might change his mind."

"If there's a war on he would," Tony said hopefully.

She was irritated. All this talk of war ... and to sound so hopeful... "Don't be silly, Tony. There won't be a war. There couldn't be. No one would be so stupid."

"Don't be sure. Ask Dad. He says there will be. In which case the air force will need all the pilots it can get. The Germans are stronger than us already, and they didn't have any planes at all this time last year."

She shivered. "Don't let's talk about it. I know it's impossible, but all the same..."

"That's the trouble with people like you," he said. "You all say don't let's talk about it, so nobody does. Hitler takes over the Saar. Nobody says a word. Then he walks into the Rhineland. Still nobody says anything. But it'll come, you'll see. Mr Henderson's certain Hitler's going to send his bombers into Spain. He'll want them to get experience, Mr Henderson says."

She could feel her irritation growing. Just because he had spent the summer with adults, he thought he knew everything. "Mr Henderson this, Mr Henderson that. You're getting above yourself, Tony. You're only fourteen, you know, far too young to understand what's going on in the outside world. Just because you've been mixing with older people—"

He was indignant. "I understand much better than you do, Aunt Gwen. You haven't the faintest idea what's going on in the rest of the world because you never go out into it. You never have. You just sit here. You wouldn't even go to Greece with Mother and Father when they asked you. All you're interested in is the garden. And your orchids, of course. You can't say what will happen or what won't because you don't know."

He stopped at the sight of her face.

"And you do, I suppose," she said. "I think it's high time you went to bed, Tony. You may think you're grown up, but you're still only a schoolboy."

He opened his mouth as he stood up, thought better of whatever it was he was going to say and went out of the room without a word or a backward glance. His footsteps sounded on the stairs and along the landing.

She was shaking. How dare he speak to her so. She took refuge in the orchid house. Only her plants could soothe. The scent of the early cymbidiums hung in the air as she stood, breathing deeply. After a while she pulled up the blinds and gave the floor its final soak of the day before going back into Hillcrest.

"You know what the rector tells us," Annie said as she passed the kitchen door. "Don't let the sun go down on your wrath. It's nearly gone down, has the old sun."

"I know. I'm going up to him."

He was already in bed, lying on his back with arms folded under his head, gazing up at the ceiling. Seeing aeroplanes, no doubt. He looked younger than he had downstairs, and surprisingly vulnerable.

"I really did think it would be all right," he said, without turning his head. "I thought you'd admired Uncle Antony for deceiving Granny and Grandpa. You didn't criticize him when you told me about it. And I know Dad is disappointed I'm not more like him. I thought if I did the same thing..."

"I know." She picked up a book from the floor to put on the table. "*The Pilot's Book of Everest.* What's this?"

"Mr Henderson said I should read it. It's exciting, he said. It's about two pilots who flew over Everest."

She shivered. "Exciting, maybe, but I think you'd be wise to keep it away from your mother."

She stood at the window. Outside, the churchyard and front garden were in shadow. Only the church tower still had the sun shining on it. Wearily she rested her cheek against the cold glass, drained by the emotions of the past hours, remembering the aeroplane at Watchet.

"Everything would have been all right," Tony said from his bed, "if only they hadn't come home when they did. I couldn't have expected that."

She reached out for the curtains. "No."

"Leave them open," he said. "I'm used to the light. I like the sun waking me up."

She came slowly away from the window into the room. "Where did you stay in Suffolk?"

"In digs, first of all. They were all right. Expensive, though. And then I got frightened. The landlady kept asking me questions, you see. Where did I live, what was I doing, all that sort of thing. I was afraid she'd go to the police, so I left. By that time everyone knew me at the airfield. They let me kip down there. On the hangar floor. In the office. Anywhere, really."

"Not very comfortable," she said.

"It didn't matter. I was happy just to be there."

"I can see that." She hesitated in the doorway, realizing with a pang that he had grown too old to kiss goodnight. "Try not to worry about tomorrow, love. I'm sure things will work out in the end."

He looked up at her from the pillow. His forehead was white where his hair had protected it from the sun. "I thought you'd understand how I feel, Aunt Gwen. You, of all people."

"Why me?"

"Flying's like your orchids. Once you're involved you can't think of anything else."

Chapter Fifteen

Tony picked at his breakfast next morning; when asked what he wanted for lunch he told Annie he wouldn't be hungry and wondered, with obvious dread, what time his parents were likely to arrive. Learning from Gwen that it was unlikely to be before mid-afternoon, he gave a gusty sigh and said that he thought he was beginning to feel a bit sick. He went out to greet Waite the moment the latter arrived, and at Gwen's suggestion paid a brief visit to the Rectory. Gwen did not ask him what he told his grandparents; she would find that out later from Lucy. The self-confidence he had shown yesterday had disappeared overnight. Not until he was invited into the orchid house to admire Question Mark's developing spike did he begin to brighten.

His reaction was all that Gwen could have hoped for.

"Oh, Aunt Gwen. Isn't it wonderful! How much longer before it comes out? It's not fair that I shan't be here to see it. You couldn't possibly send me a flower, could you? Just one? After all, you couldn't have done all this if you hadn't had my help at the beginning."

"I know. And of course I'd send a flower if I could,"

Gwen said, "but you know enough about orchids by now to realize that removing even one flower ruins a spike."

He nodded, turning the pot round to admire Question Mark from every angle. "Tell you what. Why don't you send me a postcard when it comes out? Then I can take a day off school and hitch-hike down here to see it." His grin was the first she had seen since his arrival.

"That really would get you into hot water, wouldn't it? It would be more sensible if I drove up to school with it."

"Do you mean it? Will you?" He stopped, grabbed her arm. His eyes widened. "It's them."

"It can't be. It's too early."

But it was. She recognized the sound of the engine.

"What shall I tell them?"

"The truth. What else?" She looked at his white face and softened. "Go and wait in the drawing-room. I know your mother. She'll lose her temper and shout – with reason, I might add – but she's never angry for long. I'll send her in to you while I deal with your father. Whatever you do, don't answer her back. It'll make her worse."

She watched him disappear through the French windows, sighed as she removed her gardening apron and went into the house.

Frances was already at the back door. "Where is he? Just let me get my hands on the brat."

"In the drawing-room. Frances—"

"I could strangle him. I mean it. I could."

"Try not to say anything you'll regret later," Gwen begged. "And, Frances, please. Do remember. Boys will be boys. They're bound to get into trouble now and then. You'd be the first to worry if he didn't."

Frances gave her a withering look and swept into the house.

Gabriel limped down the steps into the courtyard, saw Gwen and stopped. "Well?"

"He's fine. Upset about the trouble he's caused. It never occurred to him ... well, it did, but he didn't think anyone would find out. That's what it amounts to, really."

"Where the devil's he been?"

"On an airfield. Somewhere in Suffolk. He wants to fly – he's desperate to fly." The sound of Frances's irate voice came out from the house. Not a sound from Tony, thank goodness. Gwen had suffered too much from Frances's quick temper in the past not to feel sympathetic. "Gabriel. Listen. He's all right, is Tony. He – I do think he's more sensitive than you realize. He's desperate to please you, you know. He always has been." How much could she – should she – say?

"He goes a strange way about it," Gabriel said.

"I don't think you should want him to be like you were at his age. Or Antony, for that matter. He's not academic. He never has been. To expect him to keep his head in his books is ... well, like Frances expecting Sarah to be able to paint, just because Mother and the rest of us never did anything else. You know how she crushed that poor child."

Annie's face appeared at the kitchen window. "We didn't think you'd be here this early, Mr Gabriel," she said. "Will you be staying for lunch?"

"Yes, please, Annie. We didn't intend to be so early, as a matter of fact, but as neither of us could sleep there didn't seem any point in hanging about. We set off with the dawn chorus." He turned back to Gwen. "Are you saying that I crush Tony?"

"No, of course not. I know he needs telling off – I was furious with him myself yesterday. Don't be too hard on

194

him, that's all. He has lots of good points, if only you could see them."

"I do see them. I'm not blind. What I find so unforgivable is the way he upsets Frances."

Always Frances, Gwen thought. There were others who could do with some consideration – Tony himself for one. "We were upset too," she pointed out.

"It's hardly the same, is it?"

"I suppose not." She was silent for a moment, trying to summon up courage to be frank. "What about you and your mother, Gabriel? She didn't like you wandering round the continent, did she, but you carried on doing it all the same. You used to provoke her deliberately over the Fabians and the Poor Law, all those interests you had that she hated. You must have been older than Tony then. In your twenties, I'd have said."

His expression was grim. Now I really have gone too far, she told herself. Suddenly he smiled, the old, familiar smile.

"You're right. I did. I'd forgotten. Perhaps it's a Mackenzie failing, irritating one's mother." He cocked his head, listening to Frances's voice, milder now but still raised. "Do you think I should rescue him?"

Gwen smiled back. "Yes. Do that, and I'll give Annie a hand with the food."

Frances was still flushed when she sat down to lunch, but she said nothing. Gwen suspected that she had been crying. Tony was understandably subdued. Gwen, having kept out of earshot, first in the garden and then in the kitchen, did not know what had been said between the three of them and would not ask. It was Gabriel who kept the conversation going during the meal by seeking further enlightenment.

"What happened to our letters to you? Did you get them? Aunt Mary said nothing had come for you all summer."

Tony cast a nervous glance round the table. "Hector sent everything on to me," he muttered.

"Hector? So I was right. He was in the plot too. Poor boy. He had to get up early each day to waylay the postman, did he? I hope you appreciate what a loyal friend you have there. He swore black and blue that he had no idea where you were or what you were doing. He's probably written you a panic-stricken letter, telling you that you're in deep trouble. It'll be waiting for you in Suffolk no doubt. When did you leave the airfield?"

"Three days ago. It took me longer to hitch-hike than I expected, being cross-country."

"Indeed. I can imagine you had problems, knowing your sense of geography. You'll have to do something about your map reading, won't you, if you're going to take to the air, otherwise you'll find yourself in dire straits. And another thing. I can't quite understand why you're at Hillcrest at all. It seems absurd to make such a journey for only a couple of days. Why didn't you stay in Suffolk until it was time to go home?"

Tony played with his apple crumble. "I was sort of covering my tracks," he muttered. "I thought if I spent a couple of days here, and a couple of days at Aunt Mary's, then if you all started talking together you wouldn't realize I hadn't been around for the whole summer."

"I see. Rather a forlorn hope, wasn't it?"

Tony gave a miserable nod.

Gabriel caught Gwen's eye across the table. If she hadn't known better, she would have said he was hard put to stop himself laughing.

"Meanwhile you caused chaos and confusion throughout the land. It wasn't just your mother and I, you know. Aunt Gwen and Annie have been anxious too. Aunt Gwen has enough on her mind without worrying about you. Which reminds me – how is business, Gwen? And the orchids? How remiss of me not to have asked before."

"It's all going very well," Gwen said, grateful to be able to distract attention from her nephew. "I've as much business as I can cope with at present, and as for the orchids, well, that's very exciting. The mystery cymbidium has developed a spike. You know, the one Tony christened Question Mark. We're waiting for it to flower."

"What happens when it does?"

"It depends. If it looks special I'll need advice. From the Royal Horticultural Society, probably. Or there's someone north of Bristol Mrs Whitelaw's told me about. One of his plants is a parent of Question Mark so it might be sensible to see him. I suppose you couldn't show me the best route on the map, Gabriel? You know how I hate driving when I'm not sure of the way."

"I'd be happy to. And what about Germany? I hear our orchid professor has invited you over."

"That was months ago. Before Easter. I refused. He still keeps asking me though. First of all he just wanted to show me his orchids. Now he wants me to paint them."

"Well?"

"What do you mean, well?"

"Not tempted?"

She was about to deny it, when she remembered how hurt she had been by Tony's accusation the previous day that she never went anywhere. She said, "I am, as a matter of fact."

There was a stunned silence round the table.

"Are you serious?" Gabriel said.

She wondered whether she had taken leave of her senses. "I would be if there wasn't the problem of language."

"No need to worry about that," Gabriel said. "Ebert speaks perfect English. And Thomas Cook's people are everywhere, should you need help on the journey."

"There's the difficulty of leaving the garden, as well. Not to mention the orchids."

"If you flew you'd save masses of time," Tony said. "Days, probably."

"I'm not flying. Not over water, anyway. Definitely not over water."

"Waite could cope, couldn't he?" Frances said. "How long were you thinking of going? A week? Two weeks? He and Annie could manage without you, I'm sure."

"What about Mrs Meyer and Mr Cole?"

"Tell them you won't be able to provide anything while you're away," Gabriel said. "It's not as if they pay you a retainer."

"There's still Question Mark. I can't be away when Question Mark flowers."

"You're expecting that to happen within the next few days, you said. That still leaves plenty of time before winter."

"Well," Gwen said, and tried to smile round the table, "it looks as if everything's settled."

"We'll call in at the Rectory on the way," Gabriel said when they were leaving. "Let us know what happens about Germany. I'd be happy to see to your travel arrangements if it would help."

Frances, obviously still upset, said little. Tony gave Gwen a bear hug. "Thanks," he muttered gruffly. He leant out of the window as the car turned down Tinker's Lane. "You won't forget to let me know about Question Mark, will you?"

Back in the kitchen Annie had brought out the apples she had been preparing before Tony's arrival the previous day. "Don't suppose the colour will matter," she said practically. "Chutney's brown all over when it's simmered. Give us a hand with the onions, there's a love."

Within minutes she complained. "It doesn't take much effort to chop onions, I'd have said, but we'll be here all day if you don't get a move on. Just look at you, sitting there with your eyes all glassy. In a dream, you are. 'Tis that Question Mark, I'll be bound. Them flowers are all you can think of these days."

"You must admit it is intriguing, wondering what it will look like," Gwen said. The brown skin of the onion crackled as she pulled it away from the bulb. "We don't even know what colour it will be."

"Don't see no point in wondering," Annie said, quartering an onion with an emphatic bang of the knife on the board. "We'll find out all in good time."

Good old Annie. Always so practical.

Footsteps sounded outside. Lucy's face appeared at the kitchen window. "Is Gwen...? Ah – Gwen, you're just the person I wanted to see." She came in through the back door and joined them at the table. "Gabriel was in good form, didn't you think? The other two seemed rather subdued – with us, anyway. Goodness, your onions are strong. Don't let me hold you up; I only came round to ask Gwen a favour."

"A favour?"

"We've got a problem with tomorrow's WI meeting. Miss Legge was supposed to be giving a demonstration of embroidery and knitting."

"Supposed?"

"She's lost her voice."

"It won't matter, will it? She's giving a demonstration, not a lecture."

"She planned to talk too. Anyway, she's sent a message to say she can't do it, so I wondered, well ... would you step into the breach?"

Gwen gaped. "Me?" She took a deep breath. "Doing what, may I ask?"

"Whatever you like. Mother suggested a talk about orchids. I thought if you didn't want to do that, you could talk about sending flowers up to London. People are intrigued, you know. They might even offer you things from their own gardens as a result. Personally I think something on orchids would be best, but it's up to you."

"I couldn't possibly." The mere thought of standing up in front of everyone made her hands clammy. "Couldn't we have a social instead? A whist drive, say. Or a discussion of some sort."

"We had a whist drive the time before last. A discussion's all very well, but on what? You know we like to give everyone plenty of time to think beforehand, otherwise they sit there with nothing to say. Besides, members look forward to a speaker. Don't let me down. If Julia can do it, so can you."

"Julia's different. You know how she feels about her Mothers and Babies. She'd stand up in Parliament if she thought it would do any good."

Lucy raised her eyebrows. "And you don't feel strongly

about your orchids? Come on, Gwen. You scarcely think of anything else."

"I'd bore everyone to tears."

"Why? If you find them interesting, why shouldn't we?"

"I'm sorry, Lucy, really I am, but no. I'm no good at that sort of thing."

"You've never done it, so you can't know whether you'd be good or not. All I'm asking, Gwen, is that you stand up and talk about orchids for half an hour. It's not long, is it? Tell us where they come from, how they grow – give us a bit of geography and botany. Tell us what attracts you about them. After all, you didn't want to take them on at the beginning, did you, and look at you now. You could bring one or two over to show us. Some of your paintings too, if you like, then you can tell us how you set about doing them. You could spin that out for thirty minutes, couldn't you? Please."

What could she do but agree?

"You did right, love," Annie told her after Lucy had left promising to return the following afternoon to help load up the car. "It wouldn't have done to say no."

"It's just as well you think that," Gwen told her, "because you're going to have to do the chutney yourself now, while I go and work out what on earth I'm going to say."

"It's WI this afternoon," Annie told Waite when he came in for his lunchtime soup next day to a kitchen reeking of vinegar. "I'll leave your tea in a Thermos. Miss Purcell is going to talk to us about orchids."

Waite looked across at Gwen. "Hmph" was his only comment, but later he volunteered to take anything she might need over to the parish room, and surprised her by wishing her good luck. "You'll do all right," he told her. Such assurance, she feared, was ill merited.

Committee members were already there when she arrived to help her arrange the orchids she had brought. Miss Ross, the retired schoolmistress, had borrowed a map from the school. "Miss Mackenzie thought you might need it."

"Nothing to public speaking," Miss Blake said when she saw Gwen's hands shaking. That was all very well for Miss Blake, who, rumour had it, had run her own theatre school before moving to Clay Court. "Remember to take deep breaths before you start," she advised, adding, when Gwen looked sceptical; "the best thing to do, if you really are nervous, is to pretend to be someone else. How about a learned gentleman from the Royal Horticultural Society? Or a botanical professor from Kew Gardens?"

In the end, and much to Gwen's relief, the talk went surprisingly well. She stuttered badly at the start, her voice at first too loud and then, when she realized and tried to bring it under control, too soft, but by the time she had pointed out orchid habitats on the world map her confidence began to return. The smile of encouragement from Annie, sitting in her usual chair in the back row between Mary Roberts and Bertha from the Rectory, banished the last trace of stage fright; from that moment on she talked only to her.

She had planned to show photographs of orchids in the wild, but realized in time that black and white scarcely did such exotic plants justice. Instead she brought her own paintings. It might seem self-important but she could point out in them the distinctive parts of the flower and show the different varieties. She told them about Victorian collectors ranging the globe in their search for plants to bring back to this country, talked about the pleasure and problems for amateur growers like herself, and tried to convey to her listeners the excitement she felt watching the development of Question Mark's spike.

When at last she sat down she was astonished to discover she had been speaking for over an hour. She could not imagine why she should have been so terrified at the thought of giving the talk; it was only later that she realized her careful preparation the evening before might have had something to do with its success.

Lucy, as chairman, interrupted the ripple of applause by asking for questions. One member wanted to know whether orchids were poisonous; a farmer's wife was interested in fertilization. Mrs Kirby was called upon to give a vote of thanks, which she did, scarlet-faced (Gwen felt for her), there was enthusiastic applause and the meeting adjourned for tea and home-made scones, during which Mrs Whitelaw, eyes glistening, came up to Gwen.

"Oh, Miss Purcell, I'm so glad. I always knew Mr Whitelaw did right, giving his orchids to you."

"I told you you could do it," Lucy said. "It wasn't so bad, was it?"

"It wasn't," Gwen agreed in surprise, and wondered whether perhaps her proposed trip to Germany might not be so bad either.

Chapter Sixteen

Every day Question Mark's spike pushed a little further into the air. Every day the flower buds became more pronounced. Every evening Gwen willed the flower to open overnight; every morning she crept into the glasshouse to be disappointed.

The Mackenzies were quietly amused. "Things never change," Mr Mackenzie told her. "I remember how in the old days you used to arrive at the Rectory bubbling over with excitement about the first picking of some crop or other. I'm afraid we never showed the right amount of enthusiasm."

Gwen smiled at him with affection. "Neither did Frances nor Julia. It was Annie and Sarah I had to rely on."

"This orchid," Mrs Mackenzie said. "What will you do with it if it's so special?"

"I shall paint it," Gwen said. "I shall paint it, over and over again. After that, well, I shall have to see. And of course there may be nothing special about it. It could be hideous. Misshapen. The colours could be crude." She was frightening herself with the possibilities.

She took a candle into the orchid house on her return

from the Rectory. The flame was reflected in the glass pane against the darkness of the night outside, lighting up the planes of her face, emphasizing the hollows of her eyes. Too soon. The petals had yet to drop. Question Mark was keeping its secret still.

She lay in bed, unable to sleep, wondering about the unknown flower, as she had wondered for so many weeks.

Towards dawn she dozed. When she woke the walls of her room were light. She got up, put on her dressing-gown, thrust her feet into slippers and went quietly down the stairs, past the grandfather clock on the half landing, its steady tock marking each passing minute. She lifted the bar from the living-room shutters, opened the French windows and slipped through them to the veranda. The garden was grey and mysterious as it lay waiting for the sun to rise above the trees.

Her mouth was dry as she approached the glasshouse. She could feel her heart beating. Suppose it's a freak. Suppose something is wrong.

There was nothing wrong. In the light of early morning the first flower of the first spike was revealed, round, deep, creamy white with a darker cream lip and clean cream markings. Perfection itself. Gwen gazed at it in wonder, knowing that her eyes were the first to look on it. Tears spilled onto her cheeks.

Mrs Whitelaw too cried when she saw it. "If only Alfred could be here to see it."

Gwen gave her tea on the veranda. "It's his, really, you know," she said. "I think you should have it, rather than me. Only I would be grateful if I could paint it first..." No one would know the effort needed to make such an offer, yet she knew it had to be made.

But Mrs Whitelaw was firm. "No, Miss Purcell. He gave it to you. You may not remember, but I do. I'm sure he meant it as a thank you, for taking the rest on. Don't shake your head. I know you didn't want them, but you took them just the same. As for me, I did my bit, helping out when I could over the years and when you were starting, but that's over now. I've finished with orchids. Not that I'm not glad to see this one." Her voice shook as she brought out her handkerchief again.

"Well, if you're sure," Gwen said. "I am grateful. But you must tell me if you change your mind."

"I shan't," Mrs Whitelaw said with conviction. "What will you do with it now?"

"I shall paint the spike when the flowers are all out. Then ... I don't know. Keep it. I don't want Mr Cole to have the spike, nor Maximilian's in London."

"Have you thought of taking it to Mr Alexander at Westonbirt?" Mrs Whitelaw said. "I know it's not my place to say so, it not being my orchid, but I think you should. It needs to be registered, you see, and Mr Alexander will know how to do that. I still have Mr Whitelaw's notebooks in a drawer. I'd forgotten all about them, until your talk to the WI. I looked then, and there they were, just where he left them. All the details are there. One of Mr Alexander's hybrids was a parent. That's why I think you should talk to him."

It hadn't occurred to Gwen to consider parentage. Her efforts had been devoted to growing the plants as well as Mr Whitelaw would have wished. Hybridization was outside her interests. Yet she could see that she owed it to Mr Whitelaw to ensure recognition for the part he had played in Question Mark's genesis. "I'll think about it," she promised.

Mrs Whitelaw sat with the empty cup and saucer in her lap, looking across the lawn to the rose garden. "It's strange to be here," she said. "Mr Whitelaw described it to me, a long time ago. He came to see you. You'll have forgotten, no doubt. You'd been playing croquet on the lawn, he said, you four girls and the boys from the Rectory, the poor souls. 'It must be grand to have a big family,' he said when he came back." She glanced round, at the croquet hoops and mallets piled against the wall at the far end of the veranda, at the battered cricket bat left leaning against the trunk of the wisteria by Andrew at the end of his last visit, and sighed. "It wasn't that we didn't want children, you know. They didn't come, that was all."

"I'm sorry," Gwen said.

"He was good about it, mind. There's a reason for everything, he used to say. It's not for us to question God's purpose. Not having children meant more time for spreading the Word. That was how he looked at it. And he did have his orchids."

"I suppose so."

Mrs Whitelaw put her cup and saucer down on the table. "I'd best be getting back," she said. "And no, thank you, Miss Purcell, it's kind of you to offer, but I'm happy to walk. Thank you for the tea." As Gwen went with her to the gate she said, "I'm not good at putting things into words, but I am grateful for all you've done. Mr Whitelaw would be too. I'm sure he knows, wherever he is."

"I'd like to think so," Gwen said.

Left to herself, she would probably have done nothing. She was reluctant to approach strangers, particularly one of Mr Alexander's standing. But she had grown fond of Mrs

Whitelaw over the past eighteen months and was reluctant to disappoint her. Of greater importance, she felt she owed it to Mr Whitelaw. So she wrote to Mr Alexander, explaining about Question Mark and asking his advice.

His reply was short but courteous. He remembered Mr Whitelaw well, he said, for they had met and corresponded over a number of years. He was sorry to learn of his death. As for the orchid, he would be pleased to see it and advise her, should she care to visit Westonbirt.

Gwen discussed Gabriel's suggested route round Bristol with the AA, bought a road map of Gloucestershire and took the car down to Jim Harrison for a check-up. She packed Question Mark with infinite care and stowed the notebooks that Mrs Whitelaw had given her into a basket, along with the picnic Annie had made for her.

Mist hung in the valley as she set off, but cleared as she climbed the road onto the Quantocks. Leaves were yellowing in the beech trees above Cothelstone. There was a smell of leaf mould and smoke in the air – the scents of autumn. She felt momentary depression. In the old days each season lasted for ever. Now one season seemed to run into the next with scarcely a pause.

She arrived at Westonbirt with time to spare. The school lay on one side of the road, the arboretum on the other, just as she had been told. In the distance stood a double gabled house, with glasshouses adjoining. Woodlands: her destination. She glanced at her watch. She could picture Tony's laughter at her punctuality. "Oh, Aunt Gwen, you're always so early. What did you think might happen?" A puncture, perhaps, or a wrong turning. Better to arrive early, my lad, than too late.

She got out of the car with a sigh of relief and stretched,

before taking a rug from the boot and laying it out on the verge. She nibbled without appetite at her picnic, wishing that she had Tony with her, for company as well as for moral support. How was he getting along back at school? she wondered.

Mr Alexander was older than Gwen had expected. She was intimidated by his military bearing, but his expression was friendly and he talked easily enough of Mr Whitelaw and his orchids, so that she began slowly to relax. "I visited him several times at Huish Priory. And he came here, of course. Sadly he'd become very forgetful over the past few years. Overlooked letters, forgot that he'd written, that sort of thing. I can't say I was surprised to hear that he'd died."

He offered to show Gwen round, and within minutes she was mesmerized. She had pictured orchid houses similar to those at the Manor, where plants were cultivated for decoration, for their flowers, rather than for breeding. This was a business. Looking out over the rows of blooms, all bred by the man by her side, Gwen remembered her emotion on seeing Question Mark for the first time. What must it feel like to look over so many plants and know that they were your own creation?

"Now," Mr Alexander said as they retraced their steps to the entrance. "We come to the reason for your visit. Let me see your cymbidium."

Nervously she fetched Question Mark from the car and unwrapped it with infinite care. He took the pot from her hands, placed it on the bench and stood back. He took a deep breath. "It looks as if we have a winner here," he said.

She watched him examine the plant, first the spike as a whole, slowly, carefully, then each individual flower, then

209

the leaves. At last he straightened and smiled at her. "As I said. A winner. Now ... what about its parents?"

She handed him the notebook that Mrs Whitelaw had given her. "It's in there. *Cymbidium* Alexanderii Westonbirt was one parent. You bred that, Mrs Whitelaw said."

He nodded. "The first tetraploid. And the other – let me see. *Cymbidium* Hester Donne."

"Mr Whitelaw bred that himself. It's further back in the book. I've marked the place. Hester Donne was the daughter of Sir James Donne, Mr Whitelaw's employer."

"So," he said. "You have sufficient information to register the plant."

"How do I do that?"

"You submit it to the Royal Horticultural Society's Orchid Committee."

"Oh." She was apprehensive. "Does that mean I have to take it to London?"

His eyes were shrewd. "I'm on the Orchid Committee. Would you like me to see to it? I shall be exhibiting my own orchids at the next fortnightly show so I could take this one with them. The Orchid Committee meets the morning of the first day..."

She hesitated, scarcely taking in all he was saying about commendations and awards and certificates, as she realized what his offer meant. He was suggesting that she should abandon the orchid she had cherished over so many months and give Question Mark into his care.

"So," he summed up. "We're agreed? You'll leave the plant with me."

It would not be for long. Question Mark must be registered. She owed that much to Mr Whitelaw. And she trusted Mr Alexander. "Would you mind doing it? It seems an awful lot to ask, but it would make things easier for me. I'd be grateful."

The sun was low in a cream and pink sky as she drove over the brow of the Quantocks. The beech woods had become shadowy and mysterious in the half-light. All day she had been buoyed up, by nerves, by interest, by excitement. Now it was over. In her mind she could see the empty space on the bench of the glasshouse where Question Mark had stood filling the air with its fragrance.

She felt an overwhelming sense of loss.

Traces of the elation she had felt while at Westonbirt remained with her and helped dissipate any fears that she might have over her visit to Germany – for now that Question Mark had flowered she had no excuse to keep her at home. She had gained real pleasure from her conversation with someone so knowledgeable about orchids. Mr Alexander was eminent, however, and though she could learn much from him she could contribute little in return. In contrast, it sounded from his letters that the professor and she had much to offer each other. Besides, she was intrigued. He was growing orchids as he remembered them from his youth, he had told her, in an attempt to recreate the surroundings of his South American childhood. What challenges to the painter lay in his glasshouses?

Much had changed at Hillcrest recently, so subtly that Gwen had scarcely been aware of it. Waite's gradual acceptance of responsibility since the arrival of the orchids meant that he no longer objected to being left in charge of the garden, and Gwen herself was happy to leave him. Ridiculous as it might seem – for he was no different from what he had been before her discovery – she had more confidence in him now she knew that he had once been an officer.

Tony was delighted to hear of Gwen's plans. She could keep an eye open for aerodromes and aircraft while she was abroad, he wrote. If she saw any planes on the ground, she was to tell him how many and of what make. He enclosed silhouettes to help with identification.

"Better not take that letter with you," Annie warned. "One look at those funny shapes and they'll take it for granted you're a spy. You'll be up in front of a firing squad before you know what's what."

"Thank you, Annie," said Gwen. "That's all the encouragement I need."

Between them Gabriel and Professor Ebert saw to her travel arrangements. The professor arranged for her to be met at Munich by his daughter, who would entertain her for two nights before putting her on the train. Magda had known Gabriel years ago, apparently, and was looking forward to entertaining his sister-in-law. The news that her host had arranged for Gwen to stay at a guest house in the village nearest his home, a guest house not at all smart but quiet and homely, he said, cheered Gwen considerably, knowing that she could have solitude when she wanted it.

The inevitable question arose: what clothes to take with her? Surely one dress, old but still serviceable, together with a couple of skirts, and two or three blouses to ring the changes, would be adequate for evening meals in a comfortable guest house. Or should she include something smart, to be on the safe side?

She spent time she could ill afford going from shop to shop in Taunton, trying on tea dresses that she was assured were just the thing, but in which she felt and looked uncomfortable. She dithered over one, wondering whether it was as bad as she feared, and thought how much easier dressing had been in her youth when she had accepted Frances's or Julia's cast-offs without protest. She could not understand why she, who never had any difficulty in taking domestic or horticultural decisions, should be so indecisive where clothes were concerned.

She was about to open her car door when she saw it, in the window of a dress shop on the opposite side of the road. She crossed over, looked, went in, tried it on, studied her reflection in the mirror. She had been wanting a dress, not a blouse, but a blouse would surely be of greater use, able to be worn with different skirts. There was something about it that wasn't quite her, somehow, but she felt that about anything unsuitable for gardening. The buttons gave it a lift, making it look smarter than it otherwise might. Besides, she was desperate. She asked the price with some apprehension, and was pleasantly surprised.

Julia was doubtful when Gwen showed it to her in London. "It's the buttons that let it down, don't you think? What Mrs Mackenzie might call a bit common. Let's see if I have any that would do better."

She fetched her button box and emptied it over Gwen's bed. "Incidentally," she said as she began sorting the buttons in their different colours. "I wanted to ask you before Gabriel and Frances arrive – there seems to be some mystery about Tony in the holidays. Frances was very strange about it. Do you know anything?"

Gwen told her. "I think Gabriel was very entertained, once Tony turned up. Apart from Frances being upset, of course. I do feel so sorry for Tony. Frances really doesn't appreciate him."

"Oh, she does, Gwen. It's just that genius is hard on those

round about. Think how poor Gabriel suffered in the old days."

Gwen poked at the buttons with her finger. "She always said she'd never have children."

"She also said she'd never marry Gabriel, but she did. Oh, there's the doorbell. It'll be them."

Gwen slowly gathered the buttons into their box. If only he'd been my child... The words hovered, unspoken, barely thought, in the air.

Gabriel was on his own.

"Isn't Frances with you?" asked Julia.

"She sends her apologies. She's had a pretty disrupted summer, one way and another, and you know how she is about her routine. She begins to feel ill if it's interrupted and she isn't able to paint for any length of time. She's just beginning to recover. I said you'd understand."

Gwen came down the stairs. "How's Tony? I've had a wonderful letter from him suggesting that I should do some spying while I'm in Germany. Did he tell you?"

Gabriel laughed. "That sounds typical of Tony. He thinks it's a poor show, by the way, your not flying to Munich. It only costs ten pounds for a six-hour flight, he told me. His knowledge – about things that don't matter, unfortunately – is really quite extraordinary. Oh yes, and he offered to escort you to Munich if I'd give him permission to miss school. He was given a short answer to that, I can tell you."

She was entertained. She did not doubt that Tony had been serious when making the suggestion. Listening to Gabriel talk, she realized with thankfulness that the summer's escapade had brought father and son together. Unknown to Frances they had even motored over to Suffolk and shared a flight. "It took some doing, getting me into the aircraft," Gabriel said, with the grin of a schoolboy. "And I don't mind admitting, I was scared out of my wits, though I hope I managed to hide that from Tony. It did help me understand why he finds it so exciting. Walking the Quantocks seems tame in comparison. Not that the RAF will welcome him with open arms," he added. "If he hopes to get to Cranwell, he's going to have to knuckle down and work a lot harder than he has in the past."

There always seemed to be constant activity in Julia's household. Tonight Gwen was grateful for the company and the conversation, which kept her thoughts off the next day's journey – Rowena and her refugees, Julia and David and theirs, Andrew's drawings, Gabriel's experiences in the air, and, of course, the story of Question Mark. It was not until she was alone in her bedroom, looking down on the darkened square gardens between the houses, that she began to feel panic. Why am I doing this? What made me agree? I never wanted to leave Hillcrest.

Part Four

Germany

Chapter Seventeen

Gwen usually breakfasted alone with Julia during her London visits, after the rest of the family's departure. Today the timing of the boat train meant that such a leisurely start was impossible. So she sat with Gabriel at one end of the table, while Julia dealt with the family at the other, trying to persuade David to have something more than cups of coffee and half a slice of toast, to keep the peace between Andrew and Rowena in an argument over a missing vocabulary book and at the same time cope with telephone calls which seemed to occur every two or three minutes.

David left for his consulting-room in Harley Street, bidding Gwen goodbye as casually as if she were going to spend the day at Kew Gardens. The children went off to school, Andrew with a plea to be sent postcards – "of mountain birds if you can find them" – and Rowena with grumbles. "Now I'm bound to get a rotten mark for French. How can I learn my words if someone's pinched my vocabulary book?"

"Don't be silly," Julia said. "No one's pinched it. If you'd done your homework last night you'd have discovered it was missing then and had time to find it. How many times do I have to tell you not to leave things to the last minute? You'll finish up under a bus one of these days if you carry on doing your homework while walking to school." She listened to the angry bang of the front door behind her daughter, gave a sigh of relief and smiled at her sister and brother-in-law. "That's them out of the way. Thank goodness. And there's still time for another cup of coffee before the taxi arrives."

"It's comforting to realize other people's children aren't perfect," Gabriel said, putting *The Times* to one side. "What are you thinking, Gwen? That in comparison breakfast at Hillcrest is so peaceful?"

"Of course not," said Gwen, who had been thinking exactly that. "I was wishing I knew more about your professor. What's he *really* like?"

Gabriel considered. "Difficult to say. You must remember that I haven't seen him since 1919. I disliked him intensely when I was a student, though I never knew him well; it was his wife and children I spent most time with. I thought he treated her abominably, but now that I'm older I can see there were faults on both sides. She was full of fun and go. He was years older than she; he probably found her frivolous. Anyway, there always seemed to be an atmosphere when he was around. I shouldn't let that worry you. You'll find him stiff, but correct – and you do have a passion for orchids in common."

He realized that he had been less than encouraging. When Julia left him with Gwen on the platform of Victoria station to buy a magazine, he put his arm round her and gave her a squeeze.

"Don't worry. You'll have a wonderful time, but, remember, if not you don't have to stay. Drop us a line and we'll send a telegram. Question Mark has caught cold and collapsed, come at once. That sort of thing. Something that Ebert will sympathize with and understand why it's so urgent that you catch the next train home."

She tried to smile. "I wish you'd be serious."

"I am. I'm full of admiration. And astonishment, I have to admit. I never ever thought I'd find myself waving you off to foreign shores."

"I do hope you're right about people speaking English," she said.

"Of course I am. And if not, all you have to say is *ich verstehe nicht*. Have you got that? *Ich* – I – *verstehe* – understand – *nicht* – not. And if they themselves don't understand, well, then, just say it a bit louder until they do." His eyes were teasing.

Julia reappeared at his shoulder. "*Good Housekeeping* was sold out," she said, "so I bought *Time & Tide* instead. On reflection, it's not your sort of magazine, but never mind, it'll give you something to read. Oh, and barley sugar to suck during the crossing, though they say it should be calm. When do you reach Munich?"

"Midday tomorrow," Gwen said, and felt cold at the thought.

Julia saw her into her seat. "Have you everything you need for the journey? Tickets? Money? Passport? For goodness' sake don't lose that. Put it somewhere safe."

Gabriel smiled up from the platform. "Terrible, isn't she? Treating you like one of the children. Now ... don't forget what I said about the telegram. And do remember. It's not done to make rude remarks about That Man in public. Or politics in general. Give my regards to Ebert. And to Magda, of course."

Comfortably settled in her corner seat, Gwen looked out on the passing scene. Grimy buildings gave way to leafy suburbs, then harvested hop fields and heavily laden orchards. The Garden of England.

She stayed on deck for the crossing, leaning over the rail to watch the water surge up from under the sharp line of the ship's bow. Creamy whites, blues and greens – the colours intermingled and changed and changed again in the autumn sunlight. Impossible to put down on paper such variations of colour, or adequately portray the feeling of power underlying the sea's movement.

She had an hour to wait at Ostend. Nervous of missing her train she did not venture into the town but remained where she was, breathing in the air and absorbing the atmosphere. It had never occurred to her that the continent might smell differently from England. She caught the smell of garlic as a man walked by. Even the tobacco smoke was more pungent. I'm abroad, she told herself. She read the destinations on the train boards, destinations that she had never thought possible to visit, and resisted the temptation to step into a train and let herself go, to Bucharest ... Istanbul ... Vienna.

A porter carried her luggage into the train and found her her seat in a small, overheated carriage smelling of dust. She wondered whether she could open the window but decided to wait until she knew her fellow passengers better before suggesting such action. The two women – thank heavens for ladies only compartments – gave the appearance of seasoned travellers, and had stowed their luggage, taken off their coats, made themselves comfortable and started a conversation – in English, Gwen was relieved to hear – while Gwen herself was still wondering what she needed to get out of her case for the journey.

She sat, made drowsy by the heat, looking out on the Flanders plain as the train passed through places whose names had become familiar during the years of the war. At least there had been sun in the eastern Mediterranean, she thought, looking out on the dour and grey landscape lying under drizzling rain.

She became aware of the woman in the opposite corner looking across at her, a questioning expression on her face.

"I'm sorry," Gwen said. "I was miles away."

"I asked whether you were holidaying in Germany?" The accent was American.

"Not holidaying exactly. I'm going to paint orchids." It seemed so mundane a reason for travel that she was taken aback by her fellow passengers' astonishment.

"Orchids?" the two women exclaimed.

She nodded. "A friend of a friend asked me to make a record of his orchid collection, so..."

"Have you painted orchids before?" Her accent reminded Gwen of Mrs Meyer.

"I paint professionally," she said. "Flowers of all kinds, but orchids in particular."

"The English are so quaint," said the German. "Only an Englishwoman would cross a continent to paint a flower."

Gwen, unwilling to discuss the peculiarities of the English character, thought it time to change the subject. "What about you? Are you on holiday?"

"I'm visiting friends," said the American. "Clearing up odds and ends. Finding out facts for my husband. He's a journalist. We were in Berlin until the Nazis threw him out of the country. They didn't like what he was writing about them."

"In Vienna we wait for the same to happen as has

223

happened in Germany," said the woman Gwen had assumed to be German but who was presumably Austrian. "Marking time, that is all. My husband is a doctor, but his practice gets smaller and smaller." She shrugged. "Who can blame people? My brother-in-law was a lawyer. Now he's training to be a poultry farmer."

"A poultry farmer?" Gwen said. "Why, if he was a lawyer?"

"Why? Because we are Jewish, of course."

Gwen was silent, not understanding the logic of such a reply. Listening to her fellow travellers discussing the situation in Europe, she wished that she had paid more attention to political discussions round the Rectory dining-table during the last couple of years. Surely Gabriel had blamed Hitler's rise on the Treaty of Versailles and the vindictiveness of the French? The journalist's wife seemed to think the French had right on their side.

The frontier came upon them without warning. Doors slammed further down the train. *"Deutsche Kontrolle. Deutsche Kontrolle."*

At least one of Gwen's fears had been unnecessary; with a German speaker in the compartment (the American also spoke German, it turned out) there should be no difficulties over language with the customs men. Strangely it was the American who was questioned, unpleasantly and at length. Gwen herself received little more than a cursory glance. The official passed over her copy of *The Daily Telegraph* but confiscated the American's *Chicago Daily News*. Finally the carriage was thoroughly searched, two men even using a torch and going on their knees to investigate under the seats.

Gwen waited until the sound of their voices had disappeared down the train. She felt a curious fluttering in the pit of her stomach. "What were they looking for?"

"My husband, I dare say," the American said with a laugh.

The Viennese shuddered. "Communists."

A train travelling in the opposite direction drew up along-side. People in the carriage beside theirs stood up, reached for cases on the luggage rack, began producing papers. A small girl, much the same age as Andrew, smiled through the window at Gwen.

Minutes ticked by. Every so often a door slammed in the distance. The heat in the compartment was stifling. Gwen could bear it no longer.

"Would you mind if I opened the window?" she asked her companions. "It really is very hot in here."

She moved to the window. Two men in brown uniforms with swastika armbands were interrogating passengers in the compartment opposite. A third watched from the door. As Gwen tried to release the window catch there was unexpected movement in the carriage. The struggle was over in seconds. The two uniformed men hauled a woman, no different from any other passenger, to her feet and dragged her to the door. As she disappeared the third man advanced into the carriage. The child leapt up, ducked under his arm and launched herself towards the window, spreadeagling herself against the glass, mouth open in a silent scream.

And at that moment the Munich train gathered itself together, lurched and drew away.

Gwen overbalanced. She sat heavily down in her seat, breathless, as if she had taken part in a race. "Did you see that?"

The Viennese opened her eyes and shook her head.

"See what?" said the American.

"In that train. They dragged a woman out of the

compartment... Men. With swastika armbands."

"Breaking currency regulations, I imagine." The American sounded unconcerned. "Smuggling money, no doubt. They're only allowed to take twenty pounds out of the country, you know."

"But there was a child..."

Neither woman was listening.

The image of that moment kept recurring for the rest of the night, caught like a photograph or a still life, the child's open-mouthed face reminiscent of a painting by Munch. She felt guilt, as if she had let down someone seeking her help. Who was the child? What would happen to her?

The Viennese left the train during the night, the American at Nuremberg, which they reached the following morning. Alone in the compartment at last, Gwen opened the window and leant out. It seemed to her scarcely credible that she, who disliked going further afield than London, should be looking out on Albrecht Dürer's birthplace. Blue and white flags hung beside the red and black. People crowded the platforms, ordinary, unsophisticated, not particularly well dressed. Few of the women wore make-up. None had short hair. Germans, all of them. No different from me, thought Gwen. With daylight the ugliness of the incident the previous evening began to fade. There would have been some explanation. She must have misunderstood what was happening. And laws were laws, not made to be broken.

Her spirits began to rise and with them an unexpected surge of confidence. The worst of the journey was over. Her time in Munich, with the professor's daughter to take her around, would be fun. She would not allow herself to worry about the professor until later.

*   *   *

Fun turned out to be an inappropriate word. Gabriel had told Gwen that Magda was the same age as Sarah, but she looked years older, older than Gwen, older even than Frances. The anxious look never left her eyes, and if she smiled Gwen did not see it. Her idea of showing Gwen Munich was to take her into the English Garden, not far from the flat in which the family lived, there to spend the afternoon walking without apparent purpose or direction. Gwen was relieved to find that Magda's English was reasonable, but apart from enquiring about Gwen's journey and informing her that the Garden had been laid out at the end of the eighteenth century by a German pupil of Capability Brown the girl scarcely spoke. Gwen, conscious of her own lack of small talk, wondered how they would get through the next twenty-four hours.

The children were no help. Gwen was baffled by their behaviour. She remembered Tony at a similar age, loud, boisterous, racing round Kensington Gardens in noisy imitation of a car. She recalled the way he chased children smaller than himself, shouted at dogs, threw balls into flower beds. At eight Tony had been an embarrassment to take anywhere. Even Andrew had chased ducks in the days before he was old enough to draw them, shouting and waving his arms in an attempt to frighten them up into the air and display the colour of their feathers. "Look, Aunt Gwen, look. *Pretty* birds." Hans and Lisl did not move from their mother's side all afternoon. If Gwen spoke to them – "They understand English. I teach them. It is important they learn English," Magda assured her – they remained silent, gazing up at her wide-eyed. Frightened, Gwen would have said, had she been able to believe that she could frighten anyone.

Supper that evening was a watery meat soup with caraway seeds and dark, sour bread. The meat in it was sliced and fatty; a layer of grease lay over the surface. There was no sign of vegetables or fruit, and the coffee afterwards had such an extraordinary taste that Gwen was reminded of Gabriel's remarks about acorn coffee long ago and wondered whether this might be a sample. Magda's husband did not join them. He was an invalid, Magda explained as she prepared a tray for his supper. Gwen could imagine Annie's comments on such food as invalid fare. She listened to the murmur of voices from the bedroom, to the sound of coughing so harsh and breathless that it made her own chest ache.

Magda put the children to bed before clearing away and washing up, refusing all Gwen's offers of help. Gwen was again baffled. Though the Purcells had had money worries after their mother's death there had always been Annie and help from the village, as well as Willis in the garden. Magda appeared to have no one. The flat must once have been elegant, with its large rooms and high, ornate ceilings, but today the paintwork was peeling and the decorations shabby, while the furniture in it was no more than basic. And it was cold. Though there were pottery stoves in every room, none had been lit. Gwen could not understand it. Surely the daughter of a one-time head of a university department should be better off than the newly orphaned Purcells had been, even if her husband were sick?

Time dragged. Gwen, pleading exhaustion from the journey and a need to write home, retired early, to Magda's obvious relief. She had intended to write to Sarah, the family member who would be most intrigued by the strangeness of Gwen's experience, but a letter to Annie telling of her safe arrival was all that she could manage before the cold of the room stiffened her fingers and forced her into bed as the only warm place. Even then she had to pull her coat over the strange eiderdown that did for both sheet and blankets, and put on walking socks and a thick jumper before she stopped shivering.

Only fourteen days, she told herself thankfully, and I shall be back in my own bed at Hillcrest.

At breakfast next morning Magda suggested that Gwen should explore Munich on her own. "I have a map. I will show you where we are and where are the museums and galleries. The railway station too. You can take a sightseeing tour from there."

Two days ago Gwen would have been horrified by Magda's suggestion. Today she greeted it with relief, well merited as it turned out. The English Garden with Magda as guide had been dreary. Munich with no guide was wonderful. She wandered through art galleries, studying Rembrandt drawings and engravings by Dürer; she walked for miles, looking at buildings and watching people, and then sat for most of the afternoon in the sun at a café on one of the tree-lined boulevards. She found her lack of German no handicap, buying herself lunch by pointing at what she required and offering a handful of coins in return, from which the smiling owner took his pick. She admired the layout of the city centre with its broad avenues, monuments and fountains and was entertained by the way people used cafés for other activities besides eating – writing letters, reading newspapers, gossiping, even playing bridge. She could happily have sat all day watching life in the streets and drawing the people around her, feeling far more at ease here than she had ever felt in London. When reluctantly she returned to the cold, unwelcoming flat she realized that she had not thought about Hillcrest once during the day, and even the incident in the train seemed more like a dream than reality.

Magda received her with more warmth than before, encouraged, perhaps, by the knowledge that Gwen would be gone by morning. For the first time Gwen wondered whether Magda had been ordered by her father to entertain her, rather than, as Gwen had understood, volunteering to do so.

The meal was no more appetizing than the previous evening, but Magda was more relaxed. After putting the children to bed and fetching the tray from her husband's room, she sat down with Gwen.

"Now we can talk," she said. "Tell me about Gabriel Mackenzie. Is it true what Father tells me? He cannot walk? I find it hard to believe."

"It's true. He was wounded in Ireland, soon after the war. He can walk, but not without sticks. He manages better than the doctors ever expected, but yes, it is hard for him. He was a great walker in the old days."

"He came to see us after the war," Magda said. "Of course he had stayed with us often before, but I was too young to remember him then. We have photographs – I shall show you the photographs. He brought us food, after the war. We were starving, you see. My mother and my eldest brother died of the flu – did you have the flu in England? And then Gabriel came, from Cologne, I think, with milk powder. Meat, in tins. And jam. Tickler's jam. I can taste that jam still."

Gwen was silent. She remembered food shortages in England during the war, but at Hillcrest they had always grown more than enough to satisfy hunger. The thought came unbidden that in this household at least, things seemed little better eighteen years on.

"I thought he was a god," Magda said. "Truly. He was my first love." It was surprising how much younger she looked when she smiled. "He talked to me. He made me feel important. That was wonderful."

Yes, Gwen thought, remembering Gabriel's first visits to Hillcrest after Mrs Purcell's death, that sounds like Gabriel. He was good at that.

"Father didn't care, you see," Magda said. "Not about us children. He loved my mother very much, and when he came home from the war and found her dead – he was much older than she was: he did not expect her to die first – he was heartbroken."

Gwen did not know how to respond. Nothing Magda said seemed to fit with what Gabriel had told her. Whose memory was at fault? "You said you had photographs," she said. "May I see them?"

Magda fetched two albums from a cupboard. The covers were of tooled leather, with dates picked out in ornate figures on the front. The earlier photographs, faded from black and white to shades of grey, went back to the turn of the century. There were few of places or scenery, the majority being of people, family presumably, and young men in what looked like student groups. Magda turned the pages. "1903, 1904. Here I am, as a baby. Not very happy, eh? I did not like the camera, even then. My two brothers smile. They like seeing their pictures." She turned the pages. "You do not know when Gabriel came for the first time? Ah. Here he is, with Mutti: 1906. He was handsome, was he not? And that is Mutti."

Mutti looked too young to be a mother. In previous photographs Gwen had taken her to be one of the students.

She had one arm round Gabriel's shoulder as she smiled at the camera. She looked – Gwen searched for the right word – possessive.

"Memory is strange, is it not?" Magda said. "I look at this photograph of me sitting on Gabriel's knee. I think I can remember it, but really it is only the photograph I remember."

"It's like that with my father," Gwen said. She was trying to work out the dates; 1906 – four years before the Purcells had first met the Mackenzies. Gabriel would have been seventeen, the same age as Antony when Antony left England for the last time.

"And your father," she said. "Have you photographs of him?"

"He was working always." She continued to turn the pages. The young playing tennis, picnicking, swimming in the river, entertaining Magda and her brothers, and always Gabriel and Mrs Ebert laughing together. The next year it was another student who was close, the year after that another.

"Every summer we had students," Magda said. "Sometimes from England. Sometimes from France. Mutti liked students, you see. She said they made her young again. She laughed when they were in the house. Such fun, she said they were. That was why she hated the war. No students."

Gwen felt unbearable sadness come over her as Magda turned the pages. So many young men, so confident of the future. What had become of them all? Dead, probably, or crippled like Gabriel, or – she looked at Magda's hollow cheeks – grown old before their time.

"What happened to your other brother?" she asked. "Is he still alive?"

"He is in Berlin. Eight years he has not written. He writes

to my father, yes. Not to me. I think families should stick together, no? We do not, neither my brother nor my father. My father does not see us. Two years since he visits. He sits up in the mountains with his orchids ... I do not know how to say it ... making again his childhood. They are all he cares about, his flowers."

"They are..." Gwen searched for words that might ease the tension that had suddenly filled the room. "They are very beautiful, orchids. It's easy to think of nothing else."

"Beautiful!" Magda spat out the word. "Beauty is a luxury. The money he spends, my father. Heating, for instance. How much does that cost? What is it *for*? For people? For children? Indeed not. It is for *flowers*."

Gwen did not know what to say, faced with such bitterness. She was conscious that the only reason for her visit, as Magda must know, was to paint the professor's orchids. He was paying her expenses – did Magda know that? Until now it had not occurred to Gwen to wonder how much those expenses might amount to.

After a moment Magda said quietly, almost apologetically, "It is not for me that I mind, you understand. It is for my children. *His* grandchildren." She closed the album on her lap, picked up its companion where it lay on the floor by her feet and returned both to the cupboard. "I am sorry," she said as she came back to Gwen. "I get angry. I know you have come for the orchids. We will go to bed now. It is late and tomorrow you have the journey. You must sleep."

Easier said than done. She could not banish the events of the day from her mind – the photographs of Gabriel, the cowed children, the sick husband, Magda's resentment over her father's orchids. "Beauty is a luxury..."

In the middle of the night she was woken by the sound of

coughing. Footsteps passed by her door. Voices murmured in an endless monotone. She lay under her coat and shivered.

She was back in the past, with Antony in the greenhouse at Hillcrest, the old greenhouse at the end of the veranda, with the vine spreading leafless branches in the shape of a fan under the roof glass. February, cold outside, but warm within, the broad beans already beginning to poke through the earth in their pots. And at the far end she saw them again. Six orchids. Her orchids. She saw herself, showing them to Antony. "Aren't they beautiful?"

And Antony standing there, fair hair cropped, blue eyes distant. Was he thinking of her? Putting words together into a poem? Or were his thoughts on the battle to come?

"A bit frippery, orchids, don't you think, in times like these?"

"Beauty is a luxury..."

Chapter Eighteen

Breakfast in Munich was very different from breakfast at Julia's. Magda said little. Gwen, still preoccupied with the unexpected surfacing last night of memories long forgotten, made only feeble attempts at conversation. The two children remained silent, gazing at Gwen with unblinking eyes. At last Lisl nudged Hans as if daring him to take action. He glanced at his mother, took a deep breath. "Hello, goodbye, hello," he said. Lisl gave a giggle, quickly subdued by her mother's frown.

"I tell them to speak English to you and what do they do?" Magda said. "They wait until you leave." She sounded exasperated.

"It's my fault," Gwen said. "I know I should have tried to learn some German, but I only decided to come on the spur of the moment. Gabriel did try to teach me one or two phrases on my last evening in London. *Ich verstehe nicht.*" She looked across the table at Hans. *"Verstehe?"*

He nodded. *"Ja."* His mouth turned up. It was the only sign of a smile that Gwen had seen during her stay. She smiled back, thinking how foolish she had been to expect children to be lively when their father was dying, their mother preoccupied and money so short.

When the time came to catch her train they went with her to the station, each holding a hand, while Magda struggled with her suitcase. Gwen looked down on them from the carriage with something like affection. A week or two at Hillcrest, with Annie's cooking to fill them out and Somerset air to bring colour into their cheeks, and they would be no different from Rowena and Andrew at the same age. "Perhaps you could come and stay with me in England one day," she said.

Hans waited for his mother's translation. "I like," he said instantly. "Please."

Magda said nothing. Gwen wished her words unspoken the moment she had said them. How could she suggest such a thing when there was insufficient money for food, let alone travel abroad?

The sight of the lake through the train windows soon distracted her thoughts from Magda and her family, however. Fiery sumachs edged the shoreline. White sails fluttered over the water. Villages of timber and stone chalets came and went; fields of maize and cabbage. After a while, but so gradually that Gwen was scarcely aware of it, the train began to climb. Sloping meadows stretched away from the track, dotted with squat, dark wooden huts. Hay was still being made, despite the lateness of the season. Pale green swaths of cut grass alternated with the dark green of that still standing. The track was steeper now, the meadows fewer. Tree branches touched, the reds and yellows of deciduous leaves bright against the evergreens. Stony gullies came close to the track, narrow streams, waterfalls, rocks, paths winding away through the woods. Hills grew bigger and steeper, until

236

in the distance the mountains became visible, unreal mountains, like stage sets, grey cut-outs with no thickness to them, placed upright one behind the other. Slowly the cut-outs darkened, gained substance. Their jagged outlines became sharply defined against the skyline. Clefts appeared in the cliff face; spurs and corries divided the scree above the tree line.

The line levelled and ran along the floor of a valley beside a river of glittering apple-green water. Beyond a lowered crossing a farm cart waited, dripping hay onto the road. Scattered chalets became more frequent, then clustered together. Above red and grey roofs stood the bulk of a church building, its onion-shaped tower capped by green tiles. The train slowed, stopped. She had arrived.

She searched the crowded platform for a professor-like figure, but in vain. Before panic could grip her a sturdy countryman wearing a battered army cap came forward to greet her. "Miss Purcell? Come with me, please. I take you to Professor Ebert."

Outside the station a pony and trap waited in the shade of the chestnut trees lining the village square. The man – he introduced himself as Hermann – helped Gwen up into the trap, as he did so dismissing her worries about her luggage. "It will go to your hotel." He climbed into his seat, cracked a whip and they set off, at such a fast pace that Gwen had time to take in little more than a muddle of streets, patches of orange flowers, and scarlet geraniums tumbling over the rims of window boxes before they left the village behind.

She clutched the side of the trap and breathed in the cool fresh air. I'm here, she thought. She could scarcely believe it. This is me, Gwen Purcell, in the Alps.

*   *   *

When Professor Ebert had told Gwen in his letters of his aim to recreate the setting of his South American childhood, she had been amused as well as touched. But nothing in his letters or her imagination had prepared her for the vision before her when he led her into his orchid house for the first time.

She was in a different country, warm, dark, damp. Trees stretched up to the roof, trunks ivy-covered, their branches dripping Spanish moss like torn cobwebs. Water trickled over a bed of pebbles beneath them, through underplantings of ferns and bromeliads, ivy and cheese plants. Orchids were everywhere, thrusting roots out into the air high up under the glass, clinging to the bark, peering between ferns – laelias, vandas, epidendrums and, more than any other variety, cattleyas, huge bloomed cattleyas, purple, white, frilled.

She was overwhelmed. "You've done all this yourself?"

"You like it?"

"It's ... oh, it's wonderful."

Her own collection paled into insignificance. Mr Alexander's was a business, no more, no less. This was something out of a fairy tale. This was magic.

"I was seven when my parents brought me to Germany. For my education, they said. My childhood ended the moment I stepped on the ship bringing us back. I won't say bringing us home, though that was what my father said. Germany was not home. South America was where I was born. Try to imagine it, Miss Purcell. An only child, indulged by my parents, it goes without saying, surrounded by female cousins all older than I, hopelessly spoilt. Oh, yes, I admit it now. I was spoilt. And my cousins – I think of them now, old women they must be, dead possibly, and see them as they were then, bending down to me, laughing and teasing, and in the evenings gossiping with their friends under my window, dancing and flirting, with orchids decorating their dresses and pinned in their hair."

He was silent. Gwen stood in the warmth, listening to the sound of water and breathing in the heavy perfume.

"Life in Germany was ... rigid. Of necessity, I don't doubt, but the shock to a seven-year-old... I pushed my old life out of my mind. In time it disappeared altogether. Life has been a disappointment, Miss Purcell, but when I was young I was happy. I remembered that happiness when I retired from the university. When I look back to my childhood it is the orchids I see. They grew everywhere, not only wild in trees and in the ground, but cultivated as well. In tubs and beds and window boxes, like geraniums do here. Magnificent blooms, wherever you looked. People say orchids are exotic. Sometimes I ask myself: was my childhood exotic and the orchids commonplace? Or was it the orchids that were exotic and my childhood commonplace? I have never found the answer."

He pulled a fern forward, moved a leaf aside to display the bloom of a cattleya to better advantage. He was absorbed. She was certain that in his mind he was thousands of miles away, back in the South America of his youth. He looked at her at last and spread out his hands, as if deprecating his foolishness. "I am sorry. You have seen enough for the time being. Let us go outside."

White painted chairs and a table stood on the terrace in front of the chalet, with a striped umbrella shading them all. Sloping meadows led across the valley to tree-covered foothills in the distance. Beyond the hills the grey face of the mountain range reared up into the sky, traces of white marking the snow on faraway peaks.

"Tell me about your collection," Professor Ebert said. "You've only recently come to orchids, Mackenzie tells me." He smiled at her. "Gabriel, I should call him. Yes?"

"Yes." She hesitated for a moment, wondering what she could say about her own plants, having seen his. She had thought her collection beautiful, but now the plants in it seemed prosaic and dull. Perhaps it was the way they were arranged, set out in rows on the shelves. Unimaginative, but practical. Like her. Yet who could have guessed that this man, sitting uncomfortably erect in his upright chair, formally dressed even in this setting, would have the inspiration to create the display she had just seen?

"They seem very ordinary when I compare them with yours," she said. "Not individually, of course, but together. That setting of yours ... I feel I must try something myself the moment I get back."

"But you have not been growing them long, I understand?"

"Eighteen months, that's all. I never intended to have orchids, you see. I was busy enough as it was; I didn't want the work, or the expense. I'd have refused them if I could. But the man who owned them was dying and there was no one else. Now, of course, I can't imagine life without them." Without them there would have been no Mrs Meyer, no Mr Cole, no challenge of the flower market; more than anything else, nothing as engrossing to paint. Nor would she be here. "It sounds silly to say they've altered my life, but it's true." She gave him a rueful smile. "It's easy to become obsessed, don't you think?"

He was considering the question when Hermann

240

appeared with lunch. Cold meats, a variety of salads, followed by apricot strudel – Gwen realized at once that she was ravenously hungry. The effect of the mountain air, perhaps, or relief at her safe arrival. Eager to start painting, fascinated by the setting in which she found herself, intrigued by the professor, she was happy.

"Hermann was my servant during the war, until he was captured," Professor Ebert explained after the man had returned to the chalet. "He learnt English – and I must tell you he understands more than he speaks – while in England. He has been with me since his return."

They lingered afterwards over their coffee. The sun was hot, despite the shade of the umbrella. Gwen began to drowse.

"I have been trying to remember what Gabriel told us about your family when he was with us," Professor Ebert said. "We had students every summer before the war. My wife liked filling the house with youth. Too much so, I always thought. The noise and high spirits made my work difficult. Mackenzie was one of them, but he had greater depth than most, I think. And he paid attention to the children, which was unusual. One year he even took my sons camping up in the hills."

"He was like that with us. His father was our guardian, you know."

"So I understand. How did that come about? Are you related?"

She shook her head. "Our families barely knew each other. He was the rector – the minister – of the village where we lived. I think that was why our mother asked him."

"And he agreed? Extraordinary. An appalling responsibility, do you not think, to take on four young girls. Did he have doubts?"

"I don't know." It had never occurred to her to look at the situation from the Mackenzies' point of view, only from hers. "Mr Mackenzie is..." She hesitated, wondering whether religion, like politics, was an unwise subject for discussion, then remembered the crucifixes she had seen in the countryside on her way here and the huge calvary in the village square. "Knowing Mr Mackenzie, I'm sure he felt it his duty as a Christian."

He acknowledged that with a barely perceptible nod. "But as a family you were extraordinary too, were you not? So single-minded over your painting, Mackenzie told us."

Gwen began to feel uncomfortable. "I think he must have been talking about Frances." Now that he had brought up the subject of painting, perhaps she should voice her doubts over the purpose of her visit. "I don't know exactly what you have in mind for your orchids, Herr Professor, but I'm not at all sure that I'm the right person. You said you wanted a record. Really Frances would do that much better than me. I'm... What I do is small scale. I'm a miniaturist more than anything else. I paint individual flowers."

"A botanical painter."

"No," she said quickly. "Not a botanical painter. A flower painter."

"There is a difference?"

"Oh, yes. A flower painter is someone who paints what she sees – what she wants to see, perhaps. Her interpretation, in other words. Whereas a botanical painter must be *exact*, because what she puts down on the paper is what will identify that plant in years to come. It's a very rigid discipline."

"And you are a romantic. Is that what you are saying?"

She smiled. "Hardly. I want to be free to paint what I

want, and how I want, to develop as a painter. That's my eldest sister's training. She's the real painter in our family."

"Please do not worry about what you paint for me," Professor Ebert said. "I have seen what you do. Mackenzie sent me examples of your work. The flower books for children, for instance, *Hedgerow Flowers*, and the others. I like them very much. It is true that I invited Frances when I heard she was a painter, but that was because I hoped to meet Mackenzie again. And I did not know then of you and your orchids. To be truthful, obtaining a record was not my only reason for the invitation. You will see how isolated I am here. I looked forward to discussing orchids with a fellow enthusiast."

She smiled at him, knowing her own reason for coming to be similar, before suggesting that they should return to the orchids to discuss what he would like her to do. He would not hear of it. She must be exhausted after the long journey and her sightseeing in Munich, he told her. Better to rest, and return refreshed in the morning.

"I trust you will find the hotel comfortable," he said, helping her up into the trap. "If not, do not hesitate to let me know. Fräulein Winkel speaks very good English. She learnt it in England, I understand."

Fräulein Winkel came out of the glass-fronted hotel office to greet Gwen, obviously delighted to have an opportunity to practise her English. She had studied it while working in a Weymouth hotel, she told her. "Mother thought it would be useful, you see. English people come to stay every summer to walk and climb in the mountains. Not many speak German."

Although summer was over, there were walkers and

climbers about still, as Gwen discovered when she left the hotel to explore her surroundings. They came down from the mountains as evening approached, striding purposefully along the paths, nails in their boots ringing against the hard earth, haversacks on their backs and rope slung round their chests, nodding in friendly fashion at Gwen as they passed. Those whom Gwen took to be local wore what she assumed was Bavarian dress – uncomfortable-looking dirty leather shorts, and extraordinary white socks. Annie would have loved the socks, for they covered only the calf and lacked all those parts that might need darning. But it was the dark wide-brimmed velour hats with fluffy white feathers that attracted Gwen the most. She could imagine Andrew in one, painted by Julia. Perhaps Fräulein Winkel would know where they could be bought.

She felt surprisingly light-hearted as she explored. Never having willingly slept away from home before, she had expected to be plagued by anxiety about Hillcrest while so far away – how was Annie managing, what was Waite doing, would the orchids be damp enough, warm enough, dry enough, what unforeseen disaster might occur? None of these now worried her. Of course Annie could manage, having done so for as long as Gwen could remember. Had Waite not proved himself competent over the years? As for disaster, that might happen equally well when she was there. As she wandered round the village in the fading light she knew that all she wanted at the moment was time – time in which to paint the orchids, portray the people about her, sketch the scenery; more than anything else, time in which to discuss the fascination of orchids with her host.

Dinner was served in the only public room in the hotel, there being no lounge or anywhere for residents to sit that she could discover. It was a solid, comfortable room rather than elegant, with a decorated wooden ceiling and knotted wood furniture. She remained in it after she had eaten, sitting unobtrusively in one corner as she watched the comings and goings of the locals. Tomorrow she would bring pen and ink and sketchbook down to supper but tonight she would write a brief note to Annie and a postcard to Tony.

In the end she wrote to Sarah too, feeling the need to write at greater length of her experiences and knowing that Sarah was the one most likely to be fascinated. She described the professor's collection of orchids, the village and the mountains around it (though the Alps would be as nothing to one whose summers were spent in the foothills of the Himalayas), before retracing her steps to Munich. Sarah, the storyteller, would be intrigued by the mystery of the invisible husband and subdued children, of the bitter wife and the inexplicable poverty.

Describing Magda's situation brought Gwen's thoughts back to her host. For the first time she realized that not once during their conversation had he enquired after his daughter and grandchildren, nor his sick son-in-law. Yet there had been warmth, even passion, in his voice when he talked of his orchids, warmth too when reminiscing about his childhood. Had he forgotten his family? Did he not care?

But when she lay drowsing in bed that night, under a magnificent duvet which warmed her as nothing else so far had done during her stay, it was orchids that filled her thoughts rather than people – the orchids in that extraordinary display hidden away up in the mountains. In her mind she was there now, marvelling at the colour, the shapes, the fascination of the flowers in their tropical setting, her senses beguiled.

Chapter Nineteen

She quickly settled into a routine. Every morning, soon after breakfast, Hermann arrived with the trap to take her up into the hills. She loved that ride, finding the air wonderfully invigorating after the stuffy atmosphere of the hotel dining-room and the views breathtaking whatever the weather.

There was hot chocolate waiting on her arrival, but she wasted little time before setting to work. She painted alone, in bursts of concentration, breaking after two or three hours when her eyes could focus no longer. Professor Ebert was surprisingly undemanding about her subjects, letting her paint what she wished. She was absorbed by her work, though in odd moments she worried. Her reason for coming was to give Professor Ebert the record he wanted, yet here she was painting whatever she chose. She was dissatisfied with the attempt she made at the overall scene, knowing that Frances's current style of painting, with its density of texture and brilliance of colour, would have given a better impression of the lush tropical setting. Then, removing her glasses for a moment's rest one afternoon, she discovered her unfocused view gave an air of mystery to the orchid house.

Faint memories surfaced of the illustrations in the fairy-tale books of her childhood, with their black outlines, smudged colours and blurred shapes, the vague sense of menace and the feeling that not all was as it seemed. They gave her the inspiration she needed. She rinsed her brushes and reached for another sheet of paper.

Every day she lunched with Professor Ebert, on the terrace if the sun was out, indoors when clouds filled the sky. He talked of his orchids and his childhood; she talked of painting, her sisters, Hillcrest and Gabriel.

After lunch she worked another session, stopping for the day as soon as her eyes tired. Professor Ebert expressed concern when on the third afternoon she told him that she would prefer to walk back to the hotel rather than ride in the trap. "You don't realize how far it is, Miss Purcell – nearly six miles. It is no trouble for Hermann, I assure you."

"It's not that. I need to do something physical, after so much close work. It helps rest my eyes." Illogically she added, "Besides, I'd like to stop and sketch on the way down. There's that lake near the bottom, for instance, which is asking to be painted. The reflections of the trees in it are wonderful now that the leaves are turning. And the walking isn't hard. It's downhill most of the way."

She was not alone on the hills. There were the locals tending their cows, others transporting their hay, long-distance hikers and crocodiles of rosy-cheeked children, escorted on nature walks by smiling young teachers with blonde plaits wound round their heads. They all greeted Gwen as they passed, some with a nod, most with a *Grüss Gott*.

There were scenes to sketch in the muddle of roads and lanes of the village itself – a cow chomping hay beyond the half door of an ordinary chalet, wood carvers and cobblers, a violin maker glimpsed through a window, shaving a block of wood. Dahlias grew in odd corners, a patch of maize by the calvary in the square, marrows over the wall by the station. As for the geraniums, so different from those grown in England, she had been promised seed heads by Fräulein Winkel to take back with her to England. Fräulein Winkel was surprised by Gwen's admiration for the murals that decorated the outside walls of so many houses, and even the church. "It is not unusual. Every village is the same. But yes, you are right. I do not remember paintings on houses in Weymouth."

Letters came from England. Annie reported that they were *managing all right,* Lucy that Waite had taken two cymbidium spikes into Taunton. A letter from Sarah, forwarded on by Annie from Hillcrest, expressed amazement at the idea of Gwen holidaying abroad. *How about India next?* she wrote.

The letter from Tony pleased Gwen the most. He wanted to thank her for all she had done, he said; he would have got nowhere with his savings without her support. He admitted that he was finding work hard – *things don't seem to stay in my brain unless I'm interested,* he said – but she mustn't worry because he was going to stick to it. *Dad was cross that I'd made you pay me but he's got over it now. He says we'll sort things out between us about flying lessons and all that, but I'd still like to work a bit in the garden when I'm staying at Hillcrest if that's all right with you.* The writing was marginally more legible and there were no spelling mistakes, so some progress had already been made.

While Tony's letter gave her pleasure, the one from Mr Alexander astonished. Question Mark had won a first class certificate. What astonished Gwen even more than the award was the offer Mr Alexander made towards the end of his letter. He wanted to buy Question Mark.

He listed the options open to her. She could keep Question Mark and enjoy the flowers every year. She could keep Question Mark, and in future years divide and sell the divisions. If she were interested in hybridizing she could propagate from it. Or she could sell Question Mark, either at a London auction or to a private buyer. He hoped she would consider the latter. He was interested himself, he said, and offered her a hundred and fifty pounds. She might get more at auction; she might not. He considered one hundred and fifty a fair price.

A fair price? It seemed like a fortune. Despite that, her immediate reaction was to refuse. She did not want to lose Question Mark. She did not need the money; she was making more than enough for her needs. Would he think a refusal ungrateful, she wondered, when the plant's first class certificate was due to his efforts?

He ended his letter by asking whether she had decided on a name for Question Mark.

She had thought about names since he had told her that it was the owner of the seed parent at pollination who chose the name. The owner then had been Mr Whitelaw, of course, but Mr Alexander considered Gwen had taken his place. She had tried several in her mind, but none had seemed quite right. Perhaps Gabriel might have some suggestions.

She would have liked to discuss Mr Alexander's offer with someone – Gabriel or his father, Mrs Whitelaw, anyone. Only Professor Ebert was available.

To her amazement he expressed distaste at her mention of a hybrid.

"I see no point in such a plant. It would be impure,

untrue to its strain."

She was taken aback. "Don't you think that that's a bit extreme?"

He raised his hand. "No, Miss Purcell. You English are a mongrel race. Saxons, Normans, Vikings, who knows what else besides? You will not view the matter as we do in Germany. Racial purity matters, Miss Purcell, believe me."

She was silent, repelled as much by his manner as by his words. Disillusion was beginning to set in. She had already realized that he lived entirely for himself and his orchids. He did not seem to have any connection with the community in the valley below. No visitors had called during her time with him. And always the picture of Magda and her children hovered at the back of her mind. She could not forget the sound of the invisible husband coughing behind the closed door. She had always understood mountain air helped tubercular patients. Why then did Professor Ebert not invite his family to stay? It could not be for lack of space.

She had discovered the extra room by chance. The orchid house was part of a glassed-in terrace divided into sections. Beyond the South American scene doors led to another area, which Professor Ebert used for working and for keeping plants not being used in his display. Here Gwen kept her paints and occasionally worked. She had been told that there was a tap. When she could not find it she pushed aside the bamboo curtain at the far end ... and found herself in a further section, glassed in like the other, but larger, and empty. North facing, it was cool despite the bright sunlight outside, and shaded. A couple of branches had been propped up against the inner wall. Moss, fragments of bark and crumbs of soil lay scattered over the floor. Orchids had been housed here once, but were no longer. Traces of their scent still

250

lingered. Her footsteps echoed in the void. There was some mystery here, something she did not understand.

She wanted to know more but there were times when she felt that Professor Ebert, courteous and friendly though he was, discouraged questions. She asked Hermann instead, on the journey up from the village.

"It's a large collection, isn't it? Of orchids, I mean."

"Ja."

"Professor Ebert used to have more, though, didn't he?"

Hermann glanced briefly round at her but made no reply.

"I was sketching in the far house yesterday and happened to see the empty one beyond," Gwen explained.

Reluctantly he agreed. "He had more plants, yes. Many more."

"What happened to them?"

"Sold."

"All of them?"

"All." There was a moment's pause. "He needed the money." Another pause. He waved the whip towards the mountains. "See those clouds? There will be a storm before nightfall." The implication was clear. No more questions.

Gwen was intrigued. Considering the professor's love of his plants – they and his childhood were his only subjects of conversation – she would have expected him to increase rather than sell. And why did he need extra money? Not for poor Magda, that was certain. To pay Gwen's expenses then? She felt instantly guilty. Should she offer to contribute?

He was offended when she did so, despite her tactful approach. "My dear Miss Purcell" – his manner contradicted the words – "there is no need, believe me. You are painting my orchids. In England you would ask for a fee. Here, I pay your expenses instead."

"In England I'd be painting my own orchids without payment," she said frankly, "whereas here I'm having a holiday too. And I know that either of my sisters would have produced paintings more suitable for what you want. The work I've done seems poor recompense for what I've received, even if you really do like it as much as you say."

"I think, Miss Purcell," he said with a smile, "you underestimate your talent. Besides, your visit has given me great pleasure. We have much in common, you and I, do you not think?"

She considered the question with some surprise. A love of orchids, yes. Friendship with Gabriel, possibly – except that Gabriel had never given the impression that he cared for the older man. What else could she and he have in common?

"You do not think that we make our home a retreat from the outside world?"

She stared at him. "What an extraordinary thing to suggest. No, of course not. Not as far as I'm concerned, anyway."

He continued to smile. "No?"

"No," she said firmly, and stood up. "I must get back to work."

He made no reference to the conversation when she said goodbye to him that afternoon. "Tomorrow is your last day. I wondered whether you would care to dine with me in the evening? It would give me much pleasure and make a fitting farewell. In the moonlight my orchids are magical."

She did not know what to say. She would much rather have dined at the hotel, talked with Fräulein Winkel and finished her pen and ink sketches, but she was reluctant to offend. "Would it be possible? What about the journey at night?"

"The moon will be full. And both Hermann and the pony know the path well. They could follow it blindfold."

"Well ... how kind of you. Thank you. I shall look forward to it."

She dressed for the evening with care. Professor Ebert was always immaculate. She had never seen him without a tie nor with his top button undone, unlike Gabriel or David on their visits to Hillcrest. She wondered about wearing the blouse, deciding at last that it was the smartest she had with her, whatever Julia's opinion of it; though she did wish there had been time to change the buttons. She peered at her reflection. The light was too dim, the mirror too small, for reassurance. She hoped she would do, that was all.

She wished now that she had had the courage to refuse the invitation. She felt that they had exhausted their conversation on orchids. His childhood in South America, fascinating at first hearing, was now tedious. She stood in her room and acknowledged the fact for the first time: she did not like him. He was too cold, too self-centred. She found it hard to accept his behaviour towards his daughter. She sighed as she left her room and went slowly downstairs.

Fräulein Winkel came out of the office as Gwen reached the hall. "Such a pity you will not be dining with us tonight, Miss Purcell. We have wild boar on the menu." Missing that treat was the only benefit Gwen could see from dining away.

The pony pricked up its ears when Gwen emerged from the hotel, as though recognizing her footsteps. The temperature had dropped considerably since the afternoon; she was glad of the rug that Hermann wrapped round her.

She was surprised by the nostalgia that swept over her as she watched the familiar landscape unroll for the last time –

the stream tumbling over the stones beside the track, the lake with its fringe of bulrushes, smooth meadows rolling away to lumpy tree-covered hills in the distance. As they climbed, those hills dropped away to reveal the soaring face of the mountain range beyond. In the fading light the grey limestone crags became suffused with the crimson glow of sunset. Every evening Gwen had marvelled at the effect from the valley below, but here, high up in the hills, it seemed as if the whole world had changed colour.

Professor Ebert was waiting outside the chalet to welcome her. He bowed over her hand, before escorting her through to his orchids. A magical world, he had said. Now he led her through it, the magician whose creation it was.

Prickles ran up and down her spine. Magic it might be, but it was the magic of the Brothers Grimm. Moonlight penetrated the heavy foliage only in thin shafts, lighting on pale petals, a ripple of water, a wet pebble. The air was warm and damp, heavy with the fetid smell of tropical flowers and manure water. She felt as though she were in a fairy-tale nightmare, faced by a jungle barrier that had been grown to keep out the world.

The brightness of the dining-room dazzled in contrast. A display of orchids stood on the sideboard. Others intertwined with ivy decorated the dining-table. Hermann served the food, a mixture of German and English, as unobtrusively as usual. There was wine for Gwen although the professor himself drank beer. He appeared not to notice her lack of conversation, but talked of his climbing experiences when young ("I could never interest Gabriel in mountaineering. Always he preferred the long-distance walking"); the delights of the Alps in winter ("so clean, so white, so *pure*");

the challenge of cross-country skiing.

As she listened to the precise voice and clipped accent, Gwen knew that she would be relieved to return home. Two weeks was long enough to be away from Hillcrest. She had no regrets. She had enjoyed the experience – the galleries in Munich, the scenery, the orchids, her painting – and recognized the effect the two weeks had had on her confidence. When Professor Ebert said that he hoped she considered her visit had been worthwhile, in the tone of voice that implied he feared she might not, she was able to answer with perfect truth, "Oh yes. It's been wonderful."

He smiled. "I am glad." He gestured to Hermann to leave the room and waited for him to do so before saying, "I must confess that I had an ulterior motive in inviting you here tonight."

"Oh?"

"I have a favour to ask."

"If there's anything I can do, you've only to say…"

"I would like to give you something to take back to England."

A present? For her, or for Gabriel? She hoped it was nothing unacceptable. "Of course, so long as it will fit in my case. I don't have much room."

"There will be no trouble. It is small." He paused, as if considering his words. "I have a problem, you see, concerning my daughter."

It was the first mention she could recall of Magda. "Yes?"

"I do not know how much she told you about herself when you were with her."

"Well, nothing, really. She talked about her childhood – as you have. She showed me a couple of photograph albums, and told me about Gabriel visiting you after the war. That

255

was all." She wanted to say something about Magda's bitterness towards her father and his orchids, but could not make herself do so.

"Her husband is dying."

"I did wonder. I'm sorry."

His face was expressionless. Did he feel any emotion at all? She tried to imagine Mr Mackenzie in the same position. "Isn't there anything you can do?" She said, almost as an accusation, "In England people with tuberculosis are sent to Switzerland to recover in the mountains. Couldn't he come here? I'm sure it would be healthier than staying in Munich."

"It is not tuberculosis."

"It isn't? What is it then?"

He shrugged. "I warned her not to marry him. My son did the same. Now he is dying and Magda has no money at all."

But you've got money, she wanted to say. Why don't you help? "What about his employer? Couldn't he do something? What did your son-in-law do when he was working?"

"He was a university lecturer. He joined my department, not long before I retired. That was how he met my daughter."

"Well, then. Couldn't he ask the university? Gabriel's college helped him after he was wounded in Ireland."

"My son-in-law is a Jew."

She swallowed. "Even so..."

"The university dismissed him. They had no choice. Jews are forbidden to work. Afterwards, of course, he was arrested for not working. For being a parasite."

Gwen stared. "But that's absurd. How could he work if he wasn't allowed?"

"Do you know Dachau?" Professor Ebert said as if she had not spoken. "It is a town north of Munich. In the old

256

days it was popular with artists. Because of the light, I understand. I remember Gabriel saying as much. Strange how one remembers things long forgotten."

He paused. She sipped her wine. It tasted like vinegar in her mouth.

"The artists left long ago," he said. "Now there is a camp. That is where my son-in-law was taken. He was made to work. Heaving stones too heavy for a man to lift, my daughter said. In the end his heart gave out. So they released him. When he has recovered sufficiently they will take him back in. My daughter does not think he will recover."

Gwen licked her lips. "Isn't there something one can do?"

"Well, yes. She can divorce him. That is what she has been advised to do. But she won't. She refuses to leave him." He shrugged. "That is her choice. If she wishes to risk her life..."

"But she's not doing that, is she? She's not Jewish."

"You have stayed with her. You must have seen the life she leads. She does all the work in the house herself. No Jewish household may employ a non-Jew under forty-five. She has no money. Being married to a Jew she cannot be employed herself. Some friends, I understand, give her help, now and then ... but she cannot earn sufficient to keep the family."

She remembered Rowena's concern for refugees and her efforts to help. She remembered discussions at the Rectory and in London. She remembered – heaven forgive her – her own lack of interest. "I ... don't know what to say."

"If she wishes to stay, that is her decision. It is her children that concern me. They are my grandchildren, even if they are half-Jewish. If he dies – when he dies – I want her to take them out of the country. To England, preferably."

The evening was assuming nightmarish qualities. For a

257

terrible moment Gwen thought he was about to ask her to take the children back with her. "But if he's no longer there, won't they be all right?"

He shook his head. "No one with Jewish blood, however young, will be safe in this country."

She said, "My sister was talking the other day about guarantors..."

"Who can I ask? No doubt I have relatives still in South America, but they are distant and we are out of touch. I do not know their names, or their addresses. I cut myself off from them long ago. No, if there is money to help Magda in England, that is where she must go. That is why I invited you here tonight, Miss Purcell, to ask for your help."

He got up from the table and went over to the desk at the far end of the room. His back was towards Gwen; she could not see what he was doing. She heard a rattle, a click. He returned to the table with a jeweller's case which he held out to her. "Open it, Miss Purcell."

She lifted the lid, removed a wad of tissue paper – and revealed a brooch.

She stared down at it aghast.

The size of it! She had never seen a brooch so huge. The many facets of the stones glittered and winked. She could not believe they were real.

"I'm asking you to take it back to England." The professor's voice was quiet. "Give it to Gabriel. Ask him to sell it. He was always resourceful. He will know what to do. He must keep the money safe. For Magda and the children. If there is money to keep them in England they will be granted a visa."

She could not take her eyes from the brooch. If the buttons of her blouse were common then this must be the ultimate in vulgarity. "It's not – it can't be – it isn't *genuine*, is it?"

"Of course it is genuine. Why else should I ask you to take it? Those are diamonds. Worth a great deal."

Her mind was paralysed. She could not think. What could she say? What should she do?

"I would write a letter of explanation for Gabriel, but it would be dangerous if your papers were searched at the border. You will have to explain."

"And this?" she said. "Suppose the customs people found this? That wouldn't be dangerous?"

"Why should it? It's only a brooch. Jewellery. Every woman wears jewellery."

"I don't. Not like this. The only jewellery I have with me is my wristwatch, and that's not valuable." The memory of the child's face in the train, which she had pushed to the back of her mind, returned with dreadful clarity. She saw the terror. "Breaking currency regulations" – wasn't that what the journalist's wife assumed the mother had done? Would she not be doing the same if she took this ... this monstrous thing with her? "No," she said. "I can't. I won't."

"I beg you to consider." His voice was quiet, so insistent that for one terrifying moment she wondered whether he would keep her prisoner until she agreed.

But as she sat, mesmerized by the glitter – even Lady Donne had not boasted diamonds of such size – another emotion began to stir besides fear. Anger.

"Is this why you asked me to come in the first place? Did you and Gabriel plan it together? Did you use the orchids as an excuse to get me to Germany?"

"Gabriel had nothing to do with it. How could he? I don't deny that I had something like this in mind when I first wrote to him after so many years. Believe me, Miss Purcell, it is happening all over the country. People write to those they once knew, friends who emigrated long ago, relations, anyone living abroad who might help in case help should be needed in the future. Can you blame them? Yes, I invited Gabriel to stay. I don't deny it. I did not know then what had happened in Ireland. I knew he liked walking. Come to walk in the Alps, I said. I remembered he had been interested in politics. If he came to stay, I thought, we could talk. I could tell him about Magda. We could come to some arrangement, perhaps. In letters I dared say nothing. He said he was unable to come but he mentioned you and your orchids. I ask you, Miss Purcell – what would you have done? Think back to your childhood. You survived because of the kindness of others. Strangers, you told me that day you arrived. I beg you..."

She could not answer. She would not listen. Uppermost in her mind was the realization that he had lied to her, had tricked her, lured her here under false pretences... She looked at the thin mouth, the cold eyes behind the steel-rimmed glasses, at the man who professed concern about his daughter yet who had visited her only once in two years. She stood up, kicked back her chair.

"I'm leaving."

The air was cold in her lungs. She had not realized how icy autumn nights in the mountains could be. Moonlight silvered the grass, cast strange shadows from the trees, made mysterious the familiar path. Distant points of light dotted the slopes of the valley below, like glow-worms in the dark.

Anger propelled her forward. How could he? How *dare* he? Why hadn't she suspected?

She had been flattered, that was why. She had been naïve,

credulous. She had been *stupid*. She had really believed that he had been impressed by her knowledge, admired her talent, wanted her paintings so much that he was prepared to pay for her to come out from England. Lies, lies, lies. An excuse, nothing more. A trick. The interest he had shown in her childhood that first day had been no more than a means to find out facts to use later on. How could he?

She stopped. The track narrowed as it entered a conifer wood. Moonlight scarcely penetrated. The air was full of unidentifiable sounds – strange rustlings, animal breathing. Who knew what lurked behind those trees? Wild boar on the hotel menu – where had that roamed when alive? The thudding of her heart sounded loud in her ears as she went slowly forward. In daylight six miles seemed no distance at all. In the darkness it stretched out for ever.

The moon welcomed her when at last she came out into the open. That same moon would be hanging in the sky above Hillcrest, shining onto the orchid house, gazing down at its reflection in the glass of the veranda roof below her bedroom window. She longed desperately to be back at Hillcrest, to be home, to be safe...

A voice called from far off. Echoes of it rolled faintly round the hills. Was it her imagination? Could she sense vibrations in the ground under her feet?

A dark shape emerged from the trees, moved steadily towards her, growing bigger minute by minute. She heard the sound of hooves on the hard earth, the jangle of bridle and bit.

Pony and trap halted beside her with a creaking of wheels. She recognized the silhouette of the army cap.

Hermann gestured behind him with his whip. "Climb in, Miss Purcell."

Chapter Twenty

The dining-room was in darkness when she reached the hotel. Fräulein Winkel and her mother were sitting in the office, with what looked like account books spread out on the desk in front of them. The photograph of Adolf Hitler on the far wall, which received as little attention as the wallpaper so far as Gwen could see, seemed in the past couple of hours to have acquired a hint of menace.

Fräulein Winkel looked up and waved, but did not come out. Her smile was preoccupied. "*Gute Nacht*, Miss Purcell."

Gwen sat on her bed without moving. Anger had gone; she felt a great weariness. She did not want to think of the professor or of his daughter and her sick husband, of the subdued children or what was happening in the country around her. She wanted to be back at Hillcrest, where life was straightforward and safe.

She stood up and slowly undressed, laying her clothes carefully over the back of her chair. Packing would have to wait until the morning; all she could think about now was getting to bed.

Downstairs the voices murmured in a never-ending monotone. She remembered similar voices long ago in the days following her mother's death, as low, as indistinct and as persistent as these – the voices of Frances, Julia and Annie discussing the Purcells' future in the living-room at Hillcrest, while Gwen lay tense in bed in her room at the top of the stairs, unable to make out the words, tormented by fears for the future. No one had told her what might happen and she was too frightened to ask. When, years later, she had referred to that time, Annie had been shocked. "Why didn't you tell us, love? Why didn't you ask? We didn't want to worry you. We thought you were safe tucked up in bed."

And at last Gwen understood the reason for the inexplicable behaviour of Magda's children. They were frightened. She remembered the way they had clung to their mother in the English Garden, refusing to leave her side. They were terrified of the unknown, of the future, as Gwen herself had been when not much older than they.

The Purcells had been fortunate. They had been surrounded by people who cared: Sir James Donne, people in the village, above all by the Mackenzies, who had cared for them as if they had been members of their own family. Who did Magda and her children have but one cold, detached man who looked on Hans and Lisl as no more than extensions of himself? "They are my grandchildren, even if they are half-Jewish." Could he really have said that?

She tossed and turned under the duvet. The clock on the church across the street marked the quarter hours with a mellow, echoing clang. Regret overwhelmed her. Why hadn't she agreed to Professor Ebert's proposal? There would have been little danger, surely; the blue passport provided protection, even against the swastika.

Regret came too late. There was no time to make the trip up into the mountains before the departure of the train connecting at Munich with the continental express.

She rose early, heavy-eyed and unrefreshed, filled with remorse, and was gathering her possessions together when there was a knock on the bedroom door.

"*Fräulein Purcell?*"

It was the little maid with no English, bobbing a curtsey. "*Guten Morgen, Fräulein.*" She gestured towards the stairs. "*Der Herr Professor ist unten.*"

Traces of stale cigarette smoke lingered in the hall. Professor Ebert came forward to greet her, immaculate as always, despite his journey and the early hour. "We did not have time to say goodbye last night, Miss Purcell. Also, you left your papers behind. I thought that you might like to take your drawings home with you. I have kept the general view, which I like very much. Please take the others as a memento of your visit." As she took them, not knowing how to respond, he added, "It is a fine day outside. Perhaps, when you have eaten, we might walk to the river."

He stayed in the hall while she picked at her breakfast, her appetite banished by tiredness and self-reproach. She could see him through the open door of the dining-room with Fräulein Winkel. Fräulein Winkel was doing most of the talking, her expression earnest and anxious. Professor Ebert said little. His face was grim.

He and Gwen walked in silence down the main street. In the square Hermann, waiting at the head of the pony, nodded as they went by. Climbers were tying their bootlaces, coiling rope and checking equipment in preparation for the day's expeditions. The morning was cool, the sun still hidden by the mountain range to the east. Dahlias under the calvary showed touches of frost on their petals and leaves.

"I think I was too hasty last night," Gwen said at last. "If only you'd given me some warning, if you'd said something about the situation before. But you didn't. We never talked about your daughter. Or your grandchildren."

He was unrepentant. "I acted as I thought best."

"Yes, well ... I'm sorry. Really I am. I wish I'd said yes. I would have done if I'd had time to think. Now it's too late."

He felt in his pocket. "It is not too late, Miss Purcell. I have the brooch here. I hoped, you see, that if we talked sensibly you would change your mind."

She looked down at the box in his hand and wondered what he would have done had she remained adamant. Slipped it into her pocket when she was not looking? For a moment she was tempted to refuse. She could not: the memory of Hans and Lisl was too vivid.

She walked with him as far as the river. He leant on the wooden balustrade of the bridge and looked down at the pale green water swirling over the stones beneath.

"Things are worse than I thought," he said. His voice was muffled by the sound of the water. "Fräulein Winkel tells me we are about to become a garrison town. I had always assumed that Magda could escape from here into Austria, if need be. Now that route will no longer be open. England is the only place left to her."

"Gabriel will be able to do something, I'm sure of it. And my other sister and her husband have already helped people to come out of Germany." Eminent scientists though, said the voice in her head, who could work for a living, not women and children with jewellery as their only means of support. "Julia said something about guarantees last time I saw her. I'll ask her advice."

He remained looking down into the water. She wondered if he remembered that she had a train to catch. "I really ought to be getting back to the hotel, Herr Professor. I still have my packing to do."

Folding her clothes in her bedroom, she tried to decide what to do with the brooch. Should she hide it away, in the toe of a shoe perhaps? But if it were found in the course of a search – and how thoroughly were searches made on outward-bound trains? – customs officials would almost certainly arrest her for smuggling. Suppose she said it was in payment for her paintings? Would that transgress currency regulations? Perhaps she could pretend it was no more than a costume piece. How expert were customs officers at judging the value of jewellery? Truth to tell she found it hard to believe herself that those large pieces of stone were genuine, for all their sparkle. Still uncertain, she folded the blouse she had been wearing the previous evening and laid it on top of the clothes in the suitcase, mentally wincing at the sight of the buttons. She must remember to change them for ones less showy once she was home.

And then it came to her. Why not be blatant?

Two Englishwomen were already installed in the ladies only compartment of the express when Gwen joined it at Munich. Countrywomen, judging by their tweedy suits and sensible brogues. If they thought her overdressed they were too polite to show it. They were retired schoolmistresses, they told her, the elder a headmistress, who had been on a walking holiday in the Alps. "Rather late in the year, as it turned out. The autumn colours have been lovely, of course, but it's the spring flowers we like. Have you seen Alpine meadows in May? My dear, you must. Such a sight. You can smell their scent in the air for miles around."

Gwen was relieved by their no-nonsense style. If she were to be dragged from the train by swastika-armbanded youths there would at least be witnesses, and witnesses competent enough to take action once they reached England. They told her that they had enjoyed their time in Germany, liked the country and the people. "A bit simple," they said, and smiled benignly. They talked with disbelief of atrocities they had read about in English newspapers. "Totally untrue, of course. We were fed similar stories during the war. All propaganda, we discovered when it was over. Don't you remember? No, of course you don't. You're much too young."

She wanted to warn them that not everything in Germany was as straightforward as it appeared, but felt it would be indiscreet. She saw in them herself as she had been only a short while ago, so certain that everything was just as she thought it. It had never occurred to her to doubt the outward appearance of the country, just as it had never occurred to her to wonder about Waite's army service or Lucy's feelings for home. Even Professor Ebert, despite his coldness and detachment, was making some effort to support his daughter and grandchildren. And she herself was not all that she seemed. She suppressed a nervous giggle at the thought. What would these schoolmistresses say if she told them that she was a lawbreaker smuggling valuables out of the country? Would they believe that the brooch on her bosom was any more valuable than the cheap buttons of the blouse onto which it was pinned?

The tidy landscape of Germany passed inexorably by the train window – forests and vineyards, rivers, a castle sitting high on a rock. The blue and white flags of Bavaria disappeared. Only the red and black swastika remained.

Fear gripped her as the frontier drew nearer. She resisted the temptation to open the window, tear the brooch from her blouse and throw it onto the track. In her mind the picture of the woman being dragged from the carriage alternated with the terrified face of the child.

"Are we coming to the frontier, do you think?" asked the younger schoolmistress brightly as the train began to slow down.

It stopped, waited for ten minutes, staggered half a mile, stopped again.

"Let's hope we don't have any bother with customs," said the headmistress.

Footsteps sounded down the corridor. Doors slid open and shut. Harsh voices barked commands. Gwen's hand on her passport grew clammy. Take deep breaths, Miss Blake had told her before her lecture to the WI. Deep breaths.

"Do you remember young Ronnie Jones?" said the headmistress. "I always thought he'd make a good customs officer."

"Oh, my goodness, yes. He used to put the fear of God into everybody. Into me too, on occasions."

The footsteps stopped in the corridor. The door of the compartment slid open. A customs officer stood in the doorway studying each passenger in turn. "English? Passports."

"Please," the headmistress corrected him automatically as she handed him hers.

His companion watched from the corridor. His eyes looked straight at the brooch, partially hidden, Gwen prayed, by the frill of her blouse. What was he thinking? Deep breaths, she told herself. Not too deep, though; not noticeably deep. She took in the blue eyes, the blond hair. Aryan. Definitely Aryan. Calm. Keep calm.

What else was it that Miss Blake had said? "Pretend you're someone else. How about a learned botanist from the Royal Horticultural Society perhaps?" All right. What should she be now? A spinster, a simple-minded English spinster, with a passion for flowers and painting, no interest in politics and dreadful taste in blouses and jewellery. She let out her breath very gently. Not far from the truth, after all.

The officer took her passport. "On holiday?" he snapped.

Say yes. Get him out of the carriage as quickly as possible.

Don't be silly. Keep calm. Remember who you are.

"I've been painting orchids. Such beautiful flowers, so delicate, so exotic, quite out of this world. These were in a private collection; I was asked to paint them. A commission. Shall I show you?"

She stood up and reached for her suitcase. He watched, not offering to help. She laid it on the seat and opened it up. As she took out the drawings Professor Ebert had returned to her, she wondered briefly whether he had foreseen such a situation when he gave them to her. "Look. A *Cattleya citrina*. Isn't it wonderful? Of course, when you come to paint a flower like this..." Was she talking too much? Or was that part of her character?

He cut into the flow in German and at length. She had no idea what he was saying but it sounded unpleasant. She peered at him through her glasses and smiled. *"Ich verstehe nicht."* Loudly, Gabriel had said. She repeated the words, loudly, before picking up another of her preliminary studies.

The man's eyes glazed over. He thrust her passport into her hand without another word. The door slid to behind him with a bang.

The headmistress tut-tutted. "Not so much as a please or

269

a thank you. Dreadful. The young have no manners these days."

Her companion was exclaiming over Gwen's drawings. "These are beautiful, really beautiful. Not that I know much about orchids; wild flowers are more my line. I hadn't realized from what you said that you were a professional. Do you come abroad often?"

"This is the first time," Gwen said.

The train lurched, began to move, slowly gathered speed. Station lights disappeared into the darkness. Germany was behind them, the Channel ports in front. She was going home. Home to Hillcrest.

She lay back in her seat, her body rocking with the movement of the train. Such weariness...

The first time, she had said. How extraordinary. Was she thinking of coming again? In her mind she could see Lisl and Hans in the English Garden in Munich. How many others were there in Germany living in fear? The brooch, when sold, would support Magda and her children, but what of those who either had no jewellery or knew of no one to take it out of the country? What of them?

She would need money if she wanted to help. Where would the money come from?

Why, from her flower selling. Where else? What had she been doing over the past eighteen months but building up an income – not a large income, true, but more than enough for her own needs and the needs of Hillcrest. Flower selling and orchids... Orchids. Mr Whitelaw's orchids. She smiled. After the early years of financial worry, how miraculous to have money to spare at a time when money was needed.

"Oh, Gwen."

She looked up. It was no longer the headmistress sitting

in the seat opposite, but Antony Mackenzie, Antony from the walk over the Quantocks. How young he looked as he sat there, hair falling over his forehead, eyes laughing and teasing. "Gwen – you are wonderful." As she looked at him he changed. The classics scholar turned into the soldier Ulysses, about to depart on his travels, Achilles off to the war. Smiling no longer. "A bit frippery, orchids, don't you think?"

Something happened. The burden lifted. She felt light-hearted. Not frippery at all, she wanted to tell him. She wanted to shout. You were wrong. Orchids aren't frippery. Orchids save lives. They rescue children, bring them out of danger to play in safety in the garden at Hillcrest. Not your children, Antony – alas, alas, not your children – but others.

He smiled at her, leant forward, put his hand on her knee.

She opened her eyes.

The headmistress made a gesture of apology as she settled back into her corner. "You were talking in your sleep," she said. "Something about orchids."

"I'm sorry. I've thought of little else in the last couple of weeks."

Professor Ebert's orchids. Not hers. For the first time for days her thoughts returned to her own flowers. In the drama of the last twenty-four hours she had forgotten about Question Mark. Once back at Hillcrest she would have to make a decision about Question Mark's future.

She gazed out at the moonlit landscape through which they were passing and knew that the decision had already been made.

She would accept Mr Alexander's offer.

Reluctant as she was to let the plant go, she knew that she must. While money from flower selling would provide a

271

steady income, the windfall Question Mark offered was too valuable to refuse. Mr Whitelaw, of all people, would understand that.

And now she knew the name she should choose. She would call it after its creator, after the man who years before had been moved by the sight of children playing on the lawn at Hillcrest, who by his bequest had begun the long train of events which had brought her to this moment and this place, sitting in a continental express with a fortune pinned to her blouse and plans in her head to give children the opportunity to play without fear.

She would name Question Mark after Mr Whitelaw.

Cymbidium Alfred G. Whitelaw. A hauntingly beautiful, life-saving orchid.

Chapter Twenty-One

Gwen had expected Julia to meet her at Victoria but it was Tony's face that she glimpsed among those waiting on the platform. He saw her at the same moment and began to run, waving frantically as he dodged in and out of the crowd.

"Aunt Gwen! Aunt Gwen!"

The train stopped. He skidded to a halt by the carriage door.

"Tony! What are you doing here? Don't say you've run away again!"

He laughed at her. "Oh, Aunt Gwen. Of course I haven't. We're staying with Aunt Julia for half-term. Have you had a splendid time? Here, let me give you a hand with your case. Dad's waiting outside with the car."

A porter opened the door. She stepped down onto the platform. English soil. No red and black flags. No Nazi armbands. English people, talking a language she understood. She was safe. She was home.

Tony banged her suitcase down from the train steps, then let it go so that he could give her a quick hug. "Isn't it exciting about Question Mark, Aunt Gwen?"

No need to worry about Tony, Gwen decided. He's back on form again. "How is school?" she asked.

He made a face. "All right. Hard, though. The Rat – he's my housemaster – says it's all my own fault, and what else could I expect when I've never done a stroke of work in my life."

"I could tell him that that's not true," Gwen said.

"Have you had a good journey?" Gabriel greeted her. "Not too tired? Julia promised to make sure the kettle was boiling by the time we got back. Is that all the luggage you've got? Stow it away in the boot then, Tony, will you? In you get, Gwen."

He waited until they were driving along Grosvenor Place before asking after Professor Ebert. "I can't wait to hear all the details."

Gwen thought of the brooch, now safely put away in her handbag. "I don't know where to begin," she said.

"Begin at the beginning," Julia suggested as she poured out the tea. "No trouble with the journey – I told you there wouldn't be, didn't I? Right. You've arrived at Munich. You didn't say much about Munich in your letters. Did you enjoy it? What was Magda really like? And the children?"

How long ago Munich seemed. So much had happened that she could scarcely believe it was only two weeks since she had been waved off at the station. "Magda? A bit stiff, I suppose. It must have been difficult for her, having a foreigner to stay."

Julia was interested in Magda, Andrew in the children. Rowena wanted to know about refugees, Tony about any military sights that she might have seen. ("I didn't, Tony. Or if I did, I didn't recognize them.") Gabriel was curious about

Professor Ebert, Frances anxious to know if Gwen had been satisfied with the work she had done during her stay. Gwen did not know which to answer first.

"I'll show you my paintings later," she told Frances. "I wish you could have come too. Your present style would have been just right for that setting. It reminded me of the jungle growing up around the Sleeping Beauty. Fairy tale-ish, in a menacing sort of way. Once or twice Professor Ebert even made me think of Bluebeard."

Andrew opened his eyes wide. "Do you mean he might have murdered his wives?"

"No, no. Well, I wouldn't think so. Though I did find a mysterious empty room." Crumbs of earth on the floor, the faint scent still lingering, orchids sold and sent away. For the first time she wondered whether there might have been another reason for Professor Ebert's invitation. Had he wanted a pictorial record of his orchids because he was planning to sell more of them to invest in other pieces of jewellery?

"What about refugees, Aunt Gwen?" Rowena asked. "Did you find any refugees?"

"Ah," Gwen said. "Refugees. I want to talk about refugees while I'm here, but I think we'd better wait till your father gets home. I need his advice."

Tony grinned as he offered her a plate of sandwiches. "Just think, Aunt Gwen. You've been further afield than me. I'm impressed."

"You're looking very well, I must say," Julia said. "I was afraid you'd be exhausted after such a long journey."

Gwen's thoughts went back to Hans and Lisl as she lay in the bath before dinner. Her intention had been to bring them to England, if Magda had insisted on staying in Munich. Now she wondered if Professor Ebert bought more jewellery, would she be prepared to smuggle that too through customs? She banished the possibility from her mind. For the time being she would concentrate on what could be achieved legally – "through the proper channels" as David phrased it, smiling at her down the dining-table.

For proper channels there were, apparently. Visas could be obtained provided there was either sufficient money for financial supportor work available to make a refugee self-supporting.

"Mrs Meyer brought over a friend of a friend who was in difficulties," Julia said. "She's working as Mrs Meyer's housekeeper. Not a very good one, I believe, but Mrs Meyer just shrugs and says what else could she have done."

"A housekeeper? Miss Blake at Clay Court is looking for a housekeeper. Mrs Simons is getting too old and rheumaticky, she says."

"There were refugees at Clay Court during the war," Frances said. "A Belgian family, weren't they? Mr Tasker gave them some rooms."

"I wonder how Magda would feel about being a housekeeper?" Gwen still could not believe that that monstrous piece of jewellery would provide sufficient money to support a family indefinitely. If Magda needed to work, Clay Court might provide the opportunity ... and the children could always come to Hillcrest to play.

"When you talk about financial support," Tony said, "what do you mean exactly?"

"If your mother and I decided the three of us should emigrate, to Canada, say," his father said, "we'd be able to take our money with us. Germans aren't allowed to do that.

The only way they can take money out of the country is to smuggle cash across the border or bring it out in some other form. Like the brooch Aunt Gwen's passed on to me. Otherwise someone here has to promise financial support. A guarantor, he's called."

"How do they find a guarantor?"

"That's the problem. Usually through interested people in this country."

Gabriel was one such person, being a member of an university organization that helped intellectuals in Germany. "A number of us at Cambridge pay part of our salary into it. They're not necessarily Jews, the people we assist, but academics, men with ideas. The sort of people Hitler doesn't want around making life awkward, so he gets rid of them. Remarkably short-sighted of him. He doesn't seem to understand that he's losing the best brains of the country."

David and Julia had helped too, through both the hospital and the Settlement. "It's the children you're really interested in, isn't it?" Julia asked Gwen.

"I think so. Lisl and Hans reminded me of what it was like when we were young. We were so lucky to have Gabriel's parents. I'd like to help those who haven't anyone. I know Lisl and Hans should be all right financially, but there must be others…"

"Lord, yes," Gabriel said. "There was one physicist who was arrested the week before he was due to leave. We still can't find out what's happened to his family."

"You don't have to pay me any more when I'm working at Hillcrest," Tony said suddenly. "I think you should keep the money for that."

"And if you send me dried flowers again we'll make more pictures to sell at the Christmas fair," Rowena offered.

"That would be wonderful. Add all that to the income I get from Mrs Meyer and Cole's, and it's a beginning. As a matter of fact, I was wondering about going round and talking about it to WIs..."

"Heavens, Gwen," David said. "What's happened to you? We'll have you standing on a soapbox in Hyde Park next."

Frances too remarked on the change when she came into Gwen's room later that evening to look at Gwen's work. "I worried about how you would manage," she said. "Unnecessarily, it seems. You didn't mind being away from Hillcrest for so long?"

Gwen shook her head, amused. Family relationships never changed, it seemed. Responsibility of the elder sister for the younger carried on into middle age. The artistic mentor was still evident too.

"Why don't you ask Denis to give you an exhibition?" Frances asked. "You've painted so many orchids over the past year you must have sufficient to choose from by now. I know he'd be interested. He was never able to understand why you wouldn't send him anything after the one he gave you."

"You know how it was. I was busy with other things at the time. Wishart's had just commissioned my first book."

She still had bad memories of that exhibition. She had hated leaving Hillcrest for the time necessary, felt out of place in the London art gallery of Frances's agent, was awkward with strangers she met. Worse, she had felt a fraud. Exhibitions were for weightier works than floral watercolours. They were meant for paintings of artists like Frances. Never again, she had told herself, and had retreated

278

to Hillcrest to bury herself in the garden and the illustrating of children's books. Had she been wrong? she wondered now. Perhaps the time had come to reconsider.

She changed the subject. "What about your work, Frances? I was surprised to find you here. Gabriel had said you found the summer difficult and needed to be on your own."

"Well ... I had to come really, for Tony's sake. He's been trying so hard this term, we felt he needed a treat. We took him to the theatre last night and out for a meal afterwards." She laid Gwen's drawings carefully on the chest and sighed. "In any case it wasn't the summer that was difficult – Provence was as wonderful as ever – but the trouble with Tony, that destroyed my concentration. It was his deceit that upset me so much, Gwen. I don't understand it. Why didn't he tell us what he wanted to do, instead of behaving in such an underhand way?"

"Because he knew you wouldn't let him do it, that's why. You know you wouldn't have. You'd have thrown up your hands in horror at the very idea, and insisted he went to France with you both. Once there you'd have spent all your time painting, Gabriel would have concentrated on his book and poor Tony would have been bored to tears. Of course he wasn't going to tell you."

Frances was silent. "You think I'm a terrible mother, don't you?" she said at last.

"No, I don't. I understand about you and your work. I always have. I admire you for it. I know it must be hard. I just don't think you should call Tony deceitful, that's all."

Frances was not listening. "I don't know where he gets it from," she said. "None of *us* were deceitful."

"We were always well behaved," Gwen agreed, "but only

because we were terrified the Mackenzies would make us leave Hillcrest if we weren't. And even then... If you'd had to deceive the Mackenzies to get to the Slade you'd have done it, wouldn't you?"

Frances was suddenly still. A faint flush crept up over her face. Goodness, Gwen thought. Did she?

"Think of Antony..." she began, after a pause during which Frances neither confirmed nor denied any deception.

"Antony wasn't deceitful," Frances said. "Oh, I know he made up stories, but that was his overactive imagination..."

"Oh, Frances, you were so wrapped up in your work you didn't know what was going on half the time. Neither did Mrs Mackenzie, for that matter. She'd have died if she had."

Frances gazed at Gwen in astonishment. "What on earth do you mean?"

"Mrs Mackenzie had no idea of the things that Antony got up to – scrumping apples, getting drunk on cider, he and George Cross always egging each other on."

"I don't believe it."

"It's true."

"How do you know?"

"Antony told me. I dare say he exaggerated sometimes – you know how he was – but he never lied. Besides, there were the times he and I ... I remember we went over to Watchet once on George's bicycle..."

"To Watchet? Whatever for?"

"To see an aeroplane. Strange that, isn't it, when you think of Tony's interest in flying."

"But I thought you never left Hillcrest." Frances was incredulous.

"Well, I did, often, but I didn't tell you, for the same reason that Tony didn't mention his flying. Because you'd have been cross. You always wanted to know what everyone was doing. I know, I know. It's been an odd feeling, this summer, remembering Antony's escapades and his secrecy, which I have to admit I admired in those days, and seeing them now from the adult point of view." She smiled ruefully at Frances. "So you see, I was deceitful too. That must be where Tony gets it from. You'd better blame me."

Next morning Gwen returned to Somerset. She sat in the Taunton train, scarcely aware of the landscape beyond the window, as she drowsed, woke and drowsed again, worn out by spent emotion and the excitement of the past days. Thoughts appeared and disappeared, like landmarks on the passing scene. Faces came into her vision – Magda, Hans, Lisl – and faded. Mr Whitelaw, the man she remembered from her youth, upright and sturdy, standing by his orchids. Antony. Tony.

How alike they were, those two, uncle and nephew. The fair hair and blue eyes, the challenging stance, the amused look. So enthusiastic, so dedicated when their interest was caught. Unalike too: one so clever, living in a world of his imagination; the other down-to-earth and practical, able to see and accept the world as it was.

What children they had been, Antony and she. So young, so innocent; thinking themselves adult, yet too inexperienced to be able to cope adequately with the difficulties of parting.

Outside, rain was slanting across the Somerset levels. She shut her eyes in an effort to blot out both view and her memories. Except that memories should not be erased. They should be faced and accepted.

Strange that the ache of childlessness should only recently

have come to the surface. The approach of middle age, no doubt – or perhaps the developing relationship with Tony had something to do with it. Tony, the child she and Antony might have had, had they been granted time together.

Yet for all his other-worldliness it had been Antony, of all those who knew her, who had understood the reason for her seclusion at Hillcrest and tempted her out of it. As Tony was to do years later, with less understanding but as effectively. Tony's need for money had sent her outside the small, protective world she had made for herself, sent her out to Mr Cole and to Mrs Meyer. Later it was Tony's scorn alone that had challenged her into accepting the invitation to Germany.

She opened her eyes. The train was approaching the outskirts of Taunton. In less than an hour she would be back at Hillcrest. Hillcrest, her home. She had been surprised by Professor Ebert's suggestion that she had made Hillcrest into a retreat from the world; surprised and, when she thought about it later, angry. Remembering his words now she saw that he had been right. In the past, yes, but not now. She needed Hillcrest as a refuge no longer.

SISTERS OF THE QUANTOCK HILLS

The Silent Shore

Sisters of the Quantock Hills is the compelling saga
of the lives and loves of four sisters – Frances, Julia,
Gwen and Sarah Purcell – and their neighbours, the
Mackenzies. *The Silent Shore* (Book One) is Sarah's
story. It begins in 1910, when Sarah is still a child,
living in a world of rural bliss, idyllic outings and
romance. But the outbreak of the Great War
brings tragedy…

"The Little Women of our times." *The Times*

"A family saga to enthral."
The Times Literary Supplement

"Vivid… Memorable." *The Guardian*

SISTERS OF THE QUANTOCK HILLS

The Beckoning Hills

Sisters of the Quantock Hills is the compelling saga
of the lives and loves of four sisters – Frances, Julia,
Gwen and Sarah Purcell – and their neighbours, the
Mackenzies. *The Beckoning Hills* (Book Two) is
Frances's story. It begins in 1910 and continues
through the years of the Great War, telling of her
colourful life at art school and her passionate
relationship with Gabriel Mackenzie.

"The Little Women of our times." *The Times*

"A family saga to enthral."
The Times Literary Supplement

"Vivid... Memorable." *The Guardian*